HE WAS EVERYTHING
SHE'D EVER WANTED IN A MAN . . .

She was suddenly at a loss for words. She wanted to shout out that he had no right to be in her home, no right to hold her the way that he was holding her. But she liked the feel of him, liked the scent of him, the nearness of him, the look of his shaven cheek, the texture of his jacket against her, the way that his gaze seemed to warm and heat her. He made her feel like a school girl again. And that was just the problem; she wanted to play. She barely knew him, and she wanted to touch him. He wasn't just a handsome man she could look at and admire with an artist's eye. She wanted to touch. And feel.

And suddenly she did.

His mouth encompassed hers, seared with passion and fury. His kiss was deep, so deep it seemed to steal her strength. It ignited fires in her, fanned them, urged them to greater heat, sent them searing throughout her. It swept into her like a jagged streak of lightning, making her tremble, making her burn . . .

Why did he have to be the one man who could destroy everything she had ever loved?

* * *

HEATHER GRAHAM POZZESSERE

Down in New Orleans

ZEBRA BOOKS
KENSINGTON PUBLISHING CORP.

To the
"Ladies of Louisiana"

Lorna Broussard
Sharon Bellard
Francis Tingler
Debby Quebedeaux
Karin David
Cindy Landry
Brenda Barrett
Janet LeBlanc
Tini Nini
Chris Barclay
Mary Womack
Vickie Broussard
and, very especially,
Connie Perry

One

Annie had been expecting to see Jon that night.

Just not the way she saw him. Staggering in. Falling to his knees. Bleeding all over her floor. Gasping out cryptic and barely intelligible words.

At first, she hadn't even heard the pounding at her door. She had gone out to her balcony to stare down at the night life in the city. It was odd that now, nearly five years after her divorce, she could actually really and truly thank Jon for something—his city. She loved New Orleans, she loved that he had found this place in the French Quarter for her, and she could even say now, without bitterness or passion, that she had come to love her ex once again. She hadn't thought it possible. Their fifteen-year relationship had been too stormy, too angry, too hateful—at times even too dangerous. But the storms were over. What he chose to do with his Saturday evenings—or mornings, for that matter—no longer concerned her. It was the most exhilarating sense of freedom she had ever imagined, not to have to care. She didn't even blame him very much anymore. The things that had happened had been unavoidable—fate, even.

They had met as children, and he had stayed a big child. He was still a big child; but now she could cope with him and love him in a different manner.

In the end, it would prove to be very odd that she was deep in retrospection that night, standing on the balcony, chicory coffee in hand, staring down at the street, listening to the jazz she loved so much—and thinking how happy she was. Divorce had originally scared her. She had held on to her marriage long after the truth of the vows had gone out of it. Until the divorce finally happened, she hadn't realized how afraid she had been of being alone. That she had made excuses to stay married not because of their daughter, as she had thought, but because she had been afraid of being alone.

Until five years ago, she had never been alone. She had been Jon's wife, Katie's mom, and before that, she had been Jeff and Cheryl's daughter. She went right from high school into college—a liberal arts school because her parents just didn't believe it was possible for the average young woman to actually make a living at art. She met Jon Marcel her freshman year; they were both eighteen. They dated right away, went to wild parties, had huge jealous fights, parted. Yet kept going back together, no matter how bad the fights got.

They both went on to grad school, and didn't marry until after they had celebrated their twenty-fifth birthdays. When they should have both been mature, responsible, well-educated adults. Ready to face the world as mature, responsible people. They had sown their wild oats. This was marriage.

She wondered why she had expected things to change.

Because they certainly didn't. Marriage didn't make them one bit different. They went on treating one another like children—fighting like children. Petty irritations continued to rise as they sulked, battled, walked away from one another—called one another names. Somewhere along the line, the names finally just became too nasty, the fights just a little vicious. Jon stayed away. She grew silent. Wondering. He began to come home later and later, and then one night, not at all. But by then, it didn't really matter. If she felt rage, she kept it bottled up inside. She didn't even want to confront him—when the time came, she quietly saw her lawyer, quietly filed papers.

At first Jon considered her actions a bluff. He threatened and pleaded. Then he cried. And she cried. And they almost made up. But that had been the pattern, and Ann realized then that she had to break that pattern. Especially because it seemed that Humpty Dumpty had fallen off the wall: she couldn't even pretend anymore that he hadn't been cheating on her, and once upon a time, even with all the fighting, she had believed that there was something golden and precious in their relationship—mutual

fidelity. So they divorced, becoming awful enemies; then, suddenly, somewhere in there, the
very best of friends. They had been living in Atlanta together; he had gone home to New Orleans when they'd split up. He coaxed her down
for Jazz Fest, then found the perfect artist's garret and home for her right next to a boulangerie
dead center in the French Quarter. And she
loved it. She lived on the second floor, while
below she opened a store that sold cards, prints,
and local crafts on consignment. She found the
perfect manager for the shop, and was able to
spend her days—and nights, when she so desired—working. She loved painting; she loved
the gallery owner next door who did well with
her vivid portraits of life in New Orleans, plants,
flowers and balustrades, old fishermen, young
children. Faces.

Faces were her favorite, and faces were her
forte. One of the nicest reviews she'd ever received had stated that decades of living and an
entire spectrum of emotions could be seen in
her faces. She was wise enough to understand
her own particular talent and love of art, however; so even though she made most of her
money on her faces done in oil, she constantly
changed both her interests and her style. She
very often did so with Jon as friend, inspiration
and critic. That was part of what they shared
now—their mutual love of art, and their respect
for one another within their chosen field and
vocation.

She glanced at her watch with a frown. Jon

had actually been due quite some time ago. He was currently into a project, doing a new series of paintings. A new gallery, opened by an old friend of theirs who'd just recently made the move to New Orleans from San Francisco, was displaying the first of this series, and Jon was coming to take her by to see his paintings. The series was called *Red Light Ladies,* and though she had to admit that she had rather high-handedly scoffed at the concept at first—all right, so she had actually snickered at the very idea of Jon doing such a series—the few paintings in his garret she had already seen were wonderful, his finest work to date. Just as she had been complimented on her faces, he was being commended for his study of women living on the edge of life. His first painting, entitled *Sweet Scarlet,* was both visually stunning and emotionally wrenching. The "Scarlet" of the painting was decked out in wondrous red, a costume startlingly sensual and oddly beautiful, and against that lay the pain and loss and wonder—and just an edge of hardness—within her eyes. Tawdry, glittering, lovely, sad, pathetic. The painting was so many things. He had asked a stripper who worked a local club to pose for the painting, and it seemed that he had summed up so much of her life, the beauty and hope of youth, the wary wisdom that encroaching age brought with it. He had captured the woman with the promise of fluid movement in her dance, a grace that defied the more elemental function of removing one's clothing. Tonight, many of Jon's "ladies" would be on display, and, Ann had to admit, she was quite eager to see them all in a gallery setting.

She sipped her coffee and glanced at her watch again, wondering what was keeping him. She didn't really feel that anxious; it was a beautiful night. Darkness had just come, settling over the last of a sunset that had just bathed the old wrought-iron lacing and balconies of pastel buildings in a patina of red. If she closed her eyes, she could dimly hear the voices, the laughter of people, tourists and natives, wandering the quaint streets. The jazz horn was their backdrop; the faint but tantalizing odors of rich coffee and always fresh-baked croissants and beignets lay hauntingly on the air.

It was then that she heard the banging.

Banging . . . or a thud, actually. As if Jon had arrived and slammed a shoulder furiously against her door. For a moment, she was irritated. They weren't married anymore. He'd often had this tendency to think that the world should stop for him, that she should open the door the second he arrived even if her hands were dripping with dish soap, paint, or tomato sauce from a casserole.

"Jon?" She set her coffee on the white wrought-iron table on the balcony. She walked through the living area to the apartment's front door. Ready to tell Jon just what she thought of his obnoxious pounding, she threw the bolt and swept the door open in a fury.

"Damn you, Jon—" she began.

He was standing there, his handsome face thin, pale, almost cadaverous in the muted light of the hallway.

Then he fell.

Dead weight.

He fell forward, crashing straight into her arms. Taken completely by surprise, Ann found herself off-balance, driven flat to the floor by the impetus of his free-fall and weight, crashing down hard beneath him.

"Jon—"

His face was on the floor, just inches from her own. His lips were moving. She'd clutched him as they had fallen. She moved her hands then, still too stunned to realize just what was happening.

Her hands . . .

His lips . . .

Her fingers were dripping blood. And there was suddenly soft, desperate sound coming from his lips.

"I didn't do it."

There was blood. On her hands. From holding him.

"Oh, God!" He wasn't really seeing her. His mouth kept forming words.

"I didn't do it. I didn't do it, I didn't do it . . ."

Blood was seeping out over the polished floorboards.

"Oh, God!" He screamed it. His eyes focused on her. "I didn't do it!"

His eyes fell shut.

And the blood continued to run.

Two

Women. Wives. They were always the last to know, Mark thought with a shake of his head and a wealth of impatience. For Christ's sake, the guy had killed the stripper he'd been with. Stripper? Sweet Jesus. That was being kind. The young woman might have had a good heart; she might have been all personality beneath the price tag she usually put on her time, but in plain language, the poor, butchered girl had been a *whore*. But it didn't seem to matter to this guy's wife that she'd been such a woman. Here this jerk's wife was, his little woman, with a tear-stained face, talking with the doctor, demanding that he save the life of a man who had just stolen the tarnished dreams of another.

"Now that's a picture, huh?" whispered Jimmy Deveaux, tall and stringy as a bean pole, a friendly fellow with shaggy brown hair and a blood hound's face. Mark held rank over Jimmy, but they often worked together. Partners. When the streets were filled with knives and gunfire, rank didn't mean squat. Jimmy, too, shook his head. "Cute as a button. Pretty woman. Great hair. Great butt."

The words were typical of his partner. The guys in the force referred to Jimmy's running commentary on the world as "gallow's humor." Tonight they were investigating a murder. It couldn't get more serious. But humor was often a cop's way of surviving the life he or she had chosen.

And usually, Mark would have played along with it—not even in a sexist manner—for when the cops on duty were females, they, too, discussed the attributes of people, male and female. Men and women had clichés, but cops had clichés, too.

It was just that tonight. . . .

"Jimmy, we're not here to assess her butt," Mark said.

Jimmy didn't seem to notice his mood. "Her boobs seem to be pretty good, too."

"Jimmy, we're not here to assess her boobs or her butt," Mark said more firmly.

"Okay, we're not here to assess them; but there they are, and they're still great. What in God's name was the guy doing killing a prostitute when he had someone like that back home?"

"Come on, now, my boy, you've been in this business long enough to know that the world is full of psychos—and that even your more normal garden-variety breed of man can behave like damned psychos at times."

"I couldn't have left her for a prostitute," Jimmy said with a sigh.

"Gina L'Aveau wasn't your usual prostitute," Mark replied casually.

Jimmy glanced at his friend long and hard. Then he shrugged and agreed, "No, Mark, she wasn't your usual prostitute. Not at all. You okay with this?"

"Of course I'm okay with this."

Mark, growing more impatient now as they waited for a conference with the doctor assigned to their murder suspect, turned away from Jimmy's inquiring eyes. He looked Jon Marcel's wife up and down again. Her name was Ann. Ann Marcel. He'd almost taken her for a kid at first. She was tiny—she'd be stretching it to claim to be five-foot-three. But she wasn't a kid. On closer inspection, she looked like she was somewhere in her early to mid thirties. Maybe even a little older. Small, compact—but he had to give Jimmy and his taste some credit—she was nicely compact. She had a beautiful shape in a small package. Her hair was shoulder length, a very light blond, her eyes were almost a startling green next to her fair skin, and her features were as fine and delicate as those of a perfectly crafted doll. She was wearing what must have once been a cool spring dress, soft fabric in earth tones that both floated and hugged her form, except that now, in most areas, the dress no longer floated; it was covered in blood. Caked with it.

"Jon Marcel is an artist," Jimmy said, as if that explained everything.

Mark arched a brow to him. "Meaning?"

Jimmy shrugged a little defensively. "Who knows? I mean, I hear some city paid a guy a fortune once to wrap some islands in pink in the name of art. I just mean that artists can be a little strange."

"Jimmy, what the hell are you getting at?"

"I—I—maybe they shared their conquests."

Mark arched a brow to him.

"Ah, come on, Mark, you know what I mean." Jimmy was just a little bit red-faced. He might be frank in his ogling of an appealing woman, but he wasn't the type to engage in too much male shop talk if the subject turned kinky.

"Ah, *ménage-à-trois?*" Mark said.

"Yeah."

"She doesn't look the type."

"How do you look a type?" Jimmy demanded defensively.

"Maybe you don't 'look' a type," Mark said. "But she still doesn't 'look' the type."

Some things defied explanation.

"Aren't the wildest thoughts supposed to lurk in the minds of the mildest people. Look at Superman's alter-ego—Clark Kent. I rest my case."

"Yeah," Mark muttered. They should be resting this case damned quickly. If just a few lab tests came back positive, there would be no doubt that Jon Marcel would be facing murder charges. He swallowed, determined not to betray how shaken he had been by the case, that he'd been entangled more than he should have been since he'd gotten the call from headquarters to head quickly for the murder scene. An hysterical tourist had called in after tripping over the body; the cops in uniform had informed him that they had arrived while the corpse was still warm.

Not so when he'd gotten there, just seconds before the guys from the coroner's office. No, she'd been cold then. Cold, lying in a pool of blood, her eyes still opened, all those dreams that had lived somewhere in her heart somehow seeming to reflect in those opened eyes. She had been a pretty woman. Pretty even in death. She might have been just lying there waiting for the life of her dreams to start, except that she lay in a pool of blood.

And the life within her had grown cold.

"Lieutenant?"

One of the uniforms had been talking to him as he knelt looking at the body. He'd gone cold himself. Had some trouble trying to get his breath. He stood. "Corby," he said, acknowledging the young beat officer. "What've we got?"

It was good as far as information went. So it seemed. There had been a trail of blood leading from the murder scene. To the residence of an Ann Marcel. And it turned out that Mrs. Ann Marcel had just put in a 911 call, and her husband, covered in blood, was in the middle of emergency surgery.

He again knelt down by the corpse of what had been a beautiful, if sad, woman. "So you fought back, baby. Good for you."

The lab techs were all there, taking samples

of anything they could, being especially careful to follow the blood trail to Ann Marcel's place.

Henry Lapp, an assistant at the coroner's office, told him, "Lee will take this one himself. I've given him a call at home; he's coming right in. You know Lee—he thinks we miss things if we take too long to get to an autopsy, so this one looks pretty pure and simple. She was cut up and she fought back and her murderer ran. We should be able to run right after him."

"Yeah," Mark had told him. "Maybe the guy will talk right away. Jimmy and I are heading straight over to the hospital. Ask Lee to hang on until I get to him."

Since then, he and Jimmy had been here. Waiting. Watching the small blond woman. Shaking their heads. Why did it seem that women fell so easily for the wrong men?

"To be fair," he heard himself say aloud, "I sure as hell don't know much about this guy. Or his wife." Again, he shook his head. She wasn't irrational; she wasn't hysterical. Her eyes occasionally filled with tears and overflowed as she listened, then spoke, then listened again. Mark was startled when his heart suddenly seemed to lurch within his chest—and tighten because of her. Fool, he warned himself impatiently. He'd been here, literally right here, in this very hospital, in somewhat similar circumstances, plenty of times before. He'd respected the pain of loved ones; but he'd kept his professional distance, and he'd been ready to question them politely, courteously—but relentlessly when necessary. He'd been here before, watching a woman sob over a man. But he'd never quite felt this absurd urge to comfort someone.

Especially when he was actually thinking she was surely more than a bit of an ass to weep over a fellow like this one.

Mark loved New Orleans. Loved it almost like a parent loves a kid. He'd grown up here; he knew the streets, knew the society, knew the dangers and the pleasures. New Orleans beckoned and harbored those from all walks of life. Crooked politicians, antiquarian belles, musicians, artists, writers, coffee connoisseurs. Sainted and very Catholic little ladies and men; street toughs with knives, guns, poison, and voodoo magic when all else failed. New Orleans could be trashy, tarnished—a place where a man needed to look over his shoulder every minute. It could be a place with a hundred people standing dead still in a square, white, black, Cajun, Hispanic, Northerner, Southerner, all mesmerized by the mournful tune of one sad old man putting his heart into a horn. It was the charming patter of patois French, the smell of delicious baking, the aroma of coffee, the charm of a wealth of flowers, the bustle of the Mississippi. To many, New Orleans could be pure charisma.

Still, he never misjudged the violence and danger of his city, yet he never forgot to love it despite that danger or violence. Back to peg one, and his odd feeling that he wanted to comfort this woman. He loved his city, but dammit, he'd been here before, waiting to talk to a perp on his deathbed, watching the tears of a wife or lover who just couldn't understand how her man had gone so bad. It wasn't that the sight didn't usually move him; it did. Pain was always hard to watch. But the years allowed a cop a certain removal. The job demanded it.

Maybe this evening just wasn't going to prove to be easy, period. It had taken an emotional toll on him since he'd first reached the scene of the crime.

Maybe things were just getting worse. He should step back. Let somebody else take on this one.

Yet he wasn't going to step back, and he knew it. So he kept standing there with Jimmy, waiting.

It didn't seem that there was really any mystery here. Gina L'Aveau was a stripper who was willing to take on a number of johns as well. She'd met up with an artist who was painting stripper/hookers, and something had gone wrong, something emotional had come up. He'd stabbed her; she'd fought back. She was dead, he was dying. Sad, plain, simple. One for the books that could be closed. God, why did he feel so damned bad? Christ, this was his job.

He was tired. He wanted to get on with it. He wanted to see if Jon Marcel had survived the surgery, and if there was a possibility that he might be able to talk. Tell them about his crime.

Now, as he watched, the doctor set a steadying hand on Ann Marcel's shoulder, then started down the hallway to Jimmy and Mark. He was a man in his mid-fifties, reeking of competence and solidity. "Gentlemen," he acknowledged, shaking their hands.

"Anything?" Mark asked.

The doctor shook his head. "It took us two hours to sew him back up. He lost a lot of blood. He's sliding in and out of consciousness right now, and I'm afraid that he's going to slip into a coma."

"You don't think there will be any way we can question him?" Mark asked.

"Certainly not tonight. We're going to have to do our best to keep him alive tonight."

"What are his chances?" Jimmy asked. Mark saw that Jimmy was staring at Ann Marcel. A nurse had come to her, and Ann Marcel was nodding her head gratefully. She started to follow the nurse.

The policewoman, Holly, started to follow Ann Marcel. The nurse halted her.

They weren't going to let the cops talk to Marcel, but they were going to let his wife in, so it seemed.

"You're letting Mrs. Marcel see him?" Mark queried politely.

"Sixty seconds' worth," the doctor said. "Sixty seconds' worth."

"Mrs. Marcel?"

The kindly nurse who had been so good to her since her frantic arrival in the ambulance with Jon was at her shoulder.

She'd come to tell her the cops were ready to talk to her, Ann thought.

She'd *felt* those cops. Since the two men had gotten there. They'd kept a courteous distance while they had all awaited word from the doctor, but still, despite the fact she'd been half insane with worry, she'd *felt* them there, watching her. She was anxious to talk to them, anxious to demand that they find Jon's attacker, because that would be doing something instead of just standing here so worried, and so powerless. . . .

Yet they watched her strangely. The one who looked like a sad and weary brown bear. And the other one. The tall fellow with the boxer's shoulders. Old eagle eye.

Well, he wasn't old. He wasn't young. Late thirties? Maybe middle forties? It was so difficult to tell with men. She thought grudgingly that men often seemed to improve with age. She suddenly had a mental image of a roomful of men wearing T-shirts with the caption "Aged to Perfection!"

Whatever his age, he did wear it well. In fact, she was horrified to realize she was wondering if he would appear as hard and rugged and tightly in shape if he wasn't wearing the jacket and trousers. She didn't think he actually worried about his physique; keeping fit was probably more of a casual thing with him, or so it appeared by the way he stood.

Nice body. Fine. The rest of him was intriguing as well.

His hair was auburn with silver streaks at the

temple, longish, brushing over his collar. He had a wonderfully masculine face, a *craggy* face, a Clint Eastwood, western-type face, all strong planes and angles, squared, firm jaw, good, high cheekbones.

It would be a great face to paint, she thought instantly. Full of character. Intelligence, strength, determination. Umm. Maybe pig-headedness. He watched her constantly. She was certain that he had her analyzed down to the bones. Maybe that was good. He'd find out what had happened to Jon.

Maybe not. Those silver eyes flicked over her with what might have been something like contempt. He'd looked at her and shaken his head a few times. It was irritating. Very irritating. Especially when she could *feel* his damned eyes, and felt compelled to watch him in return. Once, a rush of warmth had swept through her, and she'd turned to find him watching her. Up, down. Taking in details. What she looked like. What she wore. And what was she doing thinking about this?

Jon . . .

She was here because of Jon.

She didn't want to think about the cop who was watching her.

Still, wasn't it better to play twenty questions in her mind regarding a strange cop than it was to worry herself sick about Jon while she waited? Some macho by-the-book pain-in-the-ass she'd probably never have to see again. *Yes!* Yes, think about this guy. He was annoying, maybe, but he kept her from being so afraid for Jon. Don't think about Jon's injuries or his chances, think about the man.

The cop—in plainclothes. Casual tweed jacket over Dockers. They had told her he was a cop when he'd come in with his long-faced buddy, but it wouldn't have mattered. The second she'd felt those eyes, she'd known what he was. And that she was being assessed. She was anxious to say anything she could that would help with Jon; equally, she was strangely uneasy. She was drawn to the man—admittedly, he was disturbingly attractive. But she felt defensive already. Why? The cops were the good guys. On her side.

"If they're ready for me—" she began.

"No, no, dear. They're going to give you a second to see Mr. Marcel." The nurse took her hand.

"A second—"

"Well, a minute or so. He's just come out of tough surgery, and he's hanging in. He needs complete rest if he's to survive."

"But he has a good chance—"

"Now, Mrs. Marcel, you're a strong woman, and the doctor has been honest with you, right?"

"Yeah," Ann told her.

She was strong. Right.

But once she had been propelled into Jon's cubicle in recovery, Ann swallowed hard, finding it difficult to look at him. Now, she could allow her limbs to feel like Jell-O, allow her knees to give; whereas before, when he'd been bleeding everywhere, she'd had to keep her wits about her. She'd had to do her best to stop that bleeding; to warm him, to keep him from going into shock.

She was helpless now. Those who really knew what they were doing were taking care of him. He'd been sewn up. Painstakingly. Inside and out. Now, tubes brought life-giving fluid to his veins. More tubes helped him breathe. He was ashen against the white hospital sheets. She was trying so hard to be stoic and strong, but she felt a little bit like the Wicked Witch of the West—she was melting. Watching him with all his tubes and pallor, she inhaled a ragged sob. She felt the nurse's hand on her shoulder. "I'm so sorry, Mrs. Marcel, remember, I can only give you a minute. . . ."

A minute. Ann knew she couldn't waste that minute standing there like an idiot.

She hurried forward to the bed. Thoughts crowded her mind. She didn't want to lose him. She loved him, terribly. Not as a husband— they'd never been meant to be man and wife— but he was her best friend. Her toughest critic; yet, when she was down, he was the first to cheer her. When she did well, he celebrated with all his heart. She touched his ashen hand—the one without the I.V. needle in it. He looked like death, but she felt the warmth of life in him. Encouraged, she clutched his hand more tightly. "You're going to be all right, you're going to be all right. I promise. I'll see to it. And I promise, too, I'm going to make sure that whoever did this awful thing doesn't get away with it." She drew his hand to her lips, kissed the warm, dry flesh. "Jon, you will be all right. I promise."

"He's still feeling the effects of the anesthesia," the kindly, gray-haired nurse offered. "And," she added regretfully, "it's doubtful he'll regain consciousness tonight. But the *sub*conscious is a wonderful thing. He may be able to hear you, dear. We never know. But we always encourage talking to our patients."

Ann nodded, managing a smile for the nurse. "Jon—"

To her amazement, his eyes opened. They were hazy; then they seemed to focus on her.

His lips moved. Breath came from them. Breath, and some kind of a whisper.

Ann leaned closer to him. "Jon, it's all right. Jon, you're in the hospital. Wonderful people are looking after you. Wonderful doctors and nurses."

He moved his lips again. He seemed so anxious! No matter what she tried to say, no matter how she tried to reassure him, he seemed desperate to speak.

"Jon, you mustn't try so hard to speak. You need rest, you need to heal—"

"Ann—"

He was saying her name.

"I'm here, Jon."

He moved his head. *No.*

"Jon, please . . ."

The hand she held tightened. Just barely. She leaned closer to him.

"Annabella's . . ."

His eyes fell shut.

The tension left his hand.

Ann inhaled again, dizzy. He'd died on her, oh, God, he'd died . . .

"He, he . . . ," she gasped out.

"It's all right, Mrs. Marcel."

"But—"

"Honey, he's unconscious," the nurse said gently, taking her shoulders. "See all those monitors. That's his heartbeat right there, on that screen to the left of the bed by his head. His vital signs seem to be sound and stable. That's very good."

Ann nodded blindly.

"I know that you being there just now was a big help to him," the nurse continued. "What was he trying to do? Whisper your name?"

Ann turned and looked at the nurse in surprise.

"He . . . ," she began, then cut off.

No. That would have been nice, of course. Jon seeing her, recognizing her. Saying her name.

Except that he hadn't been saying her name. *Annabella's.*

He had whispered the name of the club—the strip joint—where he had gone to watch his *Red Light Ladies.*

He was savagely hurt. Possibly still dying. He had come to her, fallen into her arms.

And through it all, he had said just two things.

I didn't do it. Oh, God, I didn't do it, I didn't do it!

And now . . .

Annabella's.

She turned back to look at him, biting into her lower lip. She prayed for him.

She damned him.

Didn't do what, Jon? Look at what's happened to you, and look what you've given me to go on. What the hell didn't you do, Jon? And why the hell would you look at me and whisper, Annabella's?

Three

Jacques Moret sat at a select table at Divinity's, a man impeccably dressed in a lightweight charcoal gray suit, silk shirt, crimson vest and designer tie. He had a long, slim, aristocrat's face, bright hazel eyes, sleek dark hair, and very full, sensual lips. His smile gave away dimples in his cheeks. He was handsome and charming; his elocution was excellent, with the slightest touch of a drawl that added to his completely masculine charm. When he walked through a crowd, feminine eyes followed wherever he went. He always smelled subtly and pleasantly of expensive aftershave. He cultivated his natural ability to seduce, and had, since he first discovered the power of his charm at age twelve, wielded that power with dispassionate pleasure and amusement. Tonight, he dined with the usually level-headed CEO of a tour company, a smartly dressed and chic woman in her mid-thirties. She was the type, he had decided, who usually spat out her orders with the precision of a drill sergeant. Her perfectly tinted hair was curled fashionably at her nape; she might well have worn her custom red suit down a runway in Paris. Her makeup was perfect; her nails were perfect. She was a regal no-nonsense beauty of the contemporary business world, the type taking over the business world and sending good men out pounding the streets for a job—while crying out for the ERA—he thought a little resentfully.

But not tonight.

Tonight she was falling for him. Ms. Exec was beginning to giggle into her wine—a select chablis from a very special year and very special winery. Select not just because of its quality and age, but because of its potency. One thing he'd learned early in business was to take every advantage. He didn't think twice about getting his prospective clients drunk, nor did he suffer the slightest qualm of guilt regarding the matter of seducing them.

Ms. Ellie Exec, he thought of her, disregarding her real surname entirely. Sometime in the future, it would matter again. Tonight would be a special conquest. His secretary had learned that her coworkers considered her to be an ice queen with unbreachable defenses. She was the power behind one of the biggest travel agencies in California, and what she could do for his riverboat and hotel enterprises was phenomenal. A good night tonight and he'd not only prove himself beyond the shadow of a doubt, but after stripping her mentally throughout the day, he was truly intrigued about the possibility of discovering that her undergarments were as deliciously red and perfect as her designer nails and suit. He'd make it worthwhile for her; she'd remember New Orleans with fondness for a long, long time. By morning, he'd have a piece of both her business—and her.

He lifted his wineglass to hers, smiling. "So you are enjoying Divinity's?"

"Le poison est magnifique!" she replied. Her French was good. Better than the usual dull, stuttering typical Anglo-American slaughter of the language. She had blue eyes and that perfectly coiffed platinum hair. He liked blondes. He'd learned when he was young that there was—no matter what the century—a certain contempt among many Creoles and Anglos for the Cajuns, Creoles being descended from the French and Spanish while the Cajuns were descended from the Acadians cast out of Nova Scotia. *Coon hounds,* his people were sometimes called. *Coons.* And from the most illiterate—*coon asses.* Yet lots of people got past prejudices. He thought he had, more or less.

But most Cajuns were dark-haired. For some reason, he liked seducing blond women. Actually, he just liked seducing women. But blondes . . .

The quick and easy conquest of a basically virtuous blonde always gave him the sense of a double-edged victory.

He poured more wine into her glass from the bottle sitting in the ice bucket at his side. "I'm glad you're enjoying our famous Divinity's."

"Are you about to tell me it's not popular with the locals?"

He shook his head; his eyes locked with her blue ones. "New Orleans is world-renowned for its restaurants and food with sound good reason. The locals often come here. But there are many interesting places here. For music, for dance. Jazz. Café au lait. Beignets."

"Where is the best place for jazz?" she asked him.

He arched a brow, a subtle, half smile slipping into his features.

"A strange place."

"What do you mean, a strange place."

"You can walk down any street in the Vieux Carre and hear wonderful jazz. But the best . . ."

"Yes?" she said, leaning closer to him across the table. He spoke softly on purpose, drawing her nearer and nearer to him.

"Would you hear some of the best jazz, then?"

She frowned. "Is it in a—dangerous area?"

He shook his head. "You'd never be in danger with me."

"Then . . ."

"There is jazz . . . and there is dance."

"What kind of dance?"

She knew. Her blue eyes were wide. Her lips were slightly parted. She took a very long sip of her wine. Good. A few more sips of wine. A trip to the club. She'd be on him like a ball of fire.

"Exotic dance," he said quietly.

Her mouth formed an *O*.

"Perhaps too exotic for you. . . ."

"Do . . . nice—I mean, er regular, women go there."

He smiled. His best, most devastating smile. "Even the most chaste of the Louisiana Old

Guard go now and then. Yet, of course, it is a challenge, I imagine, for a woman like you."

"Do I look so stuffy?" she inquired.

Another smile. "You are a beautiful woman."

"But a stuffy one."

He poured her more wine. "You are beautiful."

"I'd like to see this place. What's the name of it?"

"Annabella's."

His hand had just curled over hers when he saw his secretary slipping into the restaurant, weaving his way through the tables. Ryan Martin. An earnest young man with freckles and red hair, he wore a worried look.

Jacques cursed him in silence while keeping his smile in place for Ms. Ellie Exec.

"Mr. Moret, forgive the intrusion," Ryan said, breathless as he reached the table.

Ellie Exec wrenched her hand back.

"Ryan . . . you knew I wished not to be disturbed." He kept just how much he hadn't wanted to be disturbed from his voice.

"This is incredibly important."

"Ellie . . . you will excuse me for just a moment?"

He rose. The blonde rose as well. "Actually, I should just call it a day. Thank you so much, Mr. Moret. Dinner was wonderful."

"But, wait, it's so early . . ."

"Merci, merci. We'll talk again tomorrow."

She started out. Jacques was so mad he thought he would have punched Ryan if they hadn't been in a public place. He dropped his napkin on the table and sank into his chair, rubbing his temples.

"What is it?" he snapped icily.

Ryan sat across from him. "Gina L'Aveau's body was found in a dark alley tonight."

Jacques' hand dropped. He stared at Ryan, started to reach across the table and grab him by the collar, but managed to refrain.

"What—what—"

Hell. What time had he left her?

"When?" he said.

"Right after eight. I—I didn't mean to interrupt. But she is your kin, even if distant. I—I had to tell you."

Jacques nodded. "Yes, yes, of course." He stood abruptly, no longer interested in Ryan.

"Jacques—they'd be arresting that artist fellow right now if he wasn't all cut up himself."

"What?" Jacques paused, barking out the word.

"The artist—Marcel—made it to his ex-wife's place, bleeding like a stuck pig. The cops followed him there."

"Oh?"

"He may not make it through the night."

"Ah." Jacques stared at Ryan. "You did right. You did right to come to me. Keep up on the situation. And pay my tab. Tip well."

He left the restaurant. Miss Ellie Exec had surely had plenty of time to catch a cab by now.

But she hadn't. She was sauntering down the street. He watched her for a moment.

He was a gambling man. One in a wild, tormented mood. He hurried down the street, catching up with her. He grabbed her arm, spun her around. Before she could speak or protest, he kissed her with hot, open-mouthed fury and passion. He held her close, hands slipping beneath her hem and cupping her buttocks, pressing her against his sex. She was stiff for a second; then she melted like butter. He'd judged right. She'd spent so long proving herself untouchable that she was desperate for a man.

She finally managed to break her lips from his. "Jacques, we're on the street, for God's sake!"

"We can remedy that."

He hailed a cab quickly, urging her into the vehicle. While the driver brought them to their destination, he discreetly slid his hand between her thighs. She was wearing a garter belt.

It was probably red. He liked garter belts, and he liked red. But it didn't matter. Gina was dead. It didn't matter who this woman was anymore. She was going to get what she wanted.

Gina was dead.

And it looked like an artist was going to fry for it. If he lived.

He turned to his Ellie Exec again and started kissing her passionately.

She was going to like it hard and dirty.

Exactly the way it would be.

The doctor was definitely a good solid man. He stood his ground while sympathizing with the difficulties of the cops. "Don't worry about Ann Marcel having a chance to see Mr. Marcel tonight. She'll get to look at him and hold his hand. I assure you, he can't help you find his attacker tonight, fellows. He's not going to say anything lucid."

"We didn't have to have lucid," Jimmy said.

Mark cleared his throat. "You've been in surgery with Marcel, Doctor, so you may not have heard that we suspect that Marcel was wounded while he was murdering a hooker."

"I'd gotten wind from one of the nurses that there'd been a prostitute murdered in the same vicinity. And I'm not blind to the fact that the hospital is crawling with cops now."

"We really could have used a few minutes with him," Mark said.

The doctor sighed. "Look, I know you boys have a rough time trying to do your jobs, but you've got to understand mine. I'm sworn to save lives. There are already a bunch of uniforms in the hallway, watching your man. Trust me—he isn't going to get up and walk away tonight to avoid questioning."

"What is his condition?" Mark asked.

"He was stabbed several times, but no irreparable damage was done to any vital organ. The loss of blood was tremendous."

"She must have fought him fiercely," Jimmy murmured.

"Someone fought him fiercely," the doctor commented.

Jimmy made an impatient sound. "Doctor,

Jon Marcel dripped blood from the alley to the front door of that apartment! Sir—"

"The doctor's right," Mark said, his tone slightly dry. "This is America. A man is innocent until proven guilty."

"Right. Even if he's caught with a smoking gun and a dead man at his feet."

The doctor smiled wryly. "It must feel pretty rotten for you guys at times, but think back. Men—and women—have been executed in the past for crimes they didn't commit. You can't dig up a corpse and say, 'Hey, we're sorry!' Sometimes the legal system sucks, but in a way, it works better than can be expected with society what it is, huh?"

"Doctor, you're right," Mark said. "It's just been a tough night, a long night. And we risk our lives to apprehend criminals who walk—and then head right back into the street to wreak havoc. Anyway, the D.A.'s office probably will put out an arrest warrant for Marcel; I believe we've sufficient evidence to hand him over to the district attorney. Rest assured, Marcel will get a fair trial. If he lives—since it seems his fate is up to God at the moment—his future will be decided by a jury of his peers."

"She's back," Jimmy muttered suddenly.

Mark's gaze instantly followed the direction in which Jimmy stared.

"She?" the doctor queried blankly.

Mark indicated Ann Marcel, who had now returned to the waiting room. She had sunk into a chair beside the rookie policewoman whose job it was to keep her calm and mollified until the detectives had their chance to talk to her. Ann Marcel still seemed to have it together. The young policewoman looked like frazzled hell.

"Oh, my God!" the doctor said indignantly. "You don't think that—"

"No, Doctor, we don't think that the wife had anything to do with this," Mark assured him.

"Oh, thank God! She's an incredible woman," the doctor said. "But you just never know these days. I've heard of husbands who shot their wives over changing the damned channel on the television. And vice versa, of course. You just never do know. Maybe the Brits have got it right. The Brits say we've caused a lot of our own problems, with our 'right to bear arms.' They may have a good point. The London bobbies don't carry firearms, except in special cases."

Mark and Jimmy exchanged a glance. Nice thought. Mark knew he sure as hell didn't want to be sent out into the streets of New Orleans unarmed.

"Well, sir," Jimmy said to the doctor, "Jon Marcel was stabbed. No gun involved. At the moment, it appears that he slit the throat of a prostitute in a dark alley and that she had her own weapon and fought back."

"How far from the wife's place?" the doctor asked.

"Three blocks," Mark said. "You know the French Quarter. Tight spaces. Good streets right next to shady lanes."

"Amazing," the doctor murmured. "He bled all the way into her arms."

"Is there anything you can tell us about Jon Marcel's wounds, Doctor?" Mark asked.

"There were five to his abdomen and chest. Serrated knife, caused a lot of ripping. Thrust with a great deal of strength."

"She was fighting for her life," Mark muttered. Jimmy stared at him, his eyes narrowed.

"Jon Marcel has a fifty-fifty chance. As I said, no vital organ suffered irreversible damage; it's the blood loss we're fighting to combat now."

Mark produced a card. "Doctor, if there's anything—"

"Call you. Yes, Lieutenant LaCrosse, I certainly will." He inclined his head toward Ann Marcel. "If you need to talk to Mrs. Marcel, you should do so soon. The woman has gone through a lot this evening. She kept her husband alive before the paramedics responded to her 911. Gentlemen, good evening. I'll do my absolute very best to keep Marcel alive as well, I assure you."

"Thank you, Doctor," Mark said. They watched him walk back through a pair of swinging doors.

"The wife," Jimmy murmured.

"Umm," Mark agreed.

They walked forward, toward the group of hospital-generic chairs in the hospital-generic waiting room. Mark nodded imperceptibly to the young policewoman, who sighed visibly with her relief. "Mrs. Marcel, Lieutenant LaCrosse and Detective Deveaux are here now to speak with you. They'll take care of you, but if I can help you in any way . . ."

Ann Marcel's eyes were extraordinarily green—framed in red as they were from her tears. She set her small hand with its neatly clipped, filed nails on the policewoman's. "Thank you, Holly, you've been a tremendous help. I don't need anyone to take care of me—I just want to see Jon's attacker caught."

Mark and Jimmy glanced quickly at one another again. Jimmy shrugged and inched slightly to the background to watch the exchange as Mark hunkered down in front of Ann Marcel. "Mrs. Marcel, I need you to tell me exactly what happened this evening."

She swallowed, nodded. Her eyes started to fill with tears again. She blinked them away and sat tall and straight, composed. "I was waiting . . . I admit, I didn't think much of Jon's determination to paint strippers at first, but my God, his work was so good! I'm sorry, I don't mean to be rambling, but it's all important in this, I think, my point being that when tonight started, I was thinking that I had been wrong. I had been worried about him, about the people he was meeting, the places he was going, but tonight, I'd decided that his paintings of the 'ladies' are so very good, that he was perhaps right in pursuing these young women to understand more about their lives. But he must have become involved with some very wrong people while he was working on those paintings. Tonight, I was waiting for him. We were going to go and see a special showing of his *Red Light Ladies*. I thought that he was running late. The next thing I knew, he was banging on the door, falling down, bleeding . . ."

Mark cleared his throat. "So, Mrs. Marcel, you were aware of his connections with . . . er, certain club women?"

She stared at him blankly for a moment. The hint of a smile twitched at her lips. "Club women? Strippers, Lieutenant? Prostitutes?" Absurdly, he felt himself redden. She lowered her eyes for a moment, then said, "Well, of course. I've already seen some of the paintings. Oh, God, I just pray that the fact that his movements are very well known will help you catch his attacker. Jon must know who hurt him so badly, but . . ." She inhaled, a catch in her breath. Mark was afraid she'd burst into tears, but she controlled herself. "First," she said in a level tone, "I've just got to pray that he lives."

"Mrs. Marcel, did he say anything to you? Did he give you anything, drop anything in your apartment?" Mark asked.

"Give me anything? Like what?"

"He didn't give you anything?"

"Lieutenant, he fell against my door and crashed down to the floor. No, he didn't give me anything."

"Did he say anything to you when you just went in to see him?" Mark demanded.

"Say anything about what?" she queried in

turn, obviously becoming suspicious of his motives in questioning her.

"About tonight. About what happened."

She shook her head, wetting her lips. She was lying, and she wasn't good at lying. She didn't like lying. But she was like a mother bear with an injured cub. She was going to protect her man. And it appeared that she thought the police were totally out of line.

"For God's sake," Jimmy suddenly blurted out, "you must know something! You do, and he must have said something when he reached you, dropped something!"

"Like what?" she snapped.

"Jimmy!" Mark warned.

Too late. "Like a murder weapon," Jimmy said.

"Murder weapon?" she repeated, stunned. "What is the matter with the two of you!" She shook her head in disgust. "Officer—" she began angrily.

"Detective," Jimmy sighed.

"Detective, sir," she said pointedly and impatiently, "Jon came into my apartment like a spigot spewing blood. He was the one attacked—he wasn't carrying a murder weapon. You two definitely seem to be missing the main point here. Pay attention, comprehend! Jon was attacked. Nearly killed. And he's fighting for his life right now."

Jimmy was about to erupt with angry words; a glance at Mark stopped him. He lifted a hand in aggravation and defeat, leaving the explanation of the situation up to Mark.

"Mrs. Marcel, I'm afraid that you haven't been apprised of the full situation as of yet."

She was tense, careful. "What *full* situation?"

He watched her closely, pausing only a second. "Mrs. Marcel, a young woman—a stripper—was killed just a few blocks from your home. The trail of your husband's blood led from the corpse of the murdered girl straight to your doorway."

She stood, nearly knocking him backward in her abrupt movement. He just caught himself, coming to his feet as well.

"You wretched bastards!" she hissed softly. "I thought you'd come here to help apprehend the person who did this to Jon—"

"Mrs. Marcel—"

"And all you want to do is take the easy way out. Accuse him of a crime he didn't commit!"

"Mrs. Marcel!" Mark grated. "You must realize, the facts are what they are. A young woman is dead—"

"Jon is half-dead!"

"He left a trail of blood—"

"Yes! His blood."

Jimmy cleared his throat. "The blood has yet to be analyzed, but by the visual evidence, it seems that we'll be finding matches with your husband's blood and the dead woman's along the trail."

Ann Marcel's perfect porcelain-doll features were sheet white. Mark thought that she was going to fall. He reached out a hand to steady her. She slapped it away.

"Jon didn't kill anyone. Talk about your visual evidence! I haven't seen any of it, and it's plain to me that someone killed your young woman, Jon tried to stop the attack, and was nearly killed himself in the effort!"

"Mrs. Marcel—" Jimmy began placatingly.

"He didn't do it."

"If you could just help us—" Mark tried.

"The wife is always the last to know," Jimmy muttered beneath his breath. Audibly.

"Don't be such an ass, officer!" Ann Marcel said indignantly. "What, you have no interest in doing your jobs? Go for the obvious?"

Mark gave Jimmy a warning glare. She'd be complaining to the D.A.'s office about police badgering. He wanted this one by the book. "Mrs. Marcel, I'm afraid when evidence is obvious, we've no choice but to use it. We have no reason to wish Mr. Marcel any ill—I'm afraid that at the moment, evidence does point in his direction."

"You've already got him hanged."

"We don't hang people in Louisiana—they die by lethal injection!" Jimmy said indignantly.

A gasp escaped her.

"Jimmy," Mark said quietly.

The woman spun on Mark. "He's innocent, and he'll be proven innocent. You—bastard!"

"Now, wait a minute—"

"Does police brutality work two ways?" Jimmy demanded. "She's awfully damned brutal!"

"Oh, hell!" Mark muttered.

But the diminutive blonde was staring at him again, small shoulders squared, her stance rigid and proud. An absolute wall of defense and indignation. "Jon is innocent. He told me so."

"What?" Mark demanded harshly. "Then you did know—"

She shook her head, pale flesh reddening, lashes flicking over her deep green eyes. "When he reached my apartment, just before he lost consciousness, he said, 'I didn't do it.' I'd no idea what he was talking about. Of course, now I do. And he must have known that *lazy* policemen would immediately try to charge him with murder. And I'm telling you, I know Jon. He must have been trying to save her life!"

"Perhaps you could let us in on what else he said?" Jimmy drawled.

"That's it. I've told you. Oh, no, wait a minute. I think he also said, 'Oh, God! I didn't do it.' But that's it. Do you want to arrest me? I'm covered in blood."

"Mrs. Marcel—" Mark tried.

"I am covered in blood! Doesn't that make me guilty?" she demanded again.

"Mrs. Marcel, if you don't tell us everything you know, you just may be guilty of complicity in murder," Mark heard himself lash out suddenly. "And, yes, we damned well may arrest you if—"

"Mark!"

It was Jimmy's turn to caution him. What the hell was the matter with him?

Women!

Ten deep breaths. He had been at riot situations where people screamed and spit at him—he'd handled that with dead calm. Earlier he'd wanted to take this vision into his arms and comfort her; now he itched to slap her.

She stretched out her arms. "Lieutenant, go ahead. Arrest me. Cuff me." She offered him a challenging smile, her eyes bright emerald daggers. "My attorneys will have you in jail before you can blink, Lieutenant."

"Will they?"

"He didn't do it," she insisted quietly.

He exhaled, watching her. Even covered in blood, tear-stained, she was still all too appealing.

There didn't seem to be any justice in the world. He had to find a killer. The killer was most probably her husband. She was going to fight him all the way.

Gina L'Aveau had been a stripper and prostitute, yet Gina L'Aveau deserved justice the same as anyone else. And he was going to see to it that she got it.

"Did Jon Marcel say anything else to you, Mrs. Marcel?" he demanded. "Did he speak to you when you just went in to see him."

She stared at him. Green eyes wide on his. "No," she said flatly.

She was lying. He knew it.

There was no way he could prove it tonight.

"Can we see you home, Mrs. Marcel?"

"No, thank you."

"The streets can be dangerous this late at night."

"How could they be, Lieutenant, with you and your partner out in them?"

"We'll see you home—"

"I intend to sleep here."

Again, Mark produced one of his cards from the inner pocket of his jacket. "If—"

"I know. If I think of anything, call you."

He smiled grimly, staring at her. "If you think of anything in the next few hours, you can call me at the morgue. A woman is dead, you will recall."

Her lashes fell. Her cheeks whitened again. But her eyes quickly focused on his once more.

"Jon Marcel is not guilty, Lieutenant. I'm convinced Jon is where he is now because he's a good man, and he attempted to save her life."

"Your faith is quite commendable, Mrs. Marcel. But it's not enough. We need to know everything and anything. Jon Marcel said nothing more to you?"

"No."

"Absolutely nothing?"

"I told you what he said, Lieutenant."

"But he said nothing more?"

"No."

He nodded. He longed to call her a liar to her face. Not only that, she wasn't a good liar. She probably spent most of her time telling the truth.

But she was on the defensive right now. He'd probably have to resort to ancient torture—the rack, thumbscrews or the like—to get her to talk right now. And no matter what kind of bad press the force might get upon occasion, he thought dryly, they had yet to resort to thumbscrews.

"Jimmy, I think we're finished here," he said. He kept his eyes locked on Ann Marcel's. "Mrs. Marcel, it's quite obvious you're not fond of my company, nor that of my partner. Please don't behave stupidly because of that fact. You're going to want to go home. To shower and change if nothing else. Don't go home alone. Officer Holly Severt will be happy to see you back when you're ready to leave. I'm not sure if the police have finished up gathering evidence at your place or not, but Holly can stay the night as well, to look after you."

"Thank you, Lieutenant. I don't believe I need to be looked after," she said.

"No?" Mark crossed his arms over his chest. "If you're right, and your husband was attacked, you could be in very grave danger yourself, Mrs. Marcel. Especially if you're not sharing with us everything you know—everything that he might have said."

She didn't reply. She appeared somewhat pale again, but that was all.

"Good night, Mrs. Marcel. Don't go home alone."

This time, she didn't dispute him.

She stood like a regal statue, despite the fact that she was laden with dry blood. Small, delicate in face and stature, soft blond hair framing her face.

She could be hard as nails, he warned himself.

Obviously. Because when he turned to leave her, he knew for a fact that she had created a wall against him.

She was lying through her teeth.

Somewhere along the line, Marcel had said something else to her.

Something that mattered.

He knew it. Cop gut reaction.

Marcel had said something to her that would be the key to all the answers. What the hell was it?

And how in hell was he going to get it out of her?

Four

Annabella's was already in full swing for the evening when the girls began to whisper nervously back in the dressing room. "Undressing" room, Gina L'Aveau had called it. Shaking her head, Cindy McKenna wiped tears of disbelief from her face over the events of the evening.

Things had begun fairly normally at the club that night. Then an off-duty cop had brought in the word that Gina was dead. The guy who had done it was in the hospital, half-dead, probably dying himself. It was the artist, the cop had said. A New Orleans home-grown son, a fine handsome white man, apparently just freaked out over something Gina had said, something in her life. Oddly enough, the showing of Jon Marcel's paintings of his *Red Light Ladies* had just opened; if the cop had things straight, the paintings were selling like hot cakes.

Nothing like a bit of the kinky or macabre to boost sales, Cindy thought resentfully.

The painting of Gina wasn't in with the showing. Jon Marcel hadn't finished his rendition of her. Not yet. Cindy had seen it, though—and it was his best. Everything fine and beautiful about

Gina had been caught in that painting. Jon had said that he would never sell it.

Jon hadn't committed the murder. Cindy knew it. For a fact. He'd cared about Gina. He'd cared about all the girls. He'd been curious about them. Like a writer might have been curious, like any man who wanted to find out about people and tell their stories. Only Jon Marcel told his stories with his paints. So the cops had the wrong guy.

And it didn't matter if Jon Marcel was wearing Gina's blood. Marcel hadn't done it. Simple. Case closed. Cindy wondered if she'd get a chance to see Jon. Maybe she'd go to church tomorrow morning and say a few prayers. Maybe she'd go see Mama Lili Mae out in the bayou and try a potion to keep him alive. Maybe she'd try both prayers and voodoo to help with the situation. Cindy McKenna had left her home and gone for nearly four years to a good Ivy League college, but it just seemed true that you could take the girl out of the bayou, you just couldn't take the bayou out of the girl. A good Catholic bayou girl went to church.

And she went to Mama Lili Mae's.

"Cindy, you're on," April Jagger called to her, something of a warning note in her tone. April was tall, lithe, stunningly beautiful. Her skin was such a silky shade of black that almost everyone in creation felt the temptation to touch it. No one did. April was married. She danced at the club, and that was that. Dancing made her good money. She had a one-year-old baby girl and in-

tended to move far away from Louisiana within
the next few years. April hadn't had the opportunity for a college education herself, but she
was smart. Her father had died in a storm working on another man's boat; her mother had
raised eight children alone. April and her husband, Marty, one of the four male dancers at the
club, had already invested their incomes well.

"Honey, you're on!" April persisted.

Duval got ticked when his girls didn't make
their cues on time. He could be a tough boss.
Harry Duval, like a lot of his girls, had grown
up the hard way, half in the bayou, half in the
streets. Somehow, Harry had come out one strik-
ing-looking man. There was white blood in him
and there was black blood in him, and he was
copper-toned with surprising green-gold eyes
and strong, well-molded features. He kept himself up, too. At six-something, he was tall and
powerful. He'd never beat a girl, not that Cindy
had heard, and modern day as it might be, lots
of guys who ran clubs still beat their women. He
paid fair; when his girls kept men "company,"
he expected a commission. And no girl had to
take on any john. Working for Harry might be
sad, and Cindy had enjoyed her years of education enough to know that she was damned sad;
but life being what it was, she had responsibili-
ties, and Harry kept her supporting those re-
sponsibilities.

"I'm going; I'm on my way," she promised
April. Usually, they would have joked. They
would have made some silly comment to one

another. Not tonight. They were both white-faced. Gina had been murdered.

"You okay, honey?" April asked her.

"Yeah."

April shivered fiercely. "I'm not. I mean, you think a girl has met a decent guy, and . . . my God, do you think he could have done that to Gina?"

"You mean Jon?"

"Yeah, I mean Jon."

"No. No, I don't," Cindy said.

"Stranger things have happened, I suppose."

"Yeah, sure. But—"

"But what?"

Cindy shrugged. "Gina was keeping lots of company; she had lots of friends." Again, she hesitated. "Gina was a magnet. People fell for her, loved her. She made people mad because they loved her sometimes. Friends turned enemy and the like."

"Well, you be careful, do you hear? I've got Marty, and I won't be leaving here without him, I can promise you."

"I'll be careful. Very careful," Cindy promised, shivering herself.

"Get going!" April urged.

Cindy hurried from the dressing room hallway to the stage wings. She was somewhat breathless when she heard the announcer.

"Here she is, gentlemen—and you ladies out there enjoying the fine, sweet jazz sounds of Annabella's—a little bit of ever-lovin' fluff from home-grown waters, Miss Delilah Delite!"

The voice booming huskily over the speakers introduced Cindy. Some of the girls used their own names, or stage names that played off their own names. She did not. On stage, she was a different person.

The lights were down as she took her position by the long, phallic dance pole stage center. The music started with a slow gyration. She followed it with practiced undulations of her body, letting her Grecian costume—held together in strategic locations with Velcro—flow sensually.

Full house tonight. Men were packed into the tables right by the stage. All men. Women did frequent the club, many of them, as a matter of fact. Some nouveau riche, some tourists, some locals who just really knew where to find the best local jazz music. And there were, of course, the four male dancers—each guy in a different shade, built like Adonis. But despite the male appearances, women usually sat at the back tables, in the shadows. Some necked, some sipped drinks. Sometimes they watched when the girls danced; sometimes they didn't.

Cindy knew her routine. It was as natural as breathing. It was easy enough to follow with her mind engaged elsewhere.

With Gina.

Gina was dead. They'd be crucifying Jon Marcel for what had happened.

Gina's killer would walk free.

Would walk free . . . maybe. Oh, God, would they pin it on Jon? Would everyone else associated with Gina still be in danger now?

She was jarred from her thoughts at the end of her number when well-known sounds of one of the trumpets suddenly halted. The other musicians quickly picked up the sound and the beat. Someone not accustomed to the perfection of the jazz band might not have even noticed a slip in the music.

Cindy looked toward the dais across the room where the Dixie Boys played.

Crouched down on the floor, swaying her hips to the last few notes of her routine, she tossed back her hair to watch what was going on. Gregory Hanson. She had known, of course. She loved his trumpet, loved his talent, and she knew instantly that he had been the one to suddenly cease to play.

The news had just gotten to the band. Gina was dead.

Gregory was leaving the dais.

He was a huge man, muscled like a prizefighter, ebony black, sleek as a panther. Virile, striking. A power in himself. As Cindy watched, he strode across the room.

Only to be stopped by Harry Duval.

The men were probably shouting; they were both tense and fierce. Furious. Arguing.

Yet, miraculously, no one seemed to realize or notice the altercation. No one noticed because the band kept playing, and because the gentlemen in the room had burst into applause for her dance.

And her final pose, she was quite certain.

Gregory slammed a palm against Harry Duval's shoulder. Harry's eyes narrowed, sharp and glittering, but he didn't respond with violence. He set a hand on Gregory's shoulder, speaking softly and quickly.

The two men disappeared together, stepping through the crowds and outside of the club.

Cindy wondered just when Gina had been found, if the police had determined when she had been murdered. Neither man had reached the club until ten P.M. that night. She hadn't gotten there until nine, and the men had come after her.

The applause continued to crash down around her. She rose, smiled, bowed, waved. She spun around to leave the stage, exiting with all the speed that she could.

Only then did she allow the tears to slide down her cheeks. Tears of pain for a friend. And tears of . . . fear.

For herself.

Dr. Lee Minh, one of the city's top medical examiners, would perform the autopsy on Gina L'Aveau. He and Jimmy and Mark had worked together often enough to cement some strong professional bonds between them.

When they left the hospital, Mark sent Jimmy home and went on to the morgue himself. Lee had prepped the body for autopsy, then waited for Mark.

"Sure you want to be here for the whole

thing?" Lee asked him. "You know I'll give you a complete, detailed report."

Gina lay on a stainless steel gurney, naked, ready for Lee's knife.

He should go home, Mark thought. No one required him to be here. Lee would give him a detailed report. Lee missed nothing.

He walked to the gurney, looking down at Gina. The dead stripper had once been a beautiful girl, not yet too hardened by the life she had chosen to lead. Her lifeblood had drained from her through the gash at her throat; she was as pale as snow. Her eyes were now closed. Minus the gaping red gash, she might have been Snow White asleep on a pillow, dark hair still rich and lustrous, framing the white beauty of her face.

He owed her.

He backed away. "If I'm not bothering you, I'll hang around," he told Lee.

Lee nodded.

The medical examiner began without touching a knife. He commented on every scrape, bruise and tiny wound on her body, noting his findings clearly for the microphone suspended above the gurney where Gina lay. He was slow, methodical, detailed. With an assistant, he scraped underneath Gina's nails. Swabs were done of her body orifices. She'd engaged in sex during the day, but it didn't appear that the act had been forced. The sperm would be analyzed, possibly helping to pinpoint her killer.

Lee's voice droned on. None of his findings was surprising.

Yet, no matter how professional and courteous Lee's treatment of Gina's body was, Mark was forced to think of how impersonal and humiliating death could be.

He ached for the dead woman on the slab. Meat. She was dead now; her butchering was still going on.

Lines were drawn; Gina's chest was opened. More fluids were taken for the lab. Organs were removed for testing. As Mark watched and listened, Lee gave his conclusive statement at last.

"Death caused by severe loss of blood from severance of the carotid artery . . ."

No mystery. It hadn't taken a forensic genius to figure that one out.

I could have said that, Mark thought. *Any fool could have said that. . . .*

He walked out into the hallway beyond the autopsy room and leaned against the wall, exhausted. How many of these had he seen? He was accustomed to coming to the morgue. He was grateful for the pathological sciences; technicians could solve crimes now when the greatest detectives in the world would fail. Sherlock Holmes wouldn't stand a chance next to modern technology.

Death by loss of blood due to the severance of the carotid artery . . .

But there was more to the autopsy than that. And Lee Minh was a genius. His forensic findings had helped solve many a crime before. A stomach full of half-eaten fast-food french fries had once helped the police give the D.A. the materials to convict the estranged husband of the slain woman. The husband had denied seeing her, but he had been working at the place where she'd acquired the french fries. Faced with the facts, the fellow had confessed.

So no matter how obvious Lee's findings seemed so far, Mark was glad of his associate's slow care with the victim. In the end, something in the autopsy just might give them what they needed.

A cup was pressed into his hands. Hot coffee. He'd been just staring at the floor. Lee, scrubbed down now, free of his work greens, was standing next to him. "You look like shit," Lee said bluntly.

"Thanks."

"Go home. Why are you still here?"

"I don't know. I kept thinking that maybe you'd find something more."

"Something more?" Lee arched a brow. "This one looks about as good as a murder case can look, if I understand the facts correctly. Miss L'Aveau's attacker left a trail of blood all the way to the point where he collapsed. You don't have to collar him; he's in the hospital. Sad, but true—if the guy dies, he'll save the state a fortune in court costs."

"Yeah," Mark said.

"You don't think this guy did it?"

"As yet, we haven't found a murder weapon."

"They'll come up with it by morning. Wait, hell, it is morning."

"Hmm. No wonder I look like shit."

"So what's keeping you up? Cop's intuition, the guy did it, right?"

Mark hesitated. He discovered he was picturing her again. The wife. The petite dynamo with the striking eyes—so emerald against the redness of tears. *He didn't do it,* she'd insisted. She was convinced that Marcel was innocent.

Marcel had fallen at her front door.

Maybe he'd had a knife. Maybe she'd hidden it. How had Marcel been stabbed? The same knife? Maybe, he didn't want to believe this, but maybe Gina had been the one with the knife. Maybe she'd been desperate enough for some reason to attack first. Maybe Marcel had even killed her in self-defense, maybe, just maybe . . .

Maybe he was just so damned tired he couldn't think straight anymore.

"Go home, my friend," Lee persisted.

"Yeah, I guess it's time. You will tell me—"

"I will tell you anything at all that I can."

"At any time. Call me. Right?"

"Go home. If you're questioning me, you really do need some sleep." Lee Minh was smiling. He'd been at his grim work all of his adult life, but though he was forty, when he smiled, he had the look of a good-natured kid playing a prank. Lee was still blessed with a thick headful of sleek, dark hair. He was a compact, wiry man of medium height, and despite his calling, he was considered one of the city's most eligible bachelors. He and Mark spent some of their rare free evenings together, both appreciating good lager on tap and jazz music.

"Go," Lee repeated.

Mark nodded, threw his jacket over his shoulder, and started out.

He got into his car, intending to go home.

He didn't know when he changed his mind. Maybe he was driving on autopilot. But before he knew it, he was turning the wrong corners in the French Quarter.

Returning to the scene of the crime.

Ann showered until the water ran cold.

She was exhausted; she was wide awake. She would have stayed at the hospital, but the hospital staff wouldn't let her in with him that night anyway.

The night had been ungodly, all those hours spent being terrified that Jon was going to die.

Now she faced the fear of what was going to happen to Jon if he lived.

She was encouraged by Jon's stable vital signs; she was horrified by the realization that a woman had died.

A woman Jon had been painting.

A woman he had been with.

A woman he had . . .

No!

Where the hell was her faith? If nothing else, she knew the man better than anyone else on earth. He wasn't a killer.

She didn't know the circumstances, she reminded herself.

Jon wasn't a killer, not under any circumstance. She knew that, and she did have faith in him. But Jon had gripped her hand. And she had thought that he'd been about to whisper her name. But he hadn't done so. He had whispered . . .

Annabella's.

Why hadn't she told the cop what Jon had said? Because the cop had already pegged Jon, and she didn't think that it would help?

Because it might be all that she might have to help him with?

She shivered.

The cop had known she was lying. She would be seeing him again. And he would persist.

"I don't have to tell him anything!" she whispered aloud.

Well, maybe she did. She didn't know the law that well, except that she might be hindering an investigation. Didn't matter. She wasn't going to tell anyone anything. Not until she knew more about Jon's condition. Not until he could fight for himself.

And if he could never fight for himself?

She was going to have to fight for him.

That decided, she at last left the shower, shivering. She wrapped herself in an old, worn terry robe and made her way out to the living room. She hesitated, then turned off the light. It was morning. Early morning. Her balcony drapes were open; the French doors leading to the balcony were ajar. She could see the sun rising, gold and orange and beautiful, casting down delicate, soft rainbow reflections on wrought-iron filigree on the balconies across the way from her. Flowers spilled from planters, catching and playing with the light as well. She wondered how such a beautiful day could contain such pain. Such tragedy. But her husband's near death didn't change the glory of the sunrise. There was so much beauty here just in the changing colors of night and day.

She walked into the kitchen, pausing by the front door. The police had finished with her home by the time she'd returned to it. She'd been allowed to clean up Jon's blood and their fingerprint powder. She'd had a few arguments with the remaining police techs when she'd arrived. She didn't understand why they wanted samples of Jon's blood from her doorway when he'd bled all over the hospital as well. And she didn't know why they wanted his fingerprints from her doorway—no one was denying that he'd been there.

"Procedure," a pleasant, but firm, officer had told her. "We always have to go by the book, no matter how silly it seems."

"But you are done here," she persisted.

"Yes."

An officer remained in the hallway beyond the door.

For her "protection," she had been told.

Fine. She did feel a little spooked. Because the eagle-eyed cop had been right on the money about one thing. If Jon was innocent—which he had to be—then someone else had attacked him and the poor dead girl.

Annabella's.

The name he had whispered. The name of the club—the strip joint—where Gina had worked, where most of his "ladies" had worked.

I didn't do it, God, I didn't do it . . .

Annabella's. . . .

She hurried on into the kitchen, automatically reaching for the coffeepot. It was morning.

She hadn't slept, she reminded herself. She was keyed to the breaking point. She didn't need coffee. She needed a big glass of wine.

She found a bottle of chablis in the refrigerator. She didn't bother with her delicate-stemmed wineglasses—she went straight for a water tumbler. She poured herself the wine and wandered back out to the French doors that had been left ajar and stepped out onto her balcony.

I didn't do it, oh, God, I didn't do it . . .

Annabella's. . . .

"I didn't do it; Annabella's!" she breathed aloud. "Damn you, Jon!" she muttered with greater force. "Why didn't you give me a little more than that. Like the name of the person who did do it, maybe!"

She swallowed down a large gulp of wine; then, through her upraised glass, she saw a car parked across the narrow street. A man was leaned against it, looking up at her.

Not a man.

The man.

The cop. Eagle eye. Lieutenant What's-His-Name.

A warning sizzle swept through her torso and limbs, leaving her feeling oddly breathless. He wasn't the enemy, she tried to tell herself. She didn't need to be afraid. He was a cop. A good guy.

Bullshit. He was after Jon. He didn't intend to give Jon the benefit of any doubt whatsoever.

"Good morning, Mrs. Marcel," he called up to her.

"Officer," she acknowledged.

"Lieutenant," he reminded her pleasantly.

"Lieutenant."

He smiled, gray eyes already hidden by sunglasses, despite the fact that it was barely morning. He lifted a hand, indicating her wineglass. "Interesting morning brew. Even for New Orleans."

She didn't owe him any explanations regarding her choice of beverage; despite that, Ann found a flush rushing to her cheeks, and to her horror, she was explaining. "I haven't been to sleep yet, Lieutenant, and it has been a harrowing night."

"Drinking your way into oblivion, eh?"

"You might be doing the populace you serve a favor by doing something similar at this point, Lieutenant."

His lips curved into a wry half smile. He could be very handsome, she decided. And darned irritating—and perhaps incredibly dangerous as well. To Jon.

He was suspicious. Honestly, openly, regarding Jon.

But did he think that she was hiding something as well? He was parked in front of her house, watching her.

"I would do the populace a favor . . . ," he repeated, his head cocking as he looked up at her. "Are you inviting me up for a drink?" he asked, his smile broadening.

She didn't reply to his question. "Lieutenant, what are you doing down there, staring at my house?"

He shrugged. "Just making sure that everything is okay."

"I see. You're there for my protection?"

"Something like that," he said, glancing toward the rising sun, then back to her. "No, quite frankly, I'm here because my car just seemed to bring me here, Mrs. Marcel. After I stopped by the alley where Gina was found."

"Gina?"

"Miss L'Aveau. The woman who was murdered last night."

"I see," Ann said. She swallowed hard. She hadn't had much time to think about the fact that a girl was dead. Gina L'Aveau. She knew the name. Jon hadn't finished his painting of her yet; he'd still been working on it. He'd talked about Gina several times, though. "You have to meet her, Annie. She's great. I mean, normally, you'd probably never get to know one another. That's the whole strange thing about our society. We're judgmental. We fall into little cliques. Good people, bad people. Clean people, dirty people. But in truth, in essence maybe, we're all really alike. You'll meet her for me, won't you?" he'd demanded, and of course, she'd said that she would.

She'd never meet Gina now.

The cop was still staring at her. Glasses in place. But she knew what lurked behind the dark lenses. Those silver-gray, all-knowing, far-too-piercing eyes. She stepped back. "Well, Lieutenant, I'm very tired. If you'll excuse me, I'm going to get some sleep."

"You do that."

"And you're just going to stay there? Staring up at my house?"

"Something like that."

Ann started inside, then turned back. "Are you waiting for nine A.M. to roll around? Are you planning to go to the D.A. for a search warrant for my house?"

He smiled. "The wheels of justice may turn slowly, Mrs. Marcel, but I do have probable cause, don't you think?"

"The police were in here half the night."

"So I imagine. The tech boys must have been."

Aggravated, Ann grated her teeth. "Good night, Lieutenant," she said again.

"Have a nice sleep."

She was tired. So tired that her tumblerful of wine now seemed to be racing hotly through her body. That had to be her only excuse for what she was about to do.

Know your enemy. Face him! she thought, and she continued to stare down at the man. "If you want to see the place, Lieutenant, do come on up. Have a morning cup of wine."

He arched a brow to her. "You're really inviting me up, Mrs. Marcel?"

She was insane. He was definitely the enemy. He probably thought she was concealing the murder weapon under her robe.

"Yes, Lieutenant, I am inviting you up."

Idiot! she charged herself.

He hesitated just a second, eagle eyes hidden by his Ray-Bans. He shrugged, another of his wry smiles curving his lips.

And he started toward her door.

Panic seized Ann as she stared down at the street, at the spot where he had just been. What the hell was she doing? She stood there frozen as she heard him enter the main door, heard his footsteps on the stairs. Heard his voice, low, husky, well-modulated, definitely tinged with a subtle native drawl, as he spoke with the uniformed officer in the hallway.

Then he was knocking at her door.

What in God's name was she doing?

Making a big mistake. All she had to do was tell him to go away, she told herself. Tell him that she had made a mistake. Babble something about not talking to him without her attorney present.

Oh, good. Great. Make him really suspicious. Wind up getting herself arrested on the spot.

"Mrs. Marcel?" he asked from beyond the front door.

She found movement at last, spinning from the balcony and back into the house, then across the living room to the door. She opened it cautiously. Her mouth opened. Words half formed in her throat, but didn't quite make it to her lips.

He slipped off the glasses. His eyes still seemed as sharp as an eagle's—despite the fact that they were bloodshot and red-rimmed. He was exhausted, she thought. His casual suit was now somewhat rumpled, and he was gaining a hint of five o'clock about the jaw. It made him look all the more menacing, somehow. Larger. More macho-masculine. More dangerous. His mood, she thought, was as worn and reckless as her own.

"I think—" she began.

"You did invite me up," he reminded her, and before she could say more, he took matters— and the door—into his own hands.

He stepped determinedly past her, and into the living room.

Five

"Nice place," he told her, looking around.

It was a nice place. The living area/studio was quite large, twenty by forty, with a small kitchen and island backing the far end and the balcony with the French doors to the left of the entry. Near the kitchenette area, she had her easel and oils set up beneath the skylight that was beginning to spill the brighter hues of the day into the room. She'd managed to keep the feeling of spaciousness and yet add warmth, toward the French doors she had her sofa grouping—French Provincial in keeping with the aura of the city—with a modern entertainment unit set into a handsome antique wardrobe casing. There were two bedrooms opening up from the living room on the far side of the door, one for her, and one for Katie when she was home. But Katie wasn't home; thankfully, she was off on a college trek into the Amazon. A pre-med student, Katie was studying a genetic disease that was inherited by a particular tribe in the rain forest.

Katie, Ann thought with another stab of pain. If not just for herself and Jon, she had to prove him innocent for their daughter's sake. Katie adored her father.

"Would you like coffee?" she asked.

"I'd rather like a cup of that coffee you were drinking," he told her.

She pursed her lips together and walked to the kitchen area, digging the wine from the refrigerator and reaching into a pine cupboard for a wineglass. She hadn't realized that he was right behind her until he reached past her.

For a water tumbler. He took the wine from her and poured it into his glass. "When in Rome . . . ," he murmured. "Cheers!"

He swallowed her blush chablis down as if it were water.

"Are you supposed to be drinking on duty?" she demanded.

"I'm not on duty."

"So what are you doing—looking in my house for the murder weapon on your off hours?"

"Yes," he said flatly. He poured more wine, then walked out past the small island counter, pausing by her easel. He didn't ask permission, but cast back the sheet she'd had covering her most recent work. He let out a long whistle like an exhalation, studying the painting. She was nearly finished with it. It was a study of an old Cajun woman she bought flowers from down at Jackson Square each morning. The woman smiled; her warmth seemed to light her eyes. Her face was so weathered it was difficult to discern her racial makeup, but then, she might not have known her own racial makeup anyway, such was the wonder of New Orleans. She was aging, she was worn, she was beautiful within her soul. It was a good painting, Ann thought. One of her best. Nearly finished except for the background.

"I thought Jon Marcel had been working on *Red Light Ladies*," he said.

"He had."

"Then—"

She ripped the sheet from his hands, recovering her painting. "This is mine."

"Yours?"

"Yes."

He might have said something then. A compliment might have been in order. But he didn't offer one.

"Ah," he said, sipping his wine more slowly now as he moved about the room. He shook his head.

"Spacious, nice, but feminine," he said.

"Gee, I'm so sorry."

"You don't need to be sorry to me, but doesn't Jon mind?"

"The room isn't exactly filled with frills, and no, Jon doesn't mind. Why should he?"

He shrugged. "It's just that it's . . . very much your room," he said. "It even smells like your perfume."

"It's probably soap, since I just stepped from the shower. You could use some, you know."

He arched a brow to her. "Maybe I am acquiring something of an unwashed, manly smell."

"Maybe you simply need a shower."

"Is that another invitation?"

"Yes, I'm inviting you to go home, Lieutenant,

drink in your house, and bathe for your own well-being."

He smiled again, looking around the room. He walked toward the sofa.

"Thinking of lifting the cushions to look for the knife?"

"Should I?"

"Knock yourself out."

To her amazement, he grinned, and lifted the cushion next to him. Ann muttered and strode back into the kitchen, pouring herself more of the wine. If she didn't do so, he might stay until he'd consumed the rest of the bottle on his own. He was already tearing up the place on her.

"So where is hubby's work?" he asked her.

"What?"

"Your husband's work. He can't have everything in a gallery, can he? Do artists need separate space or something? Different vibes?"

Frowning, she walked slowly back out to where he sat—sprawled, rather—on the sofa.

"Hubby's work is at hubby's home," she said calmly.

His brow shot up with surprise. "You keep separate residences?"

"We do."

He shook his head. She saw that edge of contempt she had seen before at the hospital harden his steady gaze upon her. "Lady, I've got to admit it—I just don't get you. I mean, it's not as if you were a weathered old crone or the like; you're a good-looking woman."

"How kind of you, Lieutenant."

"You don't live with the guy, you don't mind

that he dates whores, you—" He broke off suddenly.

"What?"

"You're not . . ."

"What?" Ann said.

He shrugged. "He isn't into the women for you, is he?"

"For me?" Ann repeated blankly. Then she realized what he meant. She wanted to throw something at him. Thank God for her morning wine. She managed to smile instead. She strode pleasantly toward him again, pausing right in front of him.

"Lieutenant, you are an ass. How dare you?"

"Mrs. Marcel, I follow all possible leads. Actually, the idea wasn't mine. My partner—"

"Your partner, sir, is an ass. But you're the fool who is sitting here, in my house, spouting out such crude, rude, insulting words. I think it's time you got the hell off of my sofa, and out of my door."

"Ah, and without the murder weapon," he said, still staring frankly at her. He rose, walked by her, set his glass on the island counter, and turned to leave. "Well, Mrs. Marcel, I thank you for your hospitality."

"Indeed, Lieutenant."

He strode toward the door.

"Lieutenant."

He paused, turning slowly back to her, a well-defined auburn brow arching. "Mrs. Marcel?"

"You seem to know so much."

"Do I?"

She nodded. "Well, let's see, you seem to *know*

that Jon killed this woman. And you seem to know that he must have stashed the murder weapon here somewhere. You know about Jon's injuries, you know about a trail of blood, and I'm sure you know just exactly how the poor girl died."

"I do."

"Well, then, it is amazing that you don't know that Jon and I are divorced and have been for quite some time. Jon Marcel is the father of my child, Lieutenant, and my very good friend. I do love him, and I do mean to fight for him since he cannot fight for himself; but whom he chooses to date I consider to be entirely his own business. Now, if you don't mind, please do get the hell out."

Dark lashes lowered over his gray eyes. He looked up at her again, a rueful, self-mocking smile in place.

"Good morning, Mrs. Marcel. Don't forget to call me if you think of anything important."

"Certainly."

"I'm assuming I can find you at the hospital later if I need you?"

"Lieutenant, you may assume anything you wish."

"Careful. I can haul you down to the station for questioning."

"Careful. I can call in my lawyer and you'll be left holding—" She broke off, determined that she was going to be collected and mature.

An auburn brow arched high against his forehead. His smile, the one she grudgingly admitted to being attractive, slipped onto his lips once again.

"Pardon?" he queried politely. "Did you want to finish that thought."

"Good day, Lieutenant."

"I hope so, Mrs. Marcel." He still hesitated, watching her. "I'm not an art critic, but your painting . . . it's excellent, isn't it?"

She was surprised to discover that she had to smile. "It's one of my best, I think. Art is always subjective."

"And you're good."

"I make a decent living."

"What about your husband? Ex-husband," he corrected.

"He makes a very decent living. He's going to be able to afford top-notch lawyers, Lieutenant."

"He's going to need them, Mrs. Marcel."

Ann felt a heated trembling snake along her spine. He was tough, tenacious, and determined. If criminals fell through cracks in the system, they weren't going to do so through lack of effort on his part. This situation was awful enough without having such an enemy opposing her own efforts along the way.

"Has it ever occurred to you, Lieutenant, that you might be wrong?"

He looked down for a moment. She realized that he was actually trying to be gentle with her, and that was more frightening than his downright determination to be blunt. "A trail of blood led from the murder site here."

"But someone else might have attacked them both."

"From the evidence we have, such a scenario is not probable."

"But it's not impossible."

He stared at her a long moment. "If you have something to give me, I'll gladly look in another direction. Do you have something?"

"No," Ann admitted after a moment. "Not yet."

"Not yet?" he repeated with a frown. "Mrs. Marcel, don't go sticking your nose into police business—"

"I have your card, Lieutenant."

"I'm warning you—"

"Don't go sticking your nose into my business, Lieutenant."

A pulse at his throat betrayed his anger; he didn't reply at first. He managed another of his smiles. "If necessary, Mrs. Marcel, I'll see you at the station."

With that, he left at last, closing the door behind him with a quiet but definitive click.

Shaking, Ann found her way to the sofa, sinking into it. The lieutenant was dangerous. A murder had been committed; a murderer was going to have to pay. It seemed painfully obvious to everyone that Jon had committed that crime.

He hadn't.

How can you know that yourself? she cried inwardly. *How well does one human being ever know another?*

He hadn't killed the girl. Jon hadn't killed the girl; Jon wouldn't kill. She did know him.

And she didn't begin to know how, but she was going to have to prove that he hadn't done it.

He slept, but his sleep was disturbed by reckless, disjointed dreams.

Gina's face.

Gina's eyes.

It wasn't that he had known her long, but rather that he had known her well. She had been *different*. Maybe not so different. Maybe she had taught him that every poor stiff out there was some mother's child, and maybe her laughter in the face of all adversity had helped him when he had needed it most. Gina had *believed*. She had believed that her life would change, that love could fill her days. She could dance with enough sensuality for a eunuch to regrow sex organs the way a lizard regrows a tail, but all she really wanted out of life was a white picket fence, two cats in the yard, two kids, a dog, and a husband who came home nights. She had loved to cook, to sew. One day, she was going to do a tour of American amusement parks, ride every roller coaster, zoom down every slide. One day.

"One day" had seemed so very close for her!

"One day" had ended in death.

By eleven, Mark gave up on the concept of sleep. It wasn't working. He crawled out of bed and into the shower, praying the water would revive him. Scrubbed but feeling lousy, he stumbled out of the shower and headed for his drawer. He paused, seeing Maggie's picture, and sat wearily down on his bedside.

Funny how he went through life most of the time, never forgetting his wife, but realizing that life did go on, that he had an important job, and that he wasn't alone. He was lucky. Maggie had left him two boys, Michael, now twenty-six— the surprise of their lives in their junior year of college!—and Sean, twenty-two, getting ready to finish up his senior year in the film school at the University of Miami. The kids were okay; he was okay. Maybe that was Maggie's greatest legacy to him. It hadn't been a perfect marriage; no marriage was perfect. But it had been a good one, and he had realized that he loved her just as passionately on the day that he buried her as he had when he married her.

Oddly enough, though, they had been arguing on the day she'd gone to the doctor. She went in because she was getting headaches which he blamed on the fender-bender she had because she'd neglected to get her brakes checked when he'd told her to. He didn't expect anything serious when she came walking out to the waiting room; in fact, he looked up, smiling, ready to tease her. "Bad headache, huh? I know, no sex for a month, right?"

Then he saw the expression on her face, the anguish in her eyes, the tears brimming within them. She had always been a no-nonsense woman. A good wife for a cop. She had lived with the danger facing him. She was strong. So strong.

She never cried. Not when she received the

news of the tumor; not when he broke down and cried himself. The only time tears ever spilled from her eyes was once, just once, near the end. She couldn't bear to leave her sons, just coming into manhood. She couldn't bear their tears, nor Mark's, and so everyone learned to live with the days they had left. They had time, and they talked, and Mark told her once that he could never love again, and she remained quiet, ruffling his hair. "You need to love again; everyone needs to love." He denied her words, and she had smiled. "Just make sure she's a good woman, Mark. Because you're a good man. And you deserve the best. Mark, you're human. You've loved me. We've fought, we've quarreled, but it's been good. Don't punish yourself because we did love one another!" On another occasion she told him, "Don't be alone too long, Mark. God, I love you. Don't be alone. Don't hurt for me the rest of your life. Just remember, never judge a book—or a woman—by a cover!"

Near the end, she had suffered. But at the very end, she had slipped away quietly in his arms, and he and Michael and Sean had been there for one another. That had been almost seven years ago now. He still loved Maggie. And Maggie's words were what had made him realize there was so much more to Gina on that night when he had nearly arrested her. "Never judge a book—or a woman—by a cover!" Thanks to Maggie, he'd gotten to see what lay beneath Gina's veneer. And Gina, no matter what she did for a living, had been a good woman, full of life and love.

She'd died for her dreams, so it seemed.

He heard a noise at his front door and reached automatically for his police-issue gun, nestled in its holster on the chair by his bed. Then he realized that a key had turned in the lock. Michael. He rose quickly, slipping into his briefs and a pair of jeans. He was barely dressed when he heard a tapping on his bedroom door, which was standing ajar.

"Grandpa?"

"Come on in, Munchkin," he called, opening the door. Michael's daughter, Brit, just turned six, stood staring up at him with her grandmother's big blue eyes. Brit frowned, studying him. He realized his hair was still tousled from the shower. He must look like death warmed over.

"Daddy didn't think you could be home so late. I said that you were. I saw the car."

"You're a smart girl."

"I'm going to be a detective one day," she told him proudly.

He arched a brow. He opened his mouth to tell her to be something else; police work was dangerous. He didn't want her hurt.

He thought, though, that he didn't have the right to tell her such a thing. *Life* was dangerous, and he'd worry about her forever no matter what; but she had a right to choose what she wanted to do with her own life. Though he'd been the cop, Maggie was the one the family had lost.

He smoothed back her rich, strawberry blond curls, smiling. "You remember this, young lady.

You can grow up to be anything you want to be. Anything you're willing to work hard to be."

She smiled, then frowned again. "You look all tired, Grandpa."

"I just woke up and took a shower."

Brit's eyes were huge and round with sincerity. "It must have been your soap, Grandpa. Your soap couldn't have been right. You must have needed to be 'Zestfully' clean. Or maybe you needed the 'Eye Opener.' I think."

"The Eye Opener?"

Startled, Mark looked past his granddaughter to his son, who stood in the center of the living room. Michael was the spitting image of Mark in his youth. His son shrugged sheepishly. "I believe that one is Coast. I've been telling Lucy that Brit's seeing too much television lately. Our life has become one long commercial. Professional hazard."

"Hmm." He glanced down at Brit. "Honey, I'll get myself into a store today and get the right stuff. Boy, if I'd only known it was all in the soap!" He brushed her chin with his knuckles, then looked back to his son. "What are you doing here? Since when are ad execs off during the week?"

"No school and no day care this week and Stephanie had a doctor's appointment, so I took the morning off. I came over to get Brit's bathing suit bag—I left it here a couple of weeks ago with all her pool toys and such in it."

"You know you're welcome anytime."

"I didn't mean to startle you. You're not usually home now."

"I know."

"Have you had breakfast yet, Grandpa?" Brit asked anxiously. " 'Milk does a body good.' "

"Oh, boy," Mark said.

"Ask Granddad if he wants to go out for late breakfast, Brit. We'll make him put milk in his coffee."

"A quick breakfast," Mark said. "Really quick. I've got to get to work—"

"Yeah, yeah," Michael interrupted, smiling. He looked like Mark, but he had his mother's dimples. "I've seen the morning paper. The front page is all about the—" He hesitated, glancing at his daughter's head. "About the girl. Your name's all through the story."

"My name?" Mark said with a groan.

"Super-cop. Right on it in seconds. Heading up the investigation, the crime already solved. Put a shirt on. You can read it over coffee in the park."

Waking had been bad enough. She'd felt more tired than when she'd finally gone to sleep to begin with. Then she had something of a wine hangover, made worse by the dullness in her heart as she admitted to herself that what had happened last night had been real, and it wasn't going to go away.

Next, she had seen the paper. The "journalist" on the story had done a gory job of it, cleanly judging and convicting Jon, and doing macabre comparisons between the artist's favorite colors in his paintings and his favorite colors in life and death—reds and crimsons. The journalist stated that "reputable" sources had said that Jon Marcel had enjoyed a heated affair with Gina L'Aveau which had erupted in violent arguments before.

She was grateful once again that Katie was in the Amazon. And even more grateful that Jon probably had not been given a copy of the paper.

If he had regained consciousness.

Which he hadn't, she discovered when she reached the hospital.

In fact, he had slipped into a coma.

That news had sunk her into deep depression, despite the doctor's assurances that although a coma was dangerous, Jon might pull out of it at any time. He sat with her at least twenty minutes, perhaps thirty. She thought that maybe she had lost a part of her own mind because it seemed that for all his talking, she didn't comprehend one bit of his technical jargon. She'd read a Robin Cook book called *Coma*. The patients in the book had been used for body parts. There was no way they were going to tell her that a coma was okay.

She sat by Jon during the afternoon, holding his hand, talking because the nurses assured her that it would be good if she talked to him. There were police officers on duty in the hospital; one just outside the intensive care doorway, and another ready to spell him, keeping his vigil out in the most comfortable realm of the waiting room. Nurses and cops whispered; she didn't hear them.

It was around six when she became aware that someone was behind her. Someone who had been standing there, silently watching her. She was aware of a very soft and subtle scent of aftershave.

It fit him, she thought. A woodsy scent. Rugged. But not too much. Dashed on quickly.

She wasn't surprised when she turned to see that the lieutenant was behind her.

She was alarmed, however, when she felt a rush of tears rising to her eyes.

"Come on, now," he said, his voice surprisingly gentle. "It's not that bad."

She swallowed hard. "Not for you. The paper agrees with you. Jon Marcel is a monster."

"He can still make it."

"He can still make it. He's in a coma, and the papers have him convicted."

"He can come out of this and defend himself."

"Yeah," she said without conviction.

"So that's it? You're beaten? Licked?"

She spun around to stare at him. That half smile was back on his lips.

"You've decided he's innocent?"

"I haven't. Have you decided he's guilty?"

"No!"

He shrugged. "Well, it will be a battle, then. You don't look ready for it."

She arched a brow.

"You look beat. Last night I thought you were thirty. You're closer to forty this morning."

Ann stared at him, amazed. "Lieutenant, that's downright rude."

He grimaced. "Sorry."

"And by the way, you look like hell, too."

"I know. My granddaughter told me so."

"You have a *granddaughter?*"

He half smiled, nodded, and stepped closer to the bed, to Jon, with all his tubes and mechanical extensions. Despite herself, she tensed.

"Be—umm—careful," she warned.

"Mrs. Marcel, I assure you, I don't intend to pull any plugs. Whether you want to believe me or not, I'm anxious myself that this man live."

He assessed Jon, then glanced her way. "He's going to make it."

"You really want him to make it?"

"Yes, I do."

"So you can convict him."

"If he's guilty. If he's not, he may know something."

"He does know . . . something," Ann said.

"He must. He's talking already."

"He's talking already? Amazing," Ann said suspiciously. "What's he saying?"

"He's saying that you need to get out of here for a while. You need to stroll down the street, get some sunshine, smell some flowers. Sit at an outdoor cafe and have some café au lait and beignets, baguettes, cheese, protein, chocolate—food. Put some color into your cheeks, and some sustenance into your soul."

"I'm not in the mood to wander aimlessly."

"I wasn't suggesting you wander aimlessly. I'd like some café au lait."

"Is that an invitation, Lieutenant?" she inquired, surprised.

"It is."

"Are you going to grill me?"

"I think you've been grilled enough lately. I really could use some caffeine and cholesterol."

"What would your wife think of you sharing caffeine and cholesterol with the ex-wife of one of your alleged murderers?"

"If she were alive, Maggie would think you were heartily in need of something. Shall we go?"

She was still damned suspicious, and she knew that it showed. But he reached out a hand to help her rise from her chair, and though she hesitated, she took it.

His grip was strong. Powerful. Something in his hold seemed to offer her renewed strength. She did need coffee. Not hospital coffee out of a paper cup. Real, rich, New Orleans brew. Hot and mixed with steamed milk.

She stared at his hand, holding hers. Tanned, with blunt cut, clean nails.

"I—"

"Well?"

"I'm not sure. Do you know a place that's quiet, but offers a pleasant view, coffee strong enough to kill, and something incredibly sugary for dessert?"

"I do."

"You're sure."

"Mrs. Marcel, I know the city like the back of my own hand."

"Native child?"

"So damned native it hurts at times."

"There's not much by the hospital."

"I've got my car."

She must have hesitated again.

He sighed impatiently. "Mrs. Marcel, are you afraid of me?"

"Certainly not. Other than the fact that you would probably stoop to any means or measure to get me to say something that would help convict Jon, I'm sure you're a lovely man."

"That may be true, but . . ."

"But?"

"I like my opponents kicking and screaming back. You're too beat. For the moment, you're safe. Time out. Shall we go?"

She had no reason to trust him.

But he tugged on her hand, drawing her to her feet. His grip remained firm, and the warmth in it seemed to give her strength.

"Don't you have to go to work or something?" she demanded as a last out.

He hesitated, just slightly. "I've been working all afternoon," he told her. "I'll probably go back to work again later. Come on."

He released her hand and propelled her before him. She took one last look back at Jon.

He appeared to be sleeping peacefully enough.

And the hand felt oddly good.

Even if it did belong to Lieutenant Eagle Eyes.

Even if she wasn't quite sure she dared believe in this moment's truce. . . .

Six

Cindy came into the club early; she needed to do some mending on her white costume. More than that, she needed not to be alone.

The club was quiet when she came in. April, who was willing to dance for less money on the early shift in exchange for earlier nights, was on stage alone. The music was played by a DJ until nine weeknights, ten weekends, when the Dixie Boys came on. The bar was filled with nine-to-fivers who had stopped for a drink with friends on their way home, most yuppies with kids and wives at their houses. They were a laid-back, courteous crowd, and though April received a wolf whistle now and then, for the most part, the married-man types—and a few of their nine-to-five female counterparts—appreciated the music, dance and ambience, and watched with polite, low-key behavior.

Gregory was sitting at the bar, nursing a drink. He was a studious musician who came in early often enough to check on the instruments, and sometimes, to work on something new out back in what had once been a carriage house and now served as practice room cum storage for everyone who did everything at the club.

He seldom sat at the bar with a drink, unless it was a Coca-Cola.

Seeing him brooding and to a side by himself, Cindy came along and crawled up on the stool beside him.

"Gregory," she said carefully.

He nodded. "Hey, kid."

"You okay?"

He nodded. "Yeah, how about you."

"Shaken," Cindy admitted.

"Yeah, shaken. I would say that I am damned shaken. There are just no guarantees, you know." He stared at the stage unseeingly. "I miss her. I miss her already. I miss her because she was so damned happy lately. Because she—she *believed.*"

Cindy took his hand in hers and squeezed it. "I miss her, too."

"I thought she was going to be so happy. I thought she was going to have everything she wanted. She had lots of friends, lots of people who cared. Hell, she'd had lots of guys, but this one . . . I thought he was different, the artist, you know? I thought that he really loved her. That he'd see past everything she'd done in her life. I thought he was going to marry her and be decent and everything else. Hell, Cindy, I thought he was so much better than the trash she mixed up with half the time! Guys who abused her, mistreated her . . . here comes the guy with the gentle way about him, the understanding . . ." He paused, shaking his head in disbelief and utter disgust. He cast back his head and threw back what looked like bourbon on the rocks in a single swallow. The whole of his powerful frame shuddered. "The good guy kills her."

Cindy hesitated. "Maybe it's not fair to condemn him so quickly."

"Haven't you read the newspapers?"

"Yes, but someone else might have killed her, Gregory. I know that sometimes . . . well, I don't know what was going on exactly, but she was still seeing Harry Duval upon occasion."

"Yeah, she was still seeing Harry. I thought Harry might be the bastard. He never wanted anything exclusive with Gina, but then again, he never really wanted to let her go." Gregory looked at Cindy, his large, dark eyes haunted, handsome black face drawn. "I accused Harry right away."

"And?"

"He swore he didn't do it. He accused me of having done it."

"You?"

"Yeah."

"My God, what did you say?"

"Of course I swore that *I* didn't do it."

"If you were to ask Jon Marcel," Cindy said, "I betcha he'd deny that he did it as well."

"I'll betcha he would," Gregory agreed morosely. He pressed his glass toward Louis the bartender so that Louis could refill it. Jack Daniels

Black. Cindy wondered if she'd be able to get Gregory to slow down a bit.

Cindy watched him drink, gnawing on her lower lip. Gregory had been Gina's friend, no more, but he had really loved her.

"Odd thing was that . . ."

"What?" Cindy demanded.

"I had dinner with her. Just before it happened. I was with her . . . I heard her meeting someone when I left."

"Who?" Cindy gasped out, incredulous.

Gregory shrugged. "Must have been Jon Marcel."

"It might have been someone else," Cindy insisted. "It could have been Harry—"

"Right. And if the wrong people knew that I'd been with her, it could have been me. I was with her."

"That good-looking, swine-bucket kin of hers was still coming after her now and then."

"Jacques?"

"Jacques." Seeing the confusion in his eyes, Cindy sighed. "Oh, come on, Gregory! They were distant cousins. Their mothers were third cousins or the like. Gregory, she slept with him. He held something over her."

Gregory stared at her, shrugged, drank down more of his bourbon.

"It doesn't matter."

"Why not."

"They say Marcel did it, and Marcel is in a coma now."

"A coma?" Cindy whispered.

Gregory nodded sorrowfully. He sipped from his glass again, then spun around to look at her hard. "Whether we want to believe it or not, it looks like the verdict is in."

"They've proven it?"

He shrugged. "More or less. There's lots of rumor going around. Where there's smoke, you know. Oh, hell, Cindy, haven't you heard?"

"Heard what?"

He proceeded to tell her the latest.

The club's main office sat a level up from the ground floor and overlooked the stage, bar and entry from a large, see-through-one-way window. It was a spacious area with a huge modern desk, comfortable black leather sofa, numerous black leather wing chairs, refrigerator, wet bar, and complete entertainment system.

It was Harry Duval's favorite place. It was such a far cry from the mud and dirt and thatch of the poor home where he'd grown up that to this day, he still sometimes came up and just sat, and sometimes he just cried out with the pleasure of what was his—what he had done, what he had become, what he had acquired. What the snot-nosed Old Guard of Louisiana might say about him didn't matter. That some called him a pimp was foolish—those who did so too obtrusively often wound up followed by shadow-thugs and beaten in dark alleys. Never cut up, never too badly hurt, never maimed.

The poor bastards might be suspicious, but

they could never prove he'd lifted a finger against them.

Hey, it was a tough world. Shit happened.

But then . . .

Then there was what had happened to Gina.

He frowned, looking out the window, shaking his head. Gina. The brightest and the best of them. Gina, with her laughter. Her smile. The optimism that must have been with her until her dying breath.

Oh, God, yes, there was what had happened to Gina. Gina who got too involved with people. Gina who was just so blinded by her own beliefs that she couldn't see what havoc passion and emotion played upon others.

Gina. Who had refused to see evil.

April, bless her, was diligently moving on stage. Now there was a fine, good girl. More beautiful than heaven, more luscious than sin. Minding her own business, making it her own way. April was going to come out of things okay.

He walked over to his desk, ran his hand over the highly polished wood. He shrugged to himself, admitting he might be a little weird himself.

On edge.

Lascivious.

One of the last times he'd been with Gina . . .

Had been here. Feeling the imported leather beneath his flesh; watching her move on the highly polished wood. She'd caught him unaware that day. Come in when he'd just shed his clothing. He hadn't known that the door was unlocked. She hadn't expected quite what she found.

God, it had been one hell of an afternoon.

He strode to the wet bar, poured himself a bourbon. Drank it down, poured another. Hell, that was one thing he could do. Drink. When he finally died, they wouldn't need to embalm him; he'd be so completely pickled by then. Wouldn't matter none. He liked his life. He had achieved the unbelievable. The leather was his to feel against his naked skin. The girls were his, too. He didn't own them. He didn't need to. They came to him. Because they liked leather, too. Champagne, silk, and all that money had to offer. And hell, some of the girls were kinkier than the damned guys. Some of them knew how to *get down*. It was a good life. When the lights went out, he'd be ready. He wouldn't expect mercy, he wouldn't expect heaven, and he wouldn't be afraid of hell. He'd known both on earth already.

He walked back to the window, holding his drink in one hand so that he could shed his jacket and his shirt as he watched the stage.

His frown suddenly deepened.

Gregory and Cindy were at the bar, his dark head almost against her pale one. It looked like they were a pair of old geezers crying into their beers.

Talking. Still talking.

He shook his head.

Hell, some people never learned.

The cops might be holding the artist. They

might even have enough circumstantial and forensic evidence to pin it on him.

But Gina was *dead*.

And talk was dangerous.

Fools.

Talk could be just so damned dangerous. . . .

Harry Duval pondered whether or not Gregory knew anything.

If he had seen anything.

He wondered what the hell he was saying.

Indeed, if he had anything at all to say. . . .

Ann was afraid that he would take her someplace far too obvious. She was known by most of the cafe people close to her own home off of Bourbon Street, and she desperately wanted to be out without being recognized. The hospital people were all as kind as they could be to her, but they pitied her. They would fight to keep Jon alive, but they, like the rest of the city, had condemned him without a trial.

Okay, she admitted as they drove. So maybe, if you didn't know Jon, he did appear to be guilty. She could admit that much. But she could also hope that someone out there would realize that Jon had been seriously attacked as well, and that the murder weapon had yet to appear. Of course, she had supposedly hidden the murder weapon. No one had yet appeared with a search warrant for her home, but then again, she had left her house with police crawling all over it—

doors wide open—when she had gone to the hospital with Jon.

He parked his car in a private garage just outside the French Quarter, or Vieux Carre—*Old Square.* He led her along a side street she'd never seen herself, down a walkway, and back into a cafe with a private garden setting.

The waitress's name was Helena. She knew Mark; she was a pretty woman of about thirty who greeted him with a warm kiss on the cheek. "You're off the beaten path today," Helena said, leading them to a white-washed wrought-iron table to the side of a delicate little fountain featuring the Greek goddess Athena with her owl upon her shoulders.

"We need a little privacy," Mark told Helena.

"Ah," Helena said. She looked at Ann for a moment, offered her a warm smile and added, "Tough day, huh? I suggest the Duck a l'Orange. What can I get you to drink?"

"Two café au laits with a few of those great house baguettes, Helena, to start. I'll see if I can talk my friend here into the duck."

Helena smiled and disappeared through a garden trail into the old house to the side of the garden cafe setting.

"Did she recognize me?" Ann asked, curious about Helena's manner.

"Yes," he said bluntly. "You didn't read the paper today?"

"Yes, I read the paper," she said dryly.

"You must have missed your picture in the Arts section."

"My picture—"

"Jon Marcel was front page news, but he wasn't missed by the critics. That show of his work that opened last night apparently raked in a fortune. You were included in the article. There was a great photo of you in it."

"So that's why Helena recognized me."

"Unless she's a closet art critic herself and knows you from elsewhere."

"Let's hope there aren't too many critics in the city, then," Ann murmured. "I don't want to be recognized. I don't want people pitying me, or pointing at me, or whispering behind my back that Jon is a guilty sleaze-bag and that I'm a fool for defending him."

"Well, actually, *I* think you're being a fool."

"At least you say it to my face. And you don't seem to be offended—at least you don't get mad and go away—when I tell you that you're a complete ass in return."

He grinned, looking down at the table. Helena arrived with their coffees and the basket of baguettes. "Have we decided on duck yet?" she asked.

"You have to eat," he told Ann.

"I—all right, duck," Ann agreed. When the waitress was gone she told him, "Dutch treat."

"Dinner's on me."

"Or on the department and the taxpayers. Am I supposed to say something incriminating? I'm not going to. You can just save your duck if that's what you think."

"Dinner's on me. And not because I think

you're going to say something incriminating. Defense attorneys could make chopped duck out of me for plying you with food and drink to get you to say something. Entrapment, you know."

Ann bit into a baguette. It was crispy on the outside, warm, delicious, melting on the inside. She hadn't realized how hungry she was. A sip of the café au lait was delicious, too. Sustaining, somehow.

He'd been right. She needed out of the hospital.

"Can cops afford duck?" she asked. "Maybe I should be treating you if we're not dining on the taxpayers."

"I can afford dinner."

"A high-paid cop?"

"I've been in it a very long time. I've made some good investments."

"Ah." She set her bread down suddenly. She was almost enjoying herself.

And Jon was in a coma. Dying. Katie was in the Amazon, maybe losing her father. Not even knowing it.

She was startled when his fingers curled around her hand. His eyes were on hers, very intensely silver-gray. "You haven't lost him. He will most likely pull through."

"He's in a coma."

"His vital signs are good and steady; he's receiving the necessary blood. His color is good. His body sustained tremendous shock; without the immediate medical treatment he received, he would have died. But he's not going to die now."

"Did you go to medical school, Lieutenant?" she asked coolly.

His hand withdrew from hers. He sat back in his chair, watching her, the hue of his eyes taking on a steely color. "I've seen too many injured or wounded people lying in hospitals. There are things cops learn the hard way. When the victim's brain is affected, there's almost no hope. 'Brain dead,' Mrs. Marcel, and it's time to pray to heaven, and hope that the afflicted made out donor cards. Jon Marcel has slipped into a coma, but his vitals aren't just steady, they're good. He's going to pull through."

"And then you're going to arrest him."

"Probably."

She was furious. Shaking. She wasn't quite sure why his candor was making her quite so angry—it wasn't as if he was saying anything she hadn't figured out on her own. Still aware of those ruthless gray eyes watching her, she buttered her bread with a vengeance.

"Cops!" she hissed. "Aren't you supposed to be doing some kind of investigative work? You've got Jon pinned—but you don't have a murder weapon! Wouldn't it make more sense if you looked for whoever had stabbed them both?"

He hesitated a long time. "Mrs. Marcel, we've gotten some of the lab information back."

"Yes?"

"They'll be doing more thorough DNA testing, of course, but so far, the evidence suggests that your husband did have sex with Miss L'Aveau the day that she was killed. Her blood was definitely on his person; his blood was on hers."

Again, he was watching her very intently.

"Are you trying to shock me, Lieutenant, anger me?"

"I'm trying to give you the facts."

"Fact, then, Lieutenant. It's not considered a crime for a divorced man to have sex with a woman he's seeing. Actually, it's not a *crime* for a married man—or woman—to have sex with another party. Actually—"

He sighed with deep impatience. "And I don't suppose it's a crime for you to remain in love with the man, Mrs. Marcel. But you're going to have to face facts—"

"Whether I am or am not 'in love' with my ex-husband is my own concern, Lieutenant. So far, the only fact I see is that the police are being incredibly lazy. You have two stabbed people. No knife."

"The knife will turn up."

"Umm. In my apartment."

"There's no search warrant out for your apartment, Mrs. Marcel."

"Why should there be? I left that apartment with the door open and cops all over it."

"You don't have much faith in cops."

"I haven't had much experience with them. From what I am discovering, some cops seem to have the capacity to be fairly blind."

"Then again, there are those who aren't blind, but who refuse to see," he reminded her.

"Why did you bring me out if you were so determined to torture me?" Ann demanded.

"You needed to eat."

"Is it your job to make sure that the ex-wives of the murderers you're trying to arrest eat."

"*Alleged* murderers," he reminded her.

She was about to lash out an angry reply, but she bit back her words because Helena was weaving her way toward them through the cafe tables with their salads.

"I'm so sorry, I forgot to ask. Would you like wine now that you've chosen to have dinner?"

"No, thanks," Ann said.

"Yes, please," he corrected.

"I don't drink wine," Ann lied.

His smiled broadened. "The hell you don't. Helena, I'd like a half carafe of the house rosé. Mrs. Marcel can join me if the urge overtakes her."

Helena left them. Ann dug savagely into her lettuce. "Are cops supposed to drink on duty?"

"I'm not on duty."

"That's right, you're *not* grilling me."

"Right."

"But you are going back to work?"

"I am."

"Ah, I see."

"What do you see, Mrs. Marcel?"

"A cop stumbling around in the dark *blind drunk* when he should be looking for a murder weapon."

"Are you asking me back to your place?"

"What?"

"If I were planning on looking for a murder weapon tonight, that's where I'd go."

"No, you're not asked back to my place." She set her fork down. "How dare you—"

"Helena's coming."

Helena was coming. Returning with the carafe and two wineglasses. She deposited them quickly, and moved on.

And Ann wondered what the hell she cared if Helena heard her tell this cop what he should do with himself.

"Actually, I'm not really sure if I do think that you're hiding the murder weapon," he said casually when Helena had gone.

"Really? How difficult to believe."

He poured wine into his glass. "If I believed that you had that weapon and were hiding it in your place, you can bet your ass that I would have had a search warrant for your property long before now."

She swept the carafe from his hand and poured rosé into her own glass. "Remind me not to dine with you again."

"Do I drive you to drink, Mrs. Marcel? Perhaps circumstances alone are doing that."

She clunked the carafe down, picked up her glass, and nearly inhaled the contents of it. She set the glass back down, preparing to stand.

"I don't think I can wait for the duck, Lieutenant. I'm so sorry."

His hand curled over hers. "My name is Mark,

Mark LaCrosse. If you're going to walk out on me in the middle of dinner, you might want to address me by my given name."

She tried to tug her hand away. His hold was firm; his gray eyes had a tighter hold upon her. This was ridiculous; she didn't have to sit here.

"Duck!" Helena's voice suddenly boomed with enthusiasm. The waitress was accompanied by a bus boy who collected their salad plates while Helena presented their main courses with a flourish.

Ann stayed seated. He still had her hand; it lay upon the table, covered with his own.

"Enjoy!" Helena said.

She left, followed by the bus boy. The restaurant suddenly seemed to be at the end of the earth. No sounds could be heard from the busy streets that lay just feet away. A beautifully landscaped garden sufficiently buffered the din and clatter.

He withdrew his hand and cut into his duck. "You do have to eat, Mrs. Marcel. You have to rest, and eat, and maintain your strength to go to battle." He looked up at her as he cut. "Against me. You don't intend to let me win, do you?"

"You're obnoxious, Lieutenant."

"I'm afraid that it comes with the territory."

"Umm."

"You do want to keep your wits about you."

"Right. So I drink more wine in your presence."

"Drink wine, eat duck, go home, get some sleep. It will help."

She still continued to stare at him.

"Mrs. Marcel, I implore you, enjoy the duck. I will do my absolute best to refrain from being obnoxious for the next twenty minutes."

Ann cut her duck. It was delicious; she was ravenous.

She ate it all. She didn't look at him or acknowledge him in any way until she had finished with every morsel of food on her plate.

When she had eaten the last bite and sat back, she discovered that he was watching her once again. "Come on, I'll take you home," he told her.

She rose. "Aren't you required to pay a check around here, Lieutenant."

"No. This is a front for an illegal prostitution ring, and they buy my silence with duck," he told her, rising as well.

"Seriously—"

"Seriously, I run a tab. Come on, I'll take you home."

He was done with her; they had eaten dinner. He had gotten what he wanted for the day. She spun around, and felt his hand upon her back once again as he guided her along the garden path. She wanted to walk more quickly and escape that touch. At the same time . . .

It wasn't an intimate touch. They barely knew one another. It was a courteously masculine touch. She felt his warmth through it; his strength. He was, she thought, a very strong man. Strong-willed. He'd easily provide a good shoulder to cry upon.

And he'd be listening all the while.

They neared the street. Helena appeared again, her smile warm and genuine. "Did you enjoy everything?" she inquired.

"The food was excellent," Ann said.

"I'm so glad. You've got more color in your cheeks already." She flushed slightly herself. "Sorry, I didn't mean to be personal, or offensive. But the newspapers, you know. Don't be surprised when you find strangers staring. Ignore them. Time will take care of things."

"Thank you. I'll keep that in mind," Ann said.

"Bye, kid," Mark LaCrosse said to Helena. He kissed her on the cheek. The warmth between them spurred Ann into action.

"Lieutenant, thank you for the magnificent dinner—and scintillating conversation. If you don't mind, I'm not terribly far from home, and I'd like to walk—alone—for a while. Good night."

She didn't wait for a reply. She turned and walked as quickly as possible and hurried out to the street. She walked faster and faster. A block past the restaurant, she looked back.

He wasn't following her.

She was relieved.

And maybe she was just a little bit disappointed.

She paused a moment, watching, waiting. He really wasn't coming.

She was only a few blocks from Jackson

Square, and she began wandering in that direction. The clubs were beginning to grow busier with the coming of twilight; through many an open doorway, jazz strains were beginning to fill the streets, creating the unique atmosphere that was New Orleans. She turned onto Chartes Street, simply walking, aware of the city around her, paying it little heed.

She still felt so tired, yet tense. She should go back to the hospital, she thought. But she'd already spent hours with Jon, staring at Jon, and talking to Jon because the nurses were absolutely convinced that it would help if she talked.

So she had talked and stared.

And spent time eating delicious duck and *not being grilled* by Lieutenant Mark LaCrosse.

Standing up to his questions, Ann determined, was one thing. She wasn't changing the situation any. They had a dead girl, and Jon's blood. And proof that Jon had slept with the dead girl. It wouldn't have looked good in Jack the Ripper's day, and now, with modern forensic technology, it was all simply damning.

Proving Jon's innocence would be next to impossible.

Unless she could prove someone else's guilt.

She had reached Jackson Square, she realized, and was staring up at the magnificent statue of the warrior/president that graced the place.

Take Jackson, she thought.

The man had been the hero of New Orleans, rallying his own troops, city folk, and even the pirates to come to the defense of the city against the British. However, to the many Indians he subdued and decimated, he couldn't have been much better than a heinous murderer.

But Jackson's past was not disputed. It was merely varied. He had saved New Orleans; he had also ordered the slaughter and upheaval of countless Indians.

She sighed.

"Great statue."

She whirled around.

He had followed her. His hair was slightly disheveled, as if he might have had to hurry a bit to catch up with her. He didn't seem to be breathing too heavily. His silver-gray eyes were somewhat masked by twilight and the false light of street lamps that came with it. Tall, straight, hands on his hips, head slightly cocked, he stared up at the statue.

"If you like Jackson," she said.

A smile curved his lip. "Well, he was a military genius."

"He was talented and determined, but certainly not always politically popular."

"No. But he did do enough to cause the name of this common ground to be changed to Jackson Square from Place d'Armes."

"Oh?" she queried, crossing her arms over her chest.

"You're not a native child."

"No."

"You're from?"

"Atlanta."

"Good city."

"You're too kind."

"No, really."

"A good city, but not as good as New Orleans?"

"A different city." He grinned. "Nothing is as good as New Orleans." His smile broadened as he swept his arm out. "This was a military parade ground. The French and Spaniards rather resented the intrusion of the Americans after the Louisiana Purchase. Change came slowly. It hasn't come altogether yet. That's half the charm of the place. But then, sometimes that's hard to explain to non-natives."

"Ah . . ." She whirled around, looking at St. Louis Cathedral. "The cathedral! Named for the French king who undertook two Crusades! Still the oldest active cathedral in the United States. And the statue, where on the side facing the cathedral you will find printed, 'The Union must and shall be preserved!'—a message from the Yanks when they took the city. And the square—yes it was a parade ground. It was also the site of public executions, including—throughout the years—burning at the stake, hanging, beheading—and my personal favorite for most pathetic and gruesome—breaking on the wheel. Luckily, I can thank God for small favors. All that was in the past. You're not going to be able to publicly burn Jon at the stake, or chop off his head, here in this place."

She thought he would respond angrily to her taunt.

He just stared at her, eyes glittering silver in the growth of night light as the moon, nearly full, rose behind him.

But he didn't reply angrily. He didn't reply for quite a while. Then he simply shrugged and said, "Darn! No public burning at the stake?"

She turned, walking away from the statue.

"Mrs. Marcel!"

She kept walking.

"Dammit, Ann!"

She was startled when he caught her elbow, swinging her around to face him. "I'll see you to your place."

"I know the way."

"I'll see you home."

"It's easy to walk from here."

"I'll walk with you."

"Well, I won't walk with you."

"Fine, I'll walk behind you."

Ann started walking. She passed a number of artists she knew, working in the square. She offered each a forced smile and hurried on past, faster and faster, determined not to pause.

But he stayed right behind her.

"This isn't necessary."

"I think it is."

"Lieutenant, I live here. I walk these streets daily. I'm not afraid—"

"I am."

She paused, spinning back to him. He was so close, she nearly collided with him.

Instead, she smelled him. He smelled good. Darned good. Too good. She felt ridiculously dizzy, so close to the man. He set his hands on her shoulders, meeting her eyes.

"I'll see you home," he said determinedly. "And I'll check out your place."

"Lieutenant, I already left you for the evening."

"I'm back."

"And I'm out for an evening's stroll now. And you're not invited."

"It's a public street. And I intend to see you through it."

"I'm fine."

"It's just a precaution."

"I don't need—"

"I do."

"Wait a minute, you don't even know what I was going to say. What is it that I'm so certain that I don't need and you're so certain you do?"

"You."

"What?"

"I need to watch out for you, Mrs. Marcel."

"Why?"

His teeth grated. He let out a sigh of great impatience. "I need you alive."

"Oh, you do. Why, Lieutenant?"

"It's my job to keep you alive."

"I haven't been threatened."

"The situation is threatening."

"I don't need—"

"You do!"

"Why?"

"Because I am going to look after you

whether you need me to do so, want me to do so, or not!"

"Why?" she demanded one last time with total exasperation.

"Because, Mrs. Marcel, you aren't telling me the truth—the whole truth and nothing but the truth. You do know something."

"I don't."

"You do. And you're going to tell me."

"The hell I am."

"Ah," he said softly. "You admit you do know something."

She studied his eyes, so sharp and intent upon her. The breeze lifted strands of dark hair across his forehead. His shoulders seemed broad and powerful in the moonlight. She felt the most absurd temptation to lean against him.

He was trying to hang Jon.

He would probably love to see Jon burned to cinders in the middle of Jackson Square.

She smiled sweetly. "Lieutenant."

"Yes?"

"Go to hell."

She turned yet again. And walked.

And she didn't look back once.

Yet she was aware . . .

His footsteps followed her home. To her door.

She entered her second-floor dwelling from the hallway; he followed before she could close the door.

He didn't speak. He checked out the bedrooms and closets—and left again.

Yet, she remained aware.

And she knew that even when she was in bed, the doors locked, the lights out . . .

He was still with her.

He stood in the street below.

Gray eyes intently fixed upon her windows. . . .

Seven

April felt eyes.

They came out of the darkness.

Odd, she'd never felt the least unnerved leaving the club before. She knew her stomping grounds; this was her neighborhood. She and Marty had an apartment right around from the river, and she had spent her three years working at the club walking home to that apartment every time she was off duty. New Orleans could be scary; stomping grounds or not, everybody knew that. Came with the territory. New York City could be scary, L.A. could be scary, any city could be scary. Safety was in knowing the terrain. She avoided the streets the restauranteurs warned the tourists to avoid; she walked in light. She carried Mace.

She usually left the club with Marty.

Not tonight. Marty was working another few hours; she wanted to get home. Gregory had intended to leave early, she knew, and she'd planned to go the distance with him. But Harry had called Gregory back in, and she'd hesitated. When Shelly, working the bar, had told her that Gregory would be at least another twenty min-

utes, she'd weighed her fear against her urgent
desire to get home to her baby, and relieve her
sister. They had a good deal going; she watched
Jessy's baby by day, and Jessy watched her baby
by night.

Sleep was the only thing they seemed to miss
out on in the deal.

There was no reason to be more afraid than
usual—poor Gina. It was heartbreaking. But
Gina had just been playing too many places.
Falling in love with the artist, keeping Harry on
a leash, teasing Jacques Moret when either the
desire urged her or the loneliness got her down.
With everything going, she'd still call on other
friends when boredom seized her, or when she
just couldn't seem to see things straight.

Gina had played with fire. And she'd gotten
burned. Poor, sweet, confused kid. Still, her
murder had surely been personal.

There was no reason to fear the streets . . .

But she shouldn't have started walking home.
A mist was rising, dampening the streetlights,
settling over the city. Ghostly images of the old,
narrow, darkened streets hovered before her. A
dog howled; the fog seemed to whirl from the
ground, up and around old wrought-iron balconies, fences and gates. The scent of gardenias
wafted on the air, curled in with the mist. She
didn't have far to go.

The streets seemed uncannily silent. Jazz had
ceased to fill the streets with its trumpets, horns,
and saxes. She began to sing to keep herself
company.

"Goin' down by the river where it's warm and green, I got a lot to think about—" She broke off. She was singing from a Concrete Blond album. *Bloodletting.* She loved Concrete Blond. She adored that particular album, because there were direct references to New Orleans.

"O you were a vampire, and baby I'm walking dead . . ."

Oh, good, maybe now was not the time for such a song to keep haunting her.

Too bad.

The tune kept spinning through her head. The streets remained eerily silent.

Was it always this quiet this late, or this early, as it might be?

Turn . . . her street was coming up, right in front of her. She heard her own breath, heard her own footsteps. Ahead, out of the silence of the fog, a wrought-iron gate creaked.

The gate stood ajar. She felt as if she was on a movie set. More and more fog seemed to be spilling from the gate. Any minute a man in a floating black cape and top hat would take a menacing and deadly step out into the narrow streets from the field of mist and fog. The moon would rise, and light would reflect from the glittering steel blade that he carried.

"Get a grip, April!" she said aloud firmly. She slipped her hand into her shoulder bag, her fingers curling around the can of Mace there. The open gate was right in front of her. She slowed her footsteps.

She was holding her breath she realized.

"Mee-oow!"

April let out something between a gasp and a scream as a cat suddenly shot out from the garden. She was shaking, relieved. A cat. A damned black cat. She looked through the silver mist filling the garden beyond the gate. A child's swing set stood by a bird fountain. A tricycle was rolled against the fountain; a water gun lay against the tricycle. April inhaled deeply, laughing at her fears.

Then she froze once again. Chills seemed to sweep up her spine, paralyzing her momentarily.

Because *she* wasn't moving, yet she could still hear footsteps. Coming from behind her.

She spun around. There was no one there.

No one. The street was silent again. Quaint old houses on quaint narrow streets, shrouded in a blanket of mist and fog.

She turned to hurry home.

Step, step . . .

Extra steps. They were back. The footsteps. Someone else's footsteps.

Following her. Furtively.

She started to run.

And behind her . . .

Her pursuer began to run as well.

By the afternoon, Mark felt as if he'd been at the office for two days running. He couldn't seem to catch up on his sleep.

God, he was tired.

It was this case.

It was Gina.

And it was Ann Marcel.

Stop, he warned himself. He was becoming obsessed with the woman. Because she was lying. Marcel had said something to her.

What?

Damn, he just felt too tired to think straight.

Maybe Brit was right. Maybe his soap was just wrong, he thought.

He stared at his desk. It was piled high with papers to be studied, reports to fill out for the D.A.'s office. He tapped his pencil against the wood, watching the papers blur as he did so.

Jimmy came by, perching on the edge of his desk. "You with us, Mark?"

Mark glanced up at him. He nodded.

"I heard Lee Minh sent in his completed report."

"Yeah. Apparently the FBI gave him some computer help, and the DNA testing is in."

"And?"

Mark shrugged. "Jon Marcel was indisputably with Gina L'Aveau on the day she was killed."

"With her?" Jimmy said. "He had sexual intercourse with her."

"Yeah, he had sexual intercourse with her. We knew that."

"Now we know it for a certainty. Looks cut and dried. We just need to finish up the paperwork, and the D.A.'s office can charge him."

"Can't charge a guy in a coma," Mark reminded him.

"But the legal process can be prepared to

snap **him up** the minute he comes out of that coma."

Mark frowned at him.

"Well, come on, you think he's guilty, right? Mark, he was covered in her blood."

Mark pointed the pencil at Jimmy. "No murder weapon," he reminded him.

"We should have gotten a search warrant for the wife's place."

Mark shook his head determinedly. "No."

"Hell, Mark—"

"The guy was dying; Ann Marcel didn't know that there was anything to cover up. Cops were immediately all over her living room. I can guarantee you, she didn't make any decisions about whether to dial 911 or hide a knife first. She tried to save his life."

"So where's the knife?"

"I don't know."

"We've searched all over."

"Right. So that means—"

"It means Marcel was smart enough to figure out a way to get rid of the knife in a manner in which we could never find it."

"As he was bleeding nearly to death," Mark commented.

Jimmy frowned. "Mark, with all the evidence we've got, you can't mean that you're starting to believe that Ann Marcel could be right? Mark, smell the coffee, Marcel and L'Aveau were wearing each other's blood—"

"Jimmy, a good defense attorney could fight that all the way. Truthfully, I think that Jon Marcel is guilty. I think he got jealous—maybe she got jealous. Maybe they threatened each other, and things got carried away. But everything I'm saying right now is a maybe. Because we know one of two things did happen here. Either Gina stabbed Marcel and Marcel stabbed her, or there was a third party—who stabbed them both."

Jimmy shook his head, pounding with his palm on one side of it as if his brain might be waterlogged.

"Mark, they'd had lots of sex that day. They'd been together. They were both wild people who had argued rather fiercely before, according to eyewitnesses."

"Jimmy, I told you. I'm convinced that the guy is guilty as hell. But we need more. No knife, Jimmy. No murder weapon."

"We do need the damned knife," Jimmy said mournfully. He wagged a finger at Mark. "Watch out for Ann Marcel. She'll have you convinced Marcel is the friggin' pope if you're not careful."

"I think she knows something, Jimmy. Anyway, she's our only real link," Mark said.

Jimmy sniffed.

Mark's phone rang. Still staring at Jimmy, he picked up his receiver.

Captain Evers was on the line. "Tyrell just called in. We've got another dead body for you."

"Where?"

"A couple of kids playing by the river found her. The divers are on their way; I'd like you and Jimmy on this one."

"Why? What is it? Another stripper?"

"It's a Jane Doe right now. We don't have anything on her, but I'd like to know who she is as soon as possible. She's naked—no I.D."

"Give me the address; we're on our way."

He glanced at Jimmy, jotting down the captain's directions.

"Another—stripper?"

"Another dead woman. That's all we've got at the moment."

He started out. Jimmy followed behind him.

"Jesus," he said.

"Jesus—what?" Mark demanded.

"I sure hope you—I sure hope we don't know this one."

"Right."

"One thing, Mark."

"Yeah, what?"

"If it is another stripper, it means that the guy we got vegetating in the hospital is innocent."

Mark hesitated. "Yeah, it might mean that. C'mon, let's hurry."

Jon Marcel could be innocent if the murders were related. Hell, if their body had been a murder victim. He didn't know anything yet; he didn't want to speculate.

He was back to Jimmy's original thought.

He sure as hell hoped that he didn't know this one.

Eight

Walking into the club, Ann felt like a complete fool.

She'd changed five times to try and choose an inconspicuous outfit for a single woman entering a club alone where the emphasis was on the women strippers.

Actually, she didn't think such an outfit existed.

She had finally chosen a simple black cocktail dress with cap sleeves and a scoop neck. Quiet, she hoped, elegant, and dignified. Not so risque she ran the danger of appearing as if she was trying for a pickup, not so prim and proper that she would look absurd and stand out too glaringly—a fish out of water.

A fish out of water . . . she thought, entering Annabella's. She was a fish out of water, all right. A damned whale shark.

It wasn't that there weren't other women in the club. There were.

They were with men.

They tended to be in the bar area, sipping drinks, talking, not really concentrating on the stage. The men with them weren't really concentrating on the stage. They were more involved with the women in their company. The music seemed to be the main appeal; the stage a backdrop for relationships that needed little infusion.

Panic seized her as she walked in. What was she doing here? She was mad. Totally insane.

But what else could she do.

Annabella's.

It was the name Jon had whispered to her. When he should have been saying her name—as in thanks, Annie, for trying to save me. Or when he should have at least been trying to say the name of the person who had attacked him. Annabella's itself hadn't attacked him; a club couldn't walk down a street or alley wielding a knife.

So all that she could imagine was that he had said Annabella's because the answer was here. Somewhere.

Or with someone.

Fool. She couldn't find answers just by coming here.

By standing in the entry.

Feeling that . . .

She was being watched. Ah, yes, from the first seconds when she had stepped through the doorway, she had felt that she was being watched.

No great intuition. There was a strikingly handsome black man sitting at the bar. He flatly stared at her as she stood in the entry. Couples glanced up at her, and seemed momentarily amused and intrigued by her presence. There were two burly fellows near the door—bouncers, she decided. They watched her with annoyance, apparently assuming she'd be trouble.

So much for dressing carefully for the occasion. Dressing so that she'd just fit in with the clientele. It wasn't the clothing, she realized. Everyone else was relaxed. She was as tense as a piano wire.

She felt ridiculous.

She was going to do a marvelous job of trying to be a subtle snoop.

She tried not to pause after she first made it through the door. However, she had to get her bearings. To her left, once she entered, was the dais where the musicians played. Good musicians. Right now, they were involved in a medley of old show tunes. Four musicians played; Ann was certain that the dais accommodated more players. Perhaps they took turns going on break, and managed to keep the entertainment flowing more smoothly by doing so.

Straight ahead of her was a darkened area; it was filled with tables that looked upon a stage. Along the curve of the stage, chairs had been set; the outer rim of the stage itself had been set up as a bar. That would have been the place to be; it was nearly impossible to discern anything about those sitting there except that they were humanoid in form and had—in most cases—hair on their heads. But of course, those rimming the stage were all gentlemen. Or *men* of some kind or the other at the very least.

There were four dancers on stage at the minute, all in different stages of undress. Two male, two female, two black, two white. All four exquisitely perfect in their movement and form. Despite her determination not to hover obtrusively in the entryway, it was exactly what Ann did. She understood perfectly Jon's determination to try to catch some of the grace and beauty in his *Red Light Ladies.* Jon hadn't yet chosen to paint the men—but Ann imagined he would have gotten around to it. Naturally, being the healthy male heterosexual he was, he was going to find the beauty in the females first. But she knew Jon. When his one series had been completed, he would have gotten to the males. Just like the women on the stage, the men moved with fluid and mesmerizing grace. They were perfectly, beautifully, strongly formed.

She could have helped him with the men, she reflected, trying to analyze her opinion of the club.

It wasn't what she had expected, but rather, in an odd way, like Jon's paintings. There was nothing cheap here, nothing tawdry. When the dancers moved together, sensuality rather than sexuality of movement was emphasized. The dancers were intoxicating, erotic . . . and romantic. The choreography and staging, down to the colors and sexes of those involved, were beautifully planned.

A little motion distracted her from the dancers; she had that feeling of being watched again.

Of course she was being watched. She looked

ridiculously out of place, and half of the people in the club were staring at her. No. She looked up and around. This time it felt as if the very walls were watching her.

"Pardon me, but who are you and what are you doing here?"

The voice came from behind her, deep, rich and husky. She spun quickly around, startled to see that the exceedingly handsome black man had left his seat at the bar and come to talk to her.

"I'm just—I'm—"

"You don't belong here," he said matter-of-factly.

"Well, now, excuse me, but the establishment is open to the public and—"

"You're his wife."

She paused, searching out the man's face. "I'm Jon Marcel's ex-wife yes. Do you mind returning the favor? Just who the hell are you and why were you staring at me?"

He grinned. "Gregory Hanson. Friend of your husband's. Ex-husband. Casual friend. Close friend of Gina L'Aveau. The girl murdered the other night. By your husband. So they say."

Ann was pleasantly startled to realize that this man wasn't condemning Jon without a trial—no matter what kind of evidence the papers had said that the police had against him.

"Jon didn't kill her."

The man arched a brow. "He told me once that you two were friends. Best friends. That's just kind of hard to believe when a marriage splits up."

"We just got past the bitterness."

"That's even harder to believe."

Ann smiled. "Well, it's true. Maybe we're lucky. We have a daughter, and we have art in common to keep us together. Our marriage didn't make it. But I know Jon, and I know that he would never murder anyone."

"Even if he was in love with her?"

"Was he in love with her?"

"I think a lot of people were a little bit in love with her." He indicated the bar. "Have a seat with me. You won't look quite so much like a white nun in Harlem."

Ann allowed him to propel her toward the bar. "What will you drink?" he asked her. "You have to drink something. When in Rome, you know."

She glanced sideways at him. "What do women usually drink in strip joints?"

"Strip joints, Mrs. Marcel? This is a club."

"Ah. And the women never prostitute themselves; they work as escorts, right?"

"Only when they choose," Gregory replied blandly. "What will you drink?"

"A beer, please. And I don't mean to be offensive to anyone."

"I've taken no offense," Gregory said, motioning to the young woman behind the bar for a drink.

"Are you—a dancer?" Ann asked.

He grinned. "Or a male escort?"

She flushed.

He pointed to the dais. "I play the trumpet. I'm one of the best in New Orleans. In the country, maybe." He didn't brag, and he didn't offer any false modesty. He spoke quite matter-of-factly.

"Why aren't you playing your trumpet?"

"I'm on break. What are you doing here?"

"Jon is in a coma."

"Yes?"

"He can't defend himself."

"So you've come to a strip joint to defend him?"

"He didn't kill your friend."

"Maybe he didn't. Shouldn't the police be working on who did?"

"The police think that Jon is guilty."

"Foolish men. Jon was with her, their blood is mingled, they got it on sometime during the day."

"How do you know all that?"

"I read the papers."

The young woman tending the bar brought Ann's drink. She was wearing a white see-through blouse with nothing underneath. Ann couldn't find a comfortable place to focus.

"Thanks," she managed.

"Sure thing, hon," the woman said, flashed a smile to Gregory, and moved on.

Gregory lifted his own glass to her. "Salute, Mrs. Marcel."

Ann lifted her glass in return. Gregory set his glass down.

"I was in love with her," he said softly.

"Gina?"

He nodded. "And I agree with you. Your ex-husband didn't kill her."

"Thanks. It's good to have someone on my side."' She hesitated, sipping the foam off her beer. "So, who did kill her?"

Gregory shrugged. "I don't know." He looked down at his hands, at the backs first, then, turning them over, at his palms. He had very large, powerful hands. "Gina . . . I hope I can say this properly. Gina sometimes made enemies because she liked people so much."

Ann arched a brow to him.

"She liked people, she felt sorry for people. If someone needed her, she felt compelled to be there, whether she should be there or not. She—"

"She what?"

"She was seeing lots of men. Just about everybody she knew—except for me."

"I don't understand—"

"I was in love with Gina. I didn't say that she was in love with me. I think she had fallen in love with your ex-husband, Mrs. Marcel; but she hadn't managed to break off some of her previous liaisons, and I'm not sure she believed that a basically good man like Marcel could really want to marry her and give her what she honestly wanted out of life."

"Who else was she seeing?"

"Ah!" Gregory said, leaning against the bar.

"Better ask who she wasn't seeing. That list includes me."

Ann smiled at his attempt at humor. "Seriously, will you tell me what you know?"

He nodded. "Well, her family were bayou folk. Mama Lili Mae, the local voodoo guru around here, was a great-aunt to her or the like; Gina loved to visit Mama Lili Mae. She grew up out on the bayou where they have a bunch of cottages. Among the kin she grew up with was a distant cousin, Jacques Moret. She was seeing him, becoming involved with his business deals now and then. Clean deals for the most part; just shady enough to make him a fair income. Let's see, there was your husband. And . . ." He paused, looking upward where etched mirrors lined the high walls of the place. "And then there's Harry Duval."

"And he is . . . ?"

"The fellow who owns this place. She's had an ongoing relationship with him for a long time." He hesitated. "There are a few others, I guess. Friends. Friends who have been more than friends." His dark eyes touched hard upon Ann. "She had gone to see Mama Lili Mae the day she was killed. She was distressed about something she had discussed with that old voodoo witch."

"Have you talked to her?" Ann asked anxiously.

He shook his head.

"But—"

"You don't just call Mama Lili Mae. When I

say bayou, I mean you head out into the water. That's one of those places where AT&T hasn't yet managed to reach out and touch someone. No phone, no lights, no anything."

"I'd like to talk with her."

"Would you?"

"Yes. Would you consider taking me out there?"

He studied her face, then leaned toward her, suddenly angry.

"So you want to go to the bayou? To the 'squitors and the gators, the swamp, the snakessssss . . ." He hissed the last.

"Yes."

"The bayou is brutal to strangers."

"I'll be with you."

This time, he didn't get a chance to answer her. A slim brunette with huge gray eyes had come to Gregory's other side. "Hey, I'm off now, can I drown in some Scotch with you for a while? Oh!" She noticed Ann on his other side. "Hi, I'm so sorry, I didn't mean to intrude—"

"Cindy," Gregory interrupted. "This is the artist's wife."

"Ex-wife," Ann said with a smile, offering the pretty woman a hand. "Ann Marcel."

"Cindy McKenna. Nice to meet you. Your ex seems to be a great guy. Oh, wow, that sounds weird, doesn't it? He's a great guy for an alleged murderer. I mean, I—oh, God. He's your *ex*, right? What are you doing here, Mrs. Marcel? That's not what I mean—that sounds awful. I mean, this can just be such a strange place for certain people . . . ," her voice trailed away awkwardly. "I'm so sorry."

"Don't be sorry. Jon is a great guy. And he didn't do it—Jon didn't murder anybody."

Cindy McKenna's eyes widened. "Did they prove him innocent somehow? Is he out?"

Ann shook her head. "No, no one has proven anything."

"Oh, I'm sorry." She looked sorry. Her eyes remained huge and round. Staring at her, Ann realized that the woman looked familiar. Then she realized why.

"Oh, you're one of the dancers who was on stage!" Ann said.

Cindy flushed and nodded uneasily. "It's a good living," she said quietly.

Defensively.

"You all were—beautiful," Ann said. "So graceful, fluid. It was beautifully choreographed."

Cindy stared at her, then looked to Gregory. "Did you hear that?"

Ann frowned. "I meant what I said—"

"And it was really nice. So nice," Cindy said. "I'm not accustomed to comments being so nice because most of the time, well—"

"Most of the time," Gregory interjected dryly, "the comments on her dancing refer to T and A."

"Tits and ass," Cindy murmured, as if Ann might not understand.

"Well," Ann replied, "such things can be virtues as well."

Cindy laughed. "Jon always said that you were nice, and talented. And now . . . well, you're awfully loyal as well. You must be hurting very badly for him. I wish we could help you."

"I thought that I'd take her out to Mama Lili Mae's tomorrow," Gregory said.

"Out in the bayou?" Cindy said, surprised.

"Why shouldn't I take her out there?"

"Oh—just because, well . . . I mean, some folks might think the whole thing was a bit silly, reading bones, sacrificing chickens and all . . ." She smiled again, but then her smile faded; her face seemed to become a paler shade as she looked past Ann. Ann swung quickly around on her bar stool to see what had caused that reaction in Cindy.

The man who had come to stand behind her was tall, lean, and tautly muscled, handsomely dressed in a dark casual suit with a gray knit shirt beneath. His skin was a true copper; his eyes were almost gold. He was an exotic and striking individual, compelling, arresting. He smiled slowly, assessing Ann.

"Mrs. Marcel." His voice was low and well-modulated. "Welcome to Annabella's."

"You know my name."

"Most of New Orleans will know your name. There was a picture of you in the paper."

"Ah. And you, sir—"

"Ann Marcel, Harry Duval. The owner of Annabella's." Gregory performed the necessary introductions.

"All of us here are deeply disturbed by the

events of late, you understand." Harry Duval's words were saved from triteness by the incredible degree of charm behind them.

"Of course," Ann said. "If you'd rather I not be here—"

"On the contrary, we're delighted to have you here. Your ex-husband spoke of you frequently, with great warmth and enthusiasm. There were not many people he trusted with his vision when he first broached the ladies and me with his intent to paint them. We're disturbed, Mrs. Marcel, because none of us can accept what has happened. Gina was quite precious to us all; she is lost. We cannot believe what is said of Jon Marcel, but then . . ."

"He didn't do it," Ann said.

Duval's brow went up, much as Cindy's had done earlier when Ann had made her statement of faith.

"Have the police learned something new, Mrs. Marcel?"

Was there a little anxiety in his voice? As if he might be *afraid* that Jon could be innocent? Cindy had jumped on her quickly as well. Maybe, no matter how much they all said they liked Jon, they wanted him to be guilty.

Because that meant that the killer was caught; that no one else was in danger.

And that no one else was guilty.

She shook her head slowly, watching Harry Duval. "The police are going on their knowledge of their evidence; I'm going on my knowledge of Jon."

"He is a lucky man to have you. It is a . . . rare relationship, is it not?"

"I don't think that friendship is so rare."

"Why did you come here?" Duval demanded flatly.

"I—the paintings," she said quickly. "I wanted to see what had so influenced Jon to create such wonderful art. Now I know, the dancing was beautiful."

"Yes, my musicians are the best; my dancers are the most talented. Few people understand that such dancing can be like everything else in life, some exquisite, some for the gutter." He laughed suddenly, golden eyes sizzling. "Not that I pretend we don't wish to be seductive, to touch the senses, to titillate, arouse . . . we do. But the human body is beautiful, and can be a beautiful tool, and as you will note by the many different people sitting in here, sensuality belongs to all walks of life."

"It's an extraordinary place," Ann told him.

He winked at her. "And I insist you are an extraordinary woman, entering into such a den of harlots and thieves to protect your friend!" He motioned to the bartender. "A round on the house, please?" He studied Ann, smiling. "I wish that you had come here for a job, Mrs. Marcel. I believe that you would make an incredible dancer."

"You could, you know," Cindy said.

Ann smiled, shaking her head. "I'm too old, too uncoordinated, too everything."

"Too wrong," Cindy advised. "I could teach

you a dozen basic moves in two hours. Want to try sometime?"

"I—I—"

"Too exotic for you, Mrs. Marcel?" Harry Duval inched closer to her, gold eyes seeming to bathe her in a strange, compelling fire. He moved like a cat, subtle, sure. He was stalking her, she thought.

"Mr. Duval, I believe I'm past the time when I might have learned—"

"Ah, my dear Mrs. Marcel, we never pass the time when we are intrigued by what is achingly erotic, stimulating, compelling . . . just as we never lose the capacity to love, the desire to love."

Cindy laughed. "What he's trying to say, I think, is that we do want to be sexy, don't we? Most women want to be sexy to at least one man."

"Well, we'll see," Ann murmured. She was startled to feel as if her fingers were on fire. Duval had lifted her hand into his own.

"Just so long as you do come back, Mrs. Marcel. Perhaps as an artist, then, with paints, if you do not wish to use your own body in what truly is an art form. Come back with your paints. Take up where your ex-husband left off. Excuse me," he said suddenly, "I see a friend with whom I must speak."

He was looking at a man who had just come in, who stood in the entryway watching the dancers now on stage. The band was playing something with a jungle beat, and a redhead in a scanty leopard costume was sliding up and down against one of the poles. The man, however, was much more intriguing, especially to an artist, than the woman alone on the stage. He was tall; he wore Versace as if he were born to it, with an absolute casual elegance. He was a white man with slick dark hair and the fine features of an old European aristocrat. He was handsome, yet something about him made Ann think of the term "gigolo."

"Jacques Moret," Gregory murmured against Ann's ear. "Gina's lover beginning to circle . . ." He sat back, staring at someone who had come around from behind Ann.

"Mark," he said, stretching out a hand.

"Gregory, Cynthia, good evening."

Ann's head snapped around. Lieutenant Mark LaCrosse was standing right behind her.

He hadn't come through the front just now, had he? She didn't know where he'd been, only that he was suddenly there. At her side.

"Mrs. Marcel," he greeted her, silver-gray eyes as sharp as knives, his voice thick with repressed aggravation. She wasn't supposed to be here. Not in his book. And she suddenly felt as guilty as a school child.

She had a right to go anywhere she wanted! She wasn't up on murder charges.

"Lieutenant," she replied as coolly as she could manage. But of course, he was staring at her with those eagle eyes. Piercing through her with them, making her tremble inside, shake outside. She reached blindly for her beer, finished it in a swallow.

"How are things going, Mark?" Gregory asked.

Gregory was calling him by his first name; they obviously knew one another. Fairly well. Mark knew Cindy, too. Of course, he'd probably had to question people here already.

Perhaps he came here as well. As a customer. Frequently.

"Things are—just going," Mark said. He glanced at Cindy. "How're you holding up?"

"I'm fine."

"Be careful," he told her.

She shrugged, then glanced at Ann uneasily. "I understand you feel that you have the killer in the hospital."

"Maybe. And maybe Mrs. Marcel, who is surely here to delve her nose where it shouldn't be, is right. Maybe someone else is walking around out there in the shadows with a long knife—ready to strike. You be careful."

"Thanks, Mark, for the concern," Cindy said. The words were sincere.

"I won't let her head out alone," Gregory promised.

"Mrs. Marcel?" Mark LaCrosse said. She stared at him. She felt again that strange trembling.

As if she were an errant school girl, caught with her hand in the cookie jar. She felt flushed and uncomfortable, as if she had done something wrong.

Maybe there was more to it than that. This

place might be filled with erotic dancers, but it definitely had its share of exotic men as well. Gregory, like an ebony god; Duval, the striking best of two races; and Jacques Moret, handsome almost to the point of beauty. Yet, somehow, Mark LaCrosse seemed to make all those around him pale in comparison. There was something rock hard, masculine, virile and real about him. Something in his attitude, in the way he stood. He was a handsome man, but craggy. Character was worn into his face, blending with his well-cast, strong features. His eyes were the most unique she had ever known, capable of looks that spoke volumes, that seemed to rip right into the soul, and demand answers.

"I think we should go, Mrs. Marcel," he said.

She smiled, and spoke in a low, soft purr. "I didn't remember that we had come together, Lieutenant."

"Maybe we didn't. We should leave together," he replied.

"It is getting quite late," Cindy said. "Mrs. Marcel, it was great meeting you. Gregory, I'll take you up on seeing me home. You've got another set; I'll just wait in the dressing room."

"I should be getting back to the stage," Gregory said.

Ann realized that both he and Cindy were doing their best to leave her at the mercy of Lieutenant LaCrosse.

"Wait—"

"Shall we go, Mrs. Marcel?"

His hand was on her elbow; she was being

propelled off the bar stool. His grip was firm. Before she knew it, she was being led toward the door.

"You've no right to do this—"

"Do you want to be in danger, Mrs. Marcel?" he demanded.

"How can I be in danger as far as you see things, Lieutenant? Jon is in a coma, no danger to anyone."

"You're out to prove me wrong, right?"

"You bet."

"Then you're an idiot, digging into this place and playing with fire if someone else is the murderer. Now come on, I want to get you out of here!"

She gritted her teeth, fully aware that she was either going to have to go with him, or have a screaming fight at the entryway to the place. She didn't want that; she didn't want to be obvious or obnoxious.

Gregory! she thought suddenly. He'd offered to take her to Mama Lili Mae's. She had to get out to the bayou and find out what Gina L'Aveau had been discussing with the woman on the day that she had died.

"Wait—"

"We're leaving!" he insisted firmly, eyes now a smoldering gray.

"Fine, fine, we'll leave. It's just that Gregory bought me a drink; I want to say thanks."

She managed to flee his hold, hurrying to Gregory, who was already walking back to the musicians' dais. "Gregory!"

He stopped, turning back to her, catching her with firm hands when she would have slammed right into him.

"Thanks for the drink. When do I meet you to go out to the bayou and visit Mama Lili Mae?" she said in a single swift breath.

He glanced over her shoulder to Mark.

"I shouldn't—"

"Please!"

"But you could put yourself in danger—"

"You'll be with me."

"I—"

"Gregory, help me. Help Jon, and help me get real justice for Gina, please."

He glanced over her shoulder again. She turned her head quickly. Mark was coming toward her with his typical, determined long strides.

"Gina's funeral is tomorrow morning. Meet me after. Here. Outside the club. I have a black Buick sedan."

"I'll be here," she promised in a whisper.

Even as she did so, she felt a hand fall upon her shoulder. Strong, firm. Determined. "Mrs. Marcel, let's go. Gregory, good night."

"Night, Mark. Don't forget, anything at all that I can do to help—"

"Thanks, Gregory."

If they were back just a few thousand years, Ann thought, he'd hit her over her head and drag her out by the hair. As it was, he now thrust her in front of him and all but pushed her out of the club.

He didn't leave off as they left the club, but continued to propel her toward his car.

"Maybe I want to walk—"

"Fool!" he exploded.

"For being there—"

"Yes!"

"You were there."

"I'm a cop! You're just asking to put your own throat out there on the line."

She spun on him. "How could I be in danger if your killer is in the hospital?" she nearly shrieked.

He stood still in front of her, hands on his hips, staring at her. He started to speak; he went silent. "There's been another murder," he said.

Ann gasped, staring at him. "Of a—of a stripper? Does that make Jon definitely innocent?"

He shook his head. "The victim is a Jane Doe. Found naked in the Mississippi."

"But—"

"She was strangled."

"So—"

"So the murders are most probably unrelated. Hell, I wish murder was a unique thing here in New Orleans. It isn't. We don't know who she is. We don't know that she is a stripper, but then . . . we don't know that she isn't."

"Then why—why would I suddenly be in danger."

He shook his head, looking down for a minute.

"Why?"

"Cop's intuition."

"What? You can't push me around because of a cop's intuition!"

"Yes, I can."

"No—"

"Let's get out of here, shall we?"

"Now, wait a minute!" Ann persisted.

But he wasn't waiting. She found herself prodded and folded into his car.

And he was beside her. Jaw set. Eyes on the road. She was furious. She was shaking.

He was irritating beyond measure.

He smelled too pleasantly and subtly of a woodsy aftershave. She wanted to hit him; shake him.

She wanted to set her hand upon his shoulder, feel the texture of his jacket . . .

Feel the warmth of his flesh and bone and muscle and body beneath.

Nine

She didn't ask him if he'd like to come up; it didn't seem to matter. It was a very short drive from the club to her house, and when the car was barely parked he was out of it and around to the passenger's seat to let her out. She was suddenly swept into the main street entrance of the house, soaring past the door to the shop on the first floor and flying up the stairs to the second-floor apartment.

"Well, thank you, Lieutenant," she seethed, digging for her key, slipping it into the lock. "It wasn't necessary for you to see me home, but—"

The door was open; she was propelled inside. He was inside, and the door was closed behind him.

"What qualifies you to dig into this case?" he demanded.

"I don't need 'qualifications' to go to a club for a drink, Lieutenant," she returned, barely keeping her temper in check. She tossed her purse down on a chair and walked to the sofa, sitting.

It was a mistake. He followed. And towered over her.

"There are clubs all over New Orleans!"

"I heard that that particular club had the best jazz."

She wasn't sitting anymore. He'd reached for her, drawn her to her feet.

"Crime is bad enough for the police without the need to make someone babysit you."

She tried to wrench her arms free from his grasp; he was staring into her eyes and seemed unaware that she was making any effort at all.

"You don't need to babysit me—"

"I don't need for you to get yourself killed, Ann."

"I won't—" She struggled for a moment, searching for something to say. Had he called her Ann before? She didn't think so. There was suddenly something she was taking as ridiculously personal about the way he had used her given name.

"I—I won't get killed," she said. She cleared her throat. "I—"

This man was obnoxious. He was trying to fry Jon. He was authoritative, pig-headed and extremely annoying. A bully. She should call someone about police brutality.

Yet she was suddenly at a loss for words. She wanted to shout out that he had no right to be in her home, had no right to hold her the way that he was holding her. But she liked him in her home; oh, God, she liked the feel of him holding her, liked the scent of him, the nearness of him, the look of his shaven cheek, the texture of his jacket against her, the way that his gaze pierced into her and seemed to warm and heat her. Her mouth was suddenly dry; she couldn't swallow, couldn't think. Oh, God, he'd made her feel like a school girl again. Trying to play with the big boys. And oh, sweet Jesus, but that was just the problem; she wanted to play. She barely knew him, and she wanted to touch him, wanted to be touched by him in return. He wasn't just a handsome man whom she could look at and admire with an artist's eye. She wanted to touch. And feel.

It was the club. Duval had been right. It stirred the blood, scintillated, titillated, seduced. Her life had simply been too pure since she'd gotten divorced; a date here and there, friendships, fun evenings . . . but nothing like this. Nothing like this awful urge to reach out and rip the clothing off a near stranger and feel him, his chest against her own, his hands . . . those clean-shaven cheeks against her flesh.

"The club is dangerous! Something can happen to you."

She was watching his lips move. He had a great mouth. Generous. Sensual. His hands still gripped her arms. She was closer to him as he made his point. She inhaled him with each breath, and with each breath she felt absurdly weaker; the tremors within her seemed to race more hotly.

"You need to—get out," she whispered.

"You're not listening to me."

"I am. You think that the club is dangerous, and that I should stay away from it."

"What were you doing there?" A lock of hair had fallen over his forehead. His features were so intense. She felt the emotion in him making the muscles in his arms as taut as wire.

"Jon's paintings . . . ," she said vaguely.

"Paintings? You little fool—"

"Then Jon can't be guilty!"

"Whether Jon is or isn't guilty, there are undercurrents in that damned place, don't you realize it? The streets are dangerous, Ann, and you damned well know it. I'm telling you that you—"

He broke off. He was staring at her. She was closer, closer. Watching his mouth.

Suddenly, amazingly, almost savagely, it was on her own.

His hands . . .

Were moving.

His mouth encompassed hers, seared with passion and fury, invaded. She felt his tongue, hot against her lips, past her teeth, deep. So deep that it seemed to steal her strength, that it seemed a far more intimate touch than a kiss alone. So deep that it ignited fires in her, fanned them, urged them to greater heat, sent them searing throughout her. His hand cupped her cheek, fingers stroked her throat, then encompassed and cradled, teased and tormented her breasts over the sheer fabric of her black gown. His kiss . . . the depth of it swept into her like a jagged streak of lightning, making her tremble, making her shake and sear to the very intimate insides of her, throughout her limbs, down to her sex, causing her to burn. . . .

Then, as suddenly as it had come, the on-slaught ended. His mouth was parted from hers, just a breath. "Oh, God," he groaned.

Then his hold eased, and suddenly she was sitting again. He had brought her down to the sofa; maybe he had known that she would fall if he did not.

He placed her hands in her lap. Eyes still dark with passion, features far more tense than she had seen them yet, rich auburn hair tousled and mussed, he stared at her. "Dammit!" He opened his mouth to say more, but stood instead. "Shit!" he swore violently. "Shit!" He paced to the door, running his fingers through his hair. He pointed a finger at her. "Stay away from the damned club!"

And he slammed his way out of her house.

Gregory walked Cindy the few blocks to her small apartment.

"She's going to keep coming back, you know," Cindy told Gregory worriedly.

"She thinks the cops have framed the wrong man."

Cindy shook her head. "I'm afraid for her. If she is right, she'll start pushing the wrong buttons."

"The club is open to the public, and this is America; she's going to keep coming back."

"But seriously, Gregory, do you think you should be taking her to see Mama Lili Mae?"

"Might as well. She'll get out there herself if I don't."

"Yeah, maybe," Cindy agreed. "It's just that . . ."

"It's just that what?" Gregory demanded.

"Well, the swamp. God, there are so many miles of just nothing except for grass and water and snakes and alligators. And when it's dark, it's so dark. When there's a storm, it's like the ends of the earth."

"That's the nature of a bayou."

Cindy trembled. "We need to make sure that no one knows that she's going there."

"Who could know but you and me?"

"You don't think that anybody overheard you talking?"

Gregory hesitated, looking around himself. He stared down at Cindy. "No, I don't think so. Why do you care so much?"

"I don't know why, I mean, set aside Ann Marcel. Gina and Jon probably had an awful fight, and maybe neither of them ever meant it, but in the heat of fury like that . . . well, maybe he did kill her."

"Then she'd be safe."

"What if it didn't happen that way?" Cindy wailed. "What if we're all in danger."

Gregory set an arm around her shoulders. "What is that saying—'The truth will set you free.' Cindy, we're not going to be able to stop Marcel's ex-wife."

"We'll have to look out for her, though."

"Yeah, well, she will come back to the club.

She'll keep coming back until she gets what she wants."

"Maybe I can teach her to dance."

"Maybe she can do some paintings herself."

Gregory paused in the street. "What the hell are we talking about? No matter what she does at the club, she'll be there."

Cindy shivered fiercely. "Gregory, I'll come with you tomorrow, too."

"To the bayou?"

She nodded. "There's safety in numbers," she said determinedly. "I mean, what if somebody did hear you talking about taking a trip out to the bayou tomorrow?"

"Cindy—"

"Gregory, we've all gone to Mama Lili Mae's a dozen times before. We never thought a thing of it. Believe me, it will be better if we're together, don't you think?"

Gregory sighed. "If you wish." He set an arm around her shoulders. "Let me get you home, then. I have the feeling that tomorrow is going to be one hell of a long day."

Gina L'Aveau was buried in a mausoleum bearing her family name.

Ann came to the church for the service, but stayed just inside the doors, watching from a distance.

Gina's pallbearers were an interesting assortment of men: Gregory, Harry Duval, the man who had been pointed out to her as her distant kin, Jacques Moret, and, curiously enough, Lieutenant Mark LaCrosse.

Ann was fairly certain, by the time she'd followed the procession to the cemetery, that she still hadn't been seen—by Mark at least. His partner, the tall man with the basset hound face, was in attendance as well, but like her, he seemed to be hanging about in the background. Ann thought that she was staying far enough from Officer Jimmy not be seen by him as well. There were other cops there—she knew them because they had all been assigned, at different times, to watch the door to Jon's room at the hospital.

It felt very odd to be here today; she hadn't known Gina, but she was beginning to feel that she had.

It felt even stranger to be at the cemetery under the circumstances. Ann loved the cemeteries in New Orleans, and she had come to this one often enough. The first time, she had come on her own, only to be warned by a park ranger with a tour group that she was in "grave" danger, no pun intended. There'd been a shooting in the cemetery the night before she had come. She'd come with tour groups herself after that, sketching the tombs, the art, the lay of the cemetery against the city beyond. She didn't think she was particularly morbid, but funerary art was a fantastic study in itself; and though New Orleans didn't often offer the very old angels, death heads, verse, wings, Madonnas and other characters of New England and European cemeteries, the tombs, built above the ground because of the water level, were fascinating in themselves. Angels and other creatures and entities did abound, if differently. Winged griffins and wrought-iron gates guarded family tombs; vines, ivy, mosses and flowers took root in the cracks within cement and crept and crawled to create a haunting aura.

Gina's family vault appeared to date from the later half of the 1700s. The great iron gates had been opened for the delivery of her coffin into the L'Aveau crypt. The mourners were a solemn, silent crowd. A few sniffles could be heard now and then. As Ann watched, she saw Cindy McKenna, surrounded by a group of young women, crying softly. A very old woman refused assistance from any of the men who attempted to help or escort her. Ann didn't think she could be Gina's mother. Though she stood tall and firm, her face was ancient, and she had to be in her eighties, at the very least.

Gina's priest conducted the last of the service at the grave site. He offered words applauding Gina's love of life and gentle soul, and promising that she would rest easy in God's embrace, while justice was sought on earth.

Perhaps the priest didn't have a great deal of confidence in New Orleans' finest at the moment, because he promised as well that when justice wasn't found on earth, it was always found by the Almighty, and Judgment Day would come.

Ann escaped quickly to the street and her car

as the service ended; she wasn't about to be seen
now by Lieutenant LaCrosse and stopped. Not
just when she was about to go out to the bayou.
If he saw fit to drag her out of a club, he'd probably half drown her to get her out of a boat in
the swamp. Slipping behind the wheel of her
car, she felt warmth stealing over her—a now
familiar warmth, since it had been assailing her
all morning. She couldn't forget his behavior
last night. His kiss. God. She started trembling.
Fool. This wasn't what she wanted. The hell it
wasn't. He'd felt so good. Touching her, kissing
her . . .

He'd stopped.

What would she have done if he hadn't?

She'd have had no choice. Oh, God, she'd
have been so easy. Because she wanted him so
badly. That was ridiculous, surely; she just
wanted him because she'd been so busy, she
hadn't been in a relationship, she needed a relationship, just that and nothing more.

No, no, she'd never been tempted before with
other acquaintances. She'd never ached to feel
them, naked, touching her.

Her palms were sweating. Hell! She should
have jumped a stranger on the street before
now. Because she did want him; she'd wanted
to go on when he had stopped. She'd been seduced by the scent of him, the roughness of his
cheeks, of his palms, the strength in his hands.

He is the cop trying to fry Jon! she told herself
furiously.

But she could see him now. She slumped

down in her car, hoping he wouldn't recognize her little gray Mazda. He was standing there talking with his basset-faced partner and a handsome Oriental man. He wore a black suit, white shirt, black vest and tie. He was very dignified, incredibly handsome with his auburn hair, just streaked at the temples. Very grave, clean-shaven for the funeral. She felt the heat again, the trembling. She didn't really know him. She felt as if she had known him forever; he'd been in her face since the minute she had first met him. That kiss . . .

Then, of course, the way he'd sworn at her. Well, he was a cop. He wasn't supposed to be seducing his—what? Was she a suspect and accessory to murder? A possible victim, a witness, a what?

All of the above? she mocked herself.

He was going to walk right by her. She slumped down even farther in her seat. Holding her breath, then barely breathing.

As if that could keep him from seeing her!

But miraculously, he didn't notice her. He was too involved with whatever the Oriental man was saying.

"But nothing—nothing yet?" Mark LaCrosse was persisting stubbornly.

"Well, our Jane Doe was never in the military, I can tell you that. And she didn't commit any crimes—no law enforcement agency in the United States or Canada has anything on her prints. We're searching the dental records and sifting through mounds of missing person reports. But lots of single people can be missing several days before friends and family realize that they're not out with other friends and family."

"What about the club?" Mark asked gruffly.

"Well, we're kind of in the same boat there—for the next twenty-four hours at least. Harry Duval says none of his girls failed to show up for work, but then, his girls don't necessarily work every night. Naturally, I couldn't press Duval too much right now with Gina's funeral this morning, but I'll get him down to the morgue to take a look."

Mark shoved his hands into his pockets, staring back through the gates of the cemetery where the crowd was dispersing. "I should have recognized her if she'd come from the club."

"You know all the dancers?"

"No," Mark admitted.

"But what do you think? Could it have been the work of the same man?"

"Maybe."

"M.O.'s are different."

"I know that," Mark said. "But what do *you* think; that's what I want to know."

"Well . . . ," the Oriental man began.

They were past Ann's car. She strained to hear the answer, but try as she might, she couldn't hear the man's reply. She stayed sunk in her seat for several seconds, praying that there might now be some kind of forensic or circumstantial evidence that would begin to convince the police that Jon wasn't guilty. The M.O.'s were dif-

ferent. It was sad, but true. Women were murdered frequently enough that there could easily
have been two different killers.

She sat up, quickly gunned her car, and drove
away from the cemetery, headed for Annabella's.

She couldn't keep her mind from the immediate events. As she drove, she wondered how it
had happened that Mark LaCrosse had been a
pallbearer for Gina L'Aveau.

"Let me take you to lunch, Mama Lili Mae,"
Jacques Moret told his great-great-great-aunt.
He glanced sideways at the woman. She'd been
stoic throughout the services. Now, she still
stared straight ahead of herself, silent. She
didn't cry, but he knew she was mourning. Gina
had always tried to lie somewhat to Mama Lili
Mae. She'd tried to make her life seem rosier
than what it was. Mama Lili Mae was a great-
great-great-aunt to at least two dozen young men
and women who had originally sprung from the
bayou country, all stemming from the family
name L'Aveau.

And all were quick to claim her when one of
the television networks determined to do a special on the woman who, it was estimated, was
now approaching her hundred and tenth birth-
day. She remained in amazingly good health,
the usual weaknesses of old age refusing to claim
her. She walked every day, and didn't need a
cane to do so. Her eyesight continued to serve

her excellently. Occasionally, she felt a twinge of arthritis, but a pair of Advil worked the magic there.

"Mama Lili Mae?" Jacques repeated.

She shook her head.

"You shouldn't go back just yet. You should eat at a restaurant, spend a little time in New Orleans."

Mama Lili Mae fumbled in her purse for one of her hand-rolled, cigarlike cigarettes. She lit it.

Jacques didn't like smoke in his custom white Mercedes. He wouldn't tell her that. "You shouldn't smoke. It isn't good for your health," he told her.

She rolled her eyes to glance over at him. "What? I'm going to die young?"

Jacques sighed. "Fine. Light up. And fine, be stubborn, I'll take you back." He offered her one of his charming smiles. "Most women want to go to lunch with Jacques Moret, you know," he teased.

"Most women are fools," she told him, but she took the sting away from her words by patting him with an incredibly thin and bony hand on the arm. "You come home with me. Most men and women must pay to listen to Mama Lili Mae. You come and listen to the advice I give you, and I'll dish you up some of the finest crawfish you will ever have, even in New Orleans, eh, *mon fil?*"

"Sure, sure," he said with a sigh. Jacques glanced her way; she returned his stare with her steady dark eyes. They probed him. He felt as if he suddenly started to sweat inside. She saw things. Everybody knew that. She saw things.

It terrified him to wonder what she saw in him.

"Get me home quickly," she said to him.

"Yes, I'll get you there quickly, though I still say that you should—"

"I must be home," she repeated.

"Why?"

"People are coming to see me," she said complacently.

He felt himself starting to sweat again, inside and outside this time.

"People should leave you alone—"

"Gina was murdered."

"The police have spoken to you," he said, trying to be gentle. "They have the man—"

"Oh, bullshit!" Mama Lili Mae said. She looked sternly at him. "No one tells the truth to the police, eh? We never know what innocent truth may hurt us. But then . . ."

"Then what?"

"Then those who are guilty must pay, if they are blood, if they are not."

What the hell was she going on about? he wondered. He should probably drown the old bitch in the bay, save all her descendants the effort of being at her beck and call when she chose to make her appearances now and then.

"You shouldn't talk to people at all," he told her sternly. "And the police should leave you alone. You are too involved; you are too emotional." He hesitated. "You always loved Gina most, more than anyone else in the family."

"I've lived too long and seen too much death to be too emotional," she assured him. "But what about you, *mon cher*? Are you not perhaps too close to the issue, too emotional? Are you afraid for yourself when you talk to the police?"

An ash dropped on his white leather upholstery. Surely she saw it. Surely she knew how much she annoyed him.

He really wanted to strangle her.

"I've talked to the police," he told her.

"You loved her once. As more than your distant cousin."

"I loved her still, as more than my distant cousin. She did not love me."

"Passion breeds hatred?"

"Did you learn that from sacrificing chickens?"

She smiled complacently. She wasn't afraid of him; she wasn't afraid of anyone. She was old, and worn, and ready to meet her Maker when the time came.

"Passion breeds hatred, fury and tempest."

"They have the man! They have the man who was covered in her blood! Why does everyone question what is so obvious? Her murderer lies in a hospital in a coma."

"Ah, if he would conveniently die!" Mama Lili Mae mocked, calmly dusting ash from her cotton skirt. "There will always be someone to question the obvious, and there were too many men with her that night to so easily pin what happened on one, eh, *mon cher?*"

Again, he felt the sweat. *How the hell could she know what he had been doing that night? Just exactly what did she know? Not that he considered what had happened to be his fault.*

"Who is coming? Why must you rush back so quickly?" he demanded. "You already spoke to the police; they were crawling all over the cemetery today. So just who is coming?"

"I don't know exactly who. I know why."

"Why?"

"Because nothing on earth is so simple as it seems. Now, Jacques, drive. Bring me back to the bayou."

He clenched his teeth together.

And he drove.

Mama Lili Mae sat back comfortably in the car. She was an old woman. She had few pleasures left.

One was driving Jacques to distraction by smoking in his car.

Another was weighing and judging people. Testing her own abilities to judge the *insides* of those she met.

She'd seen the woman today. Watching her, watching everyone. Seeking the truth. The woman was coming. Actually, it wasn't any voodoo or magic that had told her so; Gina's one true friend, handsome young Gregory Hanson, had told her that he was bringing someone.

Intuition told her that it was the petite blond woman who would be coming.

Instinct already assured her that today would be the day when she talked herself, when she told the truth. Because the truth was not just something that had to be told to be useful.

It had to be heard as well.

Before leaving the cemetery, Mark made arrangements to meet Harry Duval at the coroner's office. During the services, he'd had an opportunity to see most of the people who had been important in Gina's life. Had there not been blood all over Jon Marcel, three of those who might have been top suspects in the case had carried Gina's coffin with him—Harry Duval, Jacques Moret, and Gregory Hanson. Mama Lili Mae had been there—she knew more than she was saying, but he'd have to get her alone to find out if she would tell him anything special or not. The Dixie Boys had all been in attendance, as had most of the dancers from the club. Gina had been loved. Not so oddly, she had probably been loved by her killer.

Now there was another murder. And one of the most important questions regarding the victim was about to be answered.

Duval was prompt. Both men were certainly dressed for the occasion of visiting the dead, as they wore their black suits from the funeral. Mark was certain they must look like a pair of penguins.

They walked down the corridor together to

meet Lee Minh at the freezer. Duval glanced Mark's way.

"I didn't kill them, you know."

"I didn't accuse you."

"We know one another well enough. You've unusual eyes, my friend. They cut into a man and condemn him quickly."

Mark arched a brow to him. "I'm a detective, Duval. I gather evidence for the D.A.'s office. I don't condemn anyone."

Duval sniffed. "Surely, if the police decide to seek further than Jon Marcel for suspects, they will look in my direction. I own the club where Gina L'Aveau worked. I deal in flesh. To the Bible thumpers, I am a devil, Satan in black and white. If it is determined that the murders are related, this strangled girl and Gina, then Jon Marcel must be innocent, unless he can rise up from his hospital bed as a spirit and commit murder by the power of his will alone."

"If the murders are related, then naturally, the case against Jon Marcel will have new light shed upon it. How many of your female dancers are unaccounted for?"

"I had not seen Judy, but she came to the funeral today. April did not show as yet; but she is married, and I have not seen or heard from her husband either. They are not due on stage until this afternoon. Renee, Samantha, Ashley and Jean have not reported to work, nor did they come to the funeral. But we will know in a matter of minutes, eh?"

"Right now," Mark agreed, opening the door for Duval.

Lee Minh was waiting for him. The corpse lay on a gurney. She had been pulled from the water. She was not beautiful in death as Gina had been.

"Do you know her?" Mark demanded as Duval stared down at the body.

Duval grated his teeth together.

He knew her.

Ten

It was a good thing they had started out fairly early.

Cindy McKenna was waiting with Gregory. They were both at the club before her, which she thought was an amazing feat until she realized that they must have slipped away from the cemetery while she was still trying to overhear Mark's words to the Oriental man—and the Oriental man's reply.

Since she had stayed in the background at the services, Ann had felt comfortable enough to wear black jeans, black Reeboks and a black pullover, ready for her excursion into the wilderness. Gregory and Cindy, who had dressed for the funeral, had both changed clothing, apparently at the club, and were prepared for a day in the wilderness, both in blue jeans and knit tops.

"Ann, we'll take your car, if that's all right," Gregory said. "No one will wonder what mine is doing at the club; they'll imagine I'm around somewhere. While your car . . ." He shrugged. "If someone is snooping around, they might recognize your car, and wonder what you're up to."

"Sure," Ann said.

Cindy slipped into the tiny backseat; Gregory sat beside her. Ann felt the slightest twinge of unease, wondering if she should be worried about what Gregory had said. If she was to become lost in the bayou . . .

No one would find her.

From the backseat, Cindy squeezed her shoulder. She glanced over at Gregory. What was human intuition and instinct worth? She felt good about Gregory. She'd felt good about him since she'd met him.

Hop out of the car, scream like a lunatic, forget meeting Mama Lili Mae and proving Jon's innocence, or go along quietly for the ride and enjoy the bayou.

They left the city behind, driving hard along the water. When a copse of trees appeared before them, Gregory had her drive off the road and park by the trees. When they got out of the car, she was surprised to see that a number of boats were tied up in the shallows.

"Come on," Gregory suggested, hopping aboard one of the small motorboats and offering her a hand.

"Is it your boat?"

"It was Gina's boat," Cindy said.

"It's all right; many of the families keep their boats here. To see them, you take a boat."

"No one steals them?"

Cindy smiled, shaking her head. "Only bayou people know that they're here. You can't see them from the road. You won't even be able to see your car from the road now."

Gregory's hand was still outstretched to her.

All right, if she was murdered—and under the circumstances it didn't seem like such a fear might be paranoia—it would be her own fault.

She wasn't going to be murdered. She knew that Gregory was innocent of hurting Gina. He wasn't passionate, he wasn't angry, he was just hurt to the core. And Cindy was with them. And she had seen Mama Lili Mae; she was even certain that Mama Lili Mae had looked right at her. The woman wasn't going to hurt her anyway.

She took Gregory's hand and settled into the boat. Cindy climbed in beside her.

"How do we know that she'll be there?" Ann shouted above the roar of the boat's motor.

"I told her we were coming," Gregory shouted back at her. "She's expecting us; I think she wants us to come."

Ann nodded.

"Sit back, enjoy the ride!" Cindy suggested. Ann swung around to see that Cindy had leaned back comfortably. The wind was rushing through her hair. She looked happier and more relaxed than Ann had yet seen her appear. The bayou, she thought, was really home to these people. The sky, the water, the dense greenery.

They didn't talk; it was too difficult to do so with the motor running. They traversed open waterways for quite some time; then Gregory cut the motor and picked up an oar as they entered into a more narrow channel where the water seemed to be quite shallow, where tree roots rose above the water level and the embankment sometimes seemed to disappear into black voids. The swamp was quiet except for the occasional cry of a bird and the slap of the oar against the water. Cindy patted her shoulder. "Look," she murmured quietly, pointing to the embankment.

An alligator—a good ten feet long—slipped into the water in a silent plunge. Its eyes remained eerily above the water.

They seemed to focus on the boat.

"Is it—safe?" Ann whispered.

Gregory chuckled softly. "That old-timer catches his fair share of birds and 'coons and the like. He ain't no man-eater."

"Well, they have killed people," Cindy said. She glanced at Ann. "Oh, but not often. And they don't charge boats or anything. At least, not that I've ever heard of."

"You're safe," Gregory assured her. "I've come here and back in this very boat with Gina dozens of times. I've come alone. So has Cindy. We've survived the alligator gauntlet every time. They make fine eating, you know, if you cook the rascals right."

"I've had alligator," Ann said, surprised to realize that she sounded a little defensive.

"Then you know the swamp, you know alligators?" Gregory said.

She shook her head. "No. I came from Atlanta straight into the French Quarter. I don't know alligators or swamps. I'm a city girl."

"Ah, you don't know alligators or swamps," Gregory teased.

"I like the swamp just fine. It's beautiful. I'd love to come here to paint one day."

"That would be great!" Cindy applauded. "Jon always said that you were wonderful with landscapes. He said that you liked faces best, but that you were wonderful with landscapes."

"He was very proud of you," Gregory said softly.

"He isn't dead yet!" Cindy hissed softly to Gregory. Then she glanced guiltily at Ann. "Is he?"

She shook her head. She'd made a stop at the hospital before heading for the funeral. Jon remained in a coma. The nurses had assured her again that he was actually in a "good" coma—which seemed extremely strange, but she was thankful for any small favors. She hadn't yet talked to her daughter; though she had put a call through to the school, and the school had promptly put out a communication to their people in the field. Katie was working with tribes in very remote regions, and it might take a few days for her to get back to her mother. Ann hadn't wanted to stress that it was an emergency; she was praying that she'd have something good to tell her daughter when she heard from her at last.

"Jon is alive. They told me again that his vitals were very good and that his color was excellent and that they think he is going to come out of it. Of course, they might just say that for my benefit. The doctor has officially given him a fifty-fifty chance."

"He'll make it," Gregory said encouragingly.

"Thanks."

"We pull in here," he said suddenly.

Ann viewed the spot Gregory indicated. There seemed to be nothing different about it from all the other stretches of embankment they had passed so far. Then she realized that beneath a cluster of gnarl-rooted trees were two more boats; surely, out here, that had to indicate something like a bayou town.

Gregory helped her out of the boat, warning her, "Watch the mud at first. The water there is only a few feet deep, but the level remains really high when you're supposedly on solid ground. Be careful—it's all firmer just up a ways."

Black mud squeaked beneath her feet. She realized that there was something similar to a trail just ahead of them. She started to follow it to the higher ground, then paused, waiting. Birds shrieked high above her. A light wind rustled the foliage that seemed to embrace her. The swamp, she discovered, had a special scent to it, the smell of the water, the damp earth, a smell that was somehow *green*.

Gregory set his arm around her shoulder. "Come on, we've a bit of a walk. The house is up there around the bend. Cindy, you coming?"

"Just pulling the boat up a bit better," Cindy called back.

"The house is a walk from here?" Ann queried.

"Yep."

"That poor old woman walks down here when she wants to come into the city?"

"That poor old woman can probably walk farther than an Olympic champion," Gregory said dryly.

"She must be at least eighty—"

"Almost one hundred and ten."

"Jesus."

Gregory grinned. "Makes you kind of believe in voodoo, eh?"

"Killing chickens and sticking pins into dolls?" Ann said skeptically.

Gregory laughed. "Ah, there's so much more to voodoo than that, in ancient times, in our current days. Mama Lili Mae is a good practicing Catholic as well as a voodoo queen."

She arched a brow to him.

"They burned witches in centuries past. Some 'witches' honor the earth, practice 'wicka.' They are gentle and kind and nurturing."

"Voodoo is gentle, kind and nurturing?"

"Mama Lili Mae's form of voodoo," he said. "She reads bones; she advises the young ones. She has second sight. Maybe there is nothing in the bones; she has just lived so long she knows what should be said. Maybe she has no second sight, just *in*sight into human nature."

"But she practices old ways."

"Old ways that have changed. You must imagine where it all began. Think of all the slaves transported from Africa, taken to the islands such as Martinique and Hispaniola, brought here then, to New Orleans. Black men and women, coming from different tribes of the Dark Continent, different beliefs, different civilizations."

"So voodoo began in the islands."

He grinned. "Yes and no. The origin of voodoo was west Africa, what they called Dahomey Land then, the People's Republic of Benin now, and Yorubaland then, Nigeria then. The white slave traders thought the black savages had no true religion, but they honored their ancestors, deities and forces of nature. They did so with their music, and their drums. They brought their religion to the New World where it was changed by native Indian cultures, and by Christianity itself. Today, voodoo is, in Mama Lili Mae's case certainly, a spirituality. There are many New Orleans Spiritual Churches. But if you think back, imagine then what it was like to be a slave. To be at the whim of an owner who may be a kind man and may be a cruel man. Women taken by their owner if they so desire. A new people coming into existence as the slave children of these unions were born. The voodoo drums scared the white people. Sometimes, the drums were all that the slaves had to use as leverage over their masters."

"Scare tactics?"

"You bet. In fact, in 1782, the governor of Louisiana was so afraid of a voodoo uprising that he clamped down on slaves being imported from Martinique, since he blamed that island in particular. Too late for New Orleans. The ground was sodden, the city was humid, and there were constant yellow fever epidemics! Life was tenuous, and the drums beat, and there were promises of what could be if the right sacrifice was made, if the proper price was paid! The mind has always been a strong friend—or foe. Belief in something can sometimes make it be. Voodoo queen Marie Laveau worked on the thought processes of others. You've heard of her."

"I live in New Orleans. Of course I've heard of her."

He grinned. "You cannot imagine how many tourists visit her grave yearly."

"Well, I admit to having done so," Ann said. She paused, wiping her face with the back of her hand. It was humid and hot. They were now away from the water. Cindy was trudging along behind them. They might well have been in the middle of nowhere. The heavy foliage and a covering of clouds was making the day dark, though it was barely three o'clock and summer, and there should have been light for hours to come. If she closed her eyes right now, she thought, she could well imagine what it had been like. The swamp, the slaves, oppressed, seeking what freedom they could, dancing wildly to a voodoo drumbeat while the blood of a chicken gushed over the hands of a voodoo priest. The rich planters would hear the drums, and know that the slaves gathered together in a frenzy. And they would be afraid.

"Marie Laveau was supposedly a woman of white, black, and Indian blood. She dressed the hair of white ladies and taught them to inflict evil upon their enemies by pricking pins into dolls depicting them. She sold magical 'gris-gris' dust as well, which was a spell-casting powder, a hex powder, or a protective powder. Her daughter, another Marie, then became famous for her machinations and power—and sex orgies. There are no more public voodoo rituals in New Orleans, you know. But in certain things, the people still believe. Right, Cindy?"

Cindy, coming up from behind them, flushed. "Well, all right, so I've asked for a love potion or two in my day. And I had a horrible teacher one year at school and I made a straw doll of the man and pricked it full of pins."

"What happened to him?" Ann asked.

"He was promoted to principal of the school," she said with a shrug. Ann laughed, Gregory snickered. The swampland didn't seem quite so forbidding or frightening. Still, Ann glanced around. And she was glad that she wasn't alone. The bayou was a haunting dark green with the clouds overhead. The occasional bird cry was unnerving. The scent of the green darkness was all around her. She could almost see it as a mossy color whirling in the air.

"I've seen things work, though," Cindy continued. Her voice was very low, almost a whisper, adding to the haunted quality of the bayou land. "I've seen Mama Lili Mae's spells work."

"On?" Ann queried.

"Men," Cindy replied flatly.

"Maybe the men were going to fall in love anyway," Ann suggested.

Cindy smiled. "Ah, but these men fell in love with the right girls and then *behaved*. Now, I assure you, that definitely takes magic!"

"Maybe you're right," Ann agreed, laughing. "The names are very similar, aren't they?"

"What names?" Cindy asked.

"Gina, and Lili Mae. The surname is L'Aveau, right? And with the infamous Marie it's Laveau, right?"

"Yes, but there's supposedly no relation. Half the people in this place have French surnames. There are dozens of families with very close spellings or grammatical variations of names," Gregory said.

Cindy giggled. "Maybe the families were related. I mean, Marie Laveau was one *bad* moma! Infamous for her sex orgies. Our L'Aveaus might not have wanted anything to do with the others."

Gregory, walking ahead, suddenly stopped. He reached up into a tree, drawing something from it.

"What is it?"

"Bad magic," he murmured, perplexed by whatever it was he had found. He turned to the two women. He held a small doll, no more than three inches in length, made of straw. It was clad in a black dress and had yellow yarn for hair, green buttons for eyes. There were pins stuck through it.

Ann had the queasy feeling that the bepinned figure was supposed to be her.

"I thought Mama Lili Mae practiced good magic," she murmured.

"She does," Gregory said firmly. He shrugged. "There are other houses out here. More of her family, and other families as well. Not a staggering population, but still . . . that area is all Cajun to our west. Lots of bayou fishermen resting from bringing in the crawfish. Then there are kids living out here, naturally. Kids play games, you know."

"Kids. They can be just terrible," Cindy agreed.

But she and Gregory were looking at one another.

Ann was convinced that they both thought that the figure was supposed to be her as well.

"Let's get on to Mama Lili Mae's," Gregory said. "The cabin is just ahead now. This is just so much rubbish!" He dropped the doll to the ground and walked ahead.

Ann paused, watching his broad back. She reached down quickly for the little doll, stuffing it carefully into her jeans pocket. She wanted to discuss it with Mama Lili Mae when she got the opportunity.

"Ann?" Gregory said, looking back for her.

"Coming!" With a smile, she hurried to catch up with him and Cindy.

"What are you up to?" Gregory asked warily. "Don't you go taking that doll seriously now."

"I'm from Atlanta, remember?" she said, and hurried on past him.

Of course she wasn't taking the doll too seriously.

She wondered if she was taking it seriously enough.

Mark stopped by the hospital, determined to find out Jon Marcel's condition. Not much changed, but Marcel was still hanging in nicely. His chances for surviving and coming out of the coma were actually looking a little better.

Marcel's wife wasn't at the hospital.

Having left the doctor, Mark drove by Ann's house. He cursed himself all the while. He was probably risking his job. His integrity. His sanity.

The sanity was already slipping.

He parked in front of her house, stepped by the pretty storefront, and took the steps to the second-floor apartment. Cops were no longer in residence, watching the door. He rang, he knocked, he called her name.

Feeling an incredible void and an odd sense of anxiety, he came back down the stairs and out to the street. He looked skyward. It was going to storm. Summer's light was already being obscured by clouds. The night, in low-lying New Orleans and environs, was going to be pure, wet hell.

What was she doing out?

Be realistic, he told himself firmly. She had

every right to be out, every right to go anywhere she so desired.

No, she didn't.

She'd answered him. She'd wanted him; he'd been the damned idiot to consider things like circumstance and what used to be a sense of integrity. Maybe he'd never had a sense of integrity; maybe he'd just never come across an Ann Marcel before. There had been other women, but . . .

Where the hell was she? What the hell was he doing here? He'd walked away last night because the urge to touch her, to taste her, had become too strong. The urge to do more had been almost overwhelming. Almost. Hell. He'd controlled it. All right, he hadn't controlled it; he'd walked away with it. So why come back? Why torture himself. Unless he had decided the hell with right or wrong, the hell with his job, the hell with his own sensibilities where this case was concerned.

A case with some of the strangest damned twists and turns he'd ever seen. Maybe they should all stop. Wait. Pray for Jon Marcel to come out of it. . . .

Come on, come on home, Ann! he thought irritably.

Again he told himself that she had a right to be out, to be anywhere she wanted to be.

The club.

He got into his car and gunned the engine.

A beep startled him. He looked up. Jimmy was driving by, pulling alongside his car.

"She's out?"

"Yeah."

"You haven't had a chance to tell her about Jane Doe, eh?"

"No."

"She was at the cemetery, you know."

"She was *what?*"

"She was at the church this morning, and at the cemetery. Oh, she didn't really come into the church; she hung around in back. She did the same thing at the cemetery, kind of hung around the tombs by the entry. She had that look about her when someone comes to a funeral because he or she feels compelled to, but doesn't want to disturb the real mourners, if you know what I mean."

"More or less," Mark said. Hell. She'd been near him all damned day and he hadn't seen her. Great detective. Well, he'd been burying Gina. He'd had another corpse on his mind as well.

And he'd still been sweating his behavior of last night. Not having the good sense to realize what a fool he'd been to start. She couldn't seem to realize that he was worried sick about her most of the time. All right, so maybe he had made it look a little cut and dried. Jon Marcel did look as guilty as all hell. The evidence was against him. But she needed to be careful. She didn't understand that. He'd been angry. Amazing what anger did. Well, anger was passion. And then passion was wanting. He should have never touched her.

He should have never left.

Now he was left with the emptiness, the burning, of so nearly having, then still wanting. Wanting so much. More of a taste of her.

God, damn, but she was affecting him. He was falling into something. Love? So quickly? Maybe he was falling into wanting. She did things to him. The sound of her voice. The flash of her smile. He liked her. Liked her talent, both her confidence and her modesty. He liked her, admired her.

Liked the way she looked, too. Her petite frame, soft, blond hair. Yep, that was it. He was falling into wanting. Spending his time fantasizing about her. About her breasts. Naked. All of her. Naked. Her flesh. Naked.

Jimmy was still talking. Grimacing. "She should be careful. She's an awfully pretty piece of bait if someone else is involved in this thing." He hesitated. "Both women killed were really beautiful. Not that that may even matter. I mean, she is involved. She does keep showing up . . ."

"I was about to check the club," Mark said.

Jimmy shook his head. "I was just there. You sent me today, remember. I was doing the question and answer thing with our Jane Doe photo and artist's rendering. Ann Marcel was not there. She . . ."

His voice trailed away suddenly, and he looked at Mark with his dark sad eyes suddenly very large. "Oh, shit."

"What?" Mark demanded. "Damn it, Jimmy, what?" The anxiety that had been growing in

him was rising uncomfortably to the surface of
any calm facade he might have pretended.

"I, uh, heard Gregory Hanson talking today
to Lili Mae L'Aveau."

"Yeah?"

"He was bringing someone out to the bayou."

"Shit!" Mark agreed. "Shit." His engine
revved, and his car jerked down the street.

Eleven

Mama Lili Mae sat on the porch of her old wooden home, rocking in a deep-cushioned, white-wicker rocking chair. Her house was a pretty place, reached by a little wooden bridge that stretched over a small pond filled with giant lily pads; Ann marvelled that they could have come upon it in the midst of what appeared to be absolute swamp.

She had apparently been waiting for them. She puffed on a long-stemmed pipe, watching the path and the bridge. When she saw them, she nodded a welcome, addressing Ann right away while ignoring both Gregory and Cindy.

"Ann Marcel, how's the boy doing tonight? Somewhat better?"

"I don't know. He's still in a coma," Ann said, crossing the bridge to come to the old woman and take the hand offered to her. Mama Lili Mae's handshake was startlingly firm. She felt the woman's vast strength in that handshake, and warned herself not to be deceived by Mama Lili Mae's fragile appearance. She was like an old reptile, Ann thought, with a hide thicker than aged leather. She had the eyes of an old reptile, too, yellowed and aging—watchful. Always watchful. Her smile was amazing, awakening her face, giving it a brilliance and beauty.

"Saw you today, hovering in the background there. Knew you'd be coming around."

"Did you?"

"Gregory, give me a hand there."

"Yes, Mama Lili Mae," Gregory said quickly. He came to her side, helping her up. Ann had the feeling that she didn't really need help getting up, but she liked the attention—and she liked the way Gregory hopped instantly to attention as well. She winked at Ann.

"You come on inside. We'll talk alone."

"But Mama Lili Mae—" Cindy protested.

"Young lady, we'll have words later," Mama Lili Mae promised. She set a hand along Gregory's handsome face. "We'll talk, too, son. Lord A'mighty, but it hurts me to see the way you're grieving, boy. She's in the Good Lord's hands, and you take comfort in that. Gina was a streak of flash and light and beauty and wildness, and she burned brighter than a Fourth of July firecracker; but she's safe now, from anyone who would hurt her. You learn to live with that, boy. God knows, I've seen enough death to know it's a part of living, and that's the way of it, and that's that. Now you get on with life, y'hear?"

Gregory took the old hand that caressed his cheek and held it tenderly. "I'm trying, Mama Lili Mae."

"You try harder!"

With that stern admonition, she moved on into the house. The others followed her.

Her living room was a strange place. Comfortable sofas draped with beautiful, handcrafted quilts were at right angles to the entry, while a small but serviceable kitchen sat at the other end with only a brick counter to separate the two rooms. Water came from a pump. Kerosene lamps burned on two end tables to give light to the room.

From the ceiling, in contrast to the old-fashioned, all-American warmth of the sofas and quilts, chimes made of small bones dangled from the ceiling in various places about the room. The breeze that now entered the opened windows caught them, creating a strange melody as bone collided with bone and more bone collided with more bone. The sound was strangely light and soft, and oddly enough, soothing.

"Don't you worry none—they're all chicken bones. I never have offered up a human being for sacrifice," Mama Lili Mae teased Ann as she watched her view the room.

"Cindy, you get Ann and me a glass of lemonade. Then you and Gregory scat."

"And do what?" Cindy demanded.

"Take a walk. Talk to Old Billy. Find some wildflowers. Search your soul, commune with your Maker. Heavens, child, I don't know. Talk to one another, you're friends, ain't ya?"

"We'll be fine," Gregory told Cindy.

"Sure," Cindy said, striding to the kitchen

area to pour the lemonade as requested. "Old Billy is a nigh-onto-fifteen-foot gator. He's just who I want to talk to!"

"He's harmless," Mama Lili Mae said. "He likes people who talk to him. Now bring us those lemonades and you two skedaddle."

Cindy brought the lemonade; Ann thanked her, grinning. Cindy grimaced. "We'll be okay, Mama Lili Mae. What about Mrs. Ann Marcel here?"

"I may be far more dangerous than that gator, child, but I'd bet Mrs. Marcel is willing to take her chances on me, else what would she be doing out here, now, hmm?"

"I think I'll be fine," Ann said.

Cindy winked. "Anything else, Mama Lili Mae?" she asked.

"Skedaddle!"

"Come on, then." Gregory rolled his eyes, caught Cindy's hand, and led her out. The screen door to the house banged and thumped as they departed.

"Well, now." Lili Mae sat back on a sofa, eyeing Ann as she relit her pipe. "It's right good to see you. It's rare a man talks about his ex-wife with such high praise. That boy set quite a store by you."

"Jon has been out here?"

Mama Lili Mae nodded her affirmation. "That he did. He told me you were a fine artist, and that you would love my face, and want to paint it."

"That's true," Ann told her with a smile. "I've

never met anyone with such a wonderful face, so completely filled with knowledge and character."

Mama Lili Mae accepted the compliment as her due. "Then one day, you'll come and paint me."

"If you allow it."

"I've just done so."

Ann found herself smiling again. She understood why people would brave the swamp to come receive advice and gris-gris dust from Mama Lili Mae.

The old woman suddenly leaned forward. "But that's to come in the future. Now we must talk about Gina."

"Apparently, she and Jon were very serious about one another."

"You knew this?"

Ann shook her head. "No. I knew about his paintings; I had seen the first and a few of the others in various stages. He talked about how much he was enjoying the people he had met; he made me see the people who worked in the clubs in a different light."

Mama Lili Mae nodded in satisfaction. "Well, he was careful about it, but he meant to marry Gina. Is that a shock to you?"

Ann shook her head. "No. Jon and I are friends. Very good friends. I keep hearing how unusual that is, and it's probably very true. We have a daughter; we both love her. And we both love art. We share a great deal, but as friends.

If he was in love and wished to marry again, I would have been very happy for him."

"That's what he said."

"So what happened?" Ann asked, lost.

Mama Lili Mae sat back, shaking her head. "I don't know. I only know that she was worried. She had become involved with someone else . . . well, honestly, Gina had become involved with many people, but whoever this person was, the involvement had gotten too serious for her. The day she died, she came to see me. She asked if she should marry Jon Marcel, if he could love her after the life she had led. She'd had so many men."

"What did you tell her?"

"I told her that the man didn't need to love her past to love her. I told her that she should marry him. Make a clean break with the past, and marry him."

"And then . . ."

"She was happy with my answer, I think. Very happy. But she was still so anxious. She was going to try to make a clean break with this other lover. I do not know who the lover was; I didn't demand an answer from her because I had no sense of her danger." She shook her head again in deep regret and confusion. "Insight . . . intuition. They are wonderful when they work. I didn't see what was about to befall her. I was blinded by the promise of happiness for her, perhaps."

"But you're as certain as I that—whether he

was doused in her blood or not—Jon did not kill Gina."

"I know that he did not. I know, too, that you feel it is up to you to prove this. You shouldn't. The police will find the answers."

"The police have Jon condemned."

Mama Lili Mae shrugged her shoulders. "The truth will tell. I think that you will put yourself into danger if you don't take a step back. Go spend your days at the hospital. Sit with Jon. Talk him back to life. Don't place yourself in this path where death threatens so freely anymore."

"So you think that I am in danger?"

"Of course you are. Jon is not guilty; someone else is."

"I wonder if that's why we found a doll on the way here."

Mama Lili Mae frowned. "A doll?"

"Yes. It was in the trees." Ann pulled the little doll out from her jeans pocket where she had stuffed it. "This doll. Is it me?"

Mama Lili Mae took the doll from her with a frown.

"Is it?"

"Yes, most probably."

"Where would it have come from? Who would have put it in the tree?"

"I don't know."

"What does it mean?"

"It's a warning. It—"

Mama Lili Mae broke off suddenly, staring toward the door. Dismayed. She slipped the little doll unobtrusively into a pocket of her skirt.

Was she frightened, perhaps?

There was someone there. Someone . . .

Menacing.

Ann felt a sensation at her nape—as if the hairs were rising there. She faced Mama Lili Mae and couldn't see the door from where she sat. She froze for a second, feeling as if she was in terrible danger, feeling as if a knife could slice into her back at any second.

She jumped up, spinning around, desperate to face whatever danger might be coming her way.

A man stood in the doorway. In the lamplight and shadows she couldn't see his face at first. Just a form, tall, powerful.

Mama Lili Mae let out her breath with a rattling sound.

And the man stepped forward.

Mark sped over the water, watching the sky as he did so. The summer sun should have lasted longer. The coming storm was snaking across the sky with billowing darkness. Already, the wind was beginning to rise.

He wasn't far. He wasn't far at all now. He could see the little alcove where the trail began. He could see the other boats drawn to the shore.

His anxiety had reached such a level that he was ready to throttle her. What in her right mind would make her come out here without a word to the police?

The fact that they hadn't been particularly willing to listen to her regarding Jon Marcel?

He still didn't know! Half truths, perhaps strange coincidences, were all that he had.

But she shouldn't be out here. He had to find her. Bring her back. He wanted to throttle her . . .

Hold her again.

The shoreline was just ahead. . . .

He should have cut the motor earlier; it was going to become entangled with the roots by the embankment. But he waited, and cut it with enough propulsion left to send his boat drifting the final distance to the shore. He hopped into the mud and pulled his boat up. Gregory should have known better than to bring her here.

Gregory would think that he could protect her. Gregory would probably think himself safe in the swamp, he knew it well enough.

It was going to be all right, Mark determined, leaving the boat to take his first quick strides through the muddy trail. The house was just ahead.

Gregory sat with Cindy by the water's edge. The sun was beginning to fall low against the horizon. The rain clouds billowing atop it seemed to be pressing it down to the earth.

"Strange, isn't it?" Cindy asked. "It seems like

Mama Lili Mae wants to tell her something that she doesn't want to tell us."

"Maybe Mama Lili Mae works on a need-to-know basis," Gregory said with a shrug. He set his arm around Cindy. "Don't you worry. She'll talk to you, too. And tell you what you need to know."

"I guess," Cindy murmured.

"You guess right," Gregory said firmly. He watched as she stood, stretching, then gave his attention to the water once more, sending a rock skipping across it.

"I'm going bonkers here."

He tossed another rock. "Cindy, you shouldn't have come with me, then. I didn't promise entertainment."

"I know. I'm just so restless. You know me. I like action. I like to keep moving."

"Pretend you're dancing for a fish out there."

"Gregory."

"Cindy, she won't be much longer."

"I think I will just move a bit. Stretch my legs. I'm going to take a little walk."

"No, Cindy, don't. Stay right here."

A few seconds later, he realized that she hadn't answered him. And she hadn't spoken again. He turned around. She was gone, as if she had disappeared cleanly into the brush.

And into the gray, billowing mist of the coming storm and darkness.

"Ah, damn it all!" Gregory swore, standing. "Cindy, damn it, come back here!"

But she didn't reply.

"Cindy, you—brat!" he muttered. "Cindy!"
Again, no reply.
Swearing, he started off after her.

The man came into the lamplight. His features were caught by it. For a moment, in stark light and shadow, he seemed to be wearing a mask of pure malevolence.

And evil.

The shadows subsided.

He wore no mask. He was, actually, a strikingly handsome man.

Yet still . . .

Something malevolent seemed to hover about him, like a spiritualist's aura. Ann chided herself for her foolishness.

Ann knew who he was.

She saw that it was the man who had been pointed out to her at Annabella's as Jacques Moret. He had come through the screen door, and now stood in the house. Staring at her.

Even here, in the swamp, he was dressed in a fastidious manner, cool linen dust-colored suit, dark silk shirt. He stared at Mama Lili Mae; she stared back at him.

His eyes, like crystals in the muted lamplight, fell to focus on Ann.

"Mrs. Marcel, I am Jacques Moret," he said smoothly. He approached her, offering his hand. She took it, and longed to wrench hers away instantly. He was too handsome, with a slick smile. Oily slick, Ann thought. His looks were

4 BESTSELLING HISTORICAL ROMANCES BY YOUR FAVORITE AUTHORS CAN BE YOURS, FREE!

Kensington Choice, our newest book club now brings you historical romances by your favorite bestselling authors including Janelle Taylor, Shannon Drake, Rosanne Bittner, Jo Beverley, and Georgina Gentry, just to name a few! Each book is filled with passion, adventure and the excitement of bygone times!

To introduce you to this great new club which is part of Zebra Home Subscription Service, we'd like to send you your first 4 bestselling historical romances, absolutely free! And once you get these 4 free books to savor at home, we'll rush you the next 4 brand-new books at the lowest prices available, as soon as they are published.

The way the club works is that after your initial FREE shipment, you will get our 4 newest bestselling historical romances delivered to your doorstep each month at the preferred subscriber's rate of only $4.20 per book, a savings of up to $7.16 per month (since these titles sell in bookstores for $4.99-$5.99)! All books are sent on a 10-day free examination basis and there is no minimum number of books to buy. (And no charge for shipping.) Plus as a regular subscriber, you'll receive our FREE monthly newsletter, *Zebra/Pinnacle Romance News*, which features author profiles, contests, subscriber benefits, book previews and more!

So start today by returning the FREE BOOK CERTIFICATE provided. We'll send you 4 FREE BOOKS with no further obligation: A FREE gift offering you hours of reading pleasure with no obligation...how can you lose?

*We have 4 FREE BOOKS for you
as your introduction to
KENSINGTON CHOICE!
To get your FREE BOOKS, worth
up to $23.96, mail the card below.*

FREE BOOK CERTIFICATE

Yes! Please send me 4 Kensington Choice (the best of Zebra and Pinnacle Books) Historical Romances without cost or obligation (worth up to $23.96). As a Kensington Choice subscriber, I will then receive 4 brand-new romances to preview each month for 10 days FREE. I can return any books I decide not to keep and owe nothing. The publisher's prices for Kensington Choice romances range from $4.99-$5.99, but as a preferred subscriber I will get these books for only $4.20 per book or $16.80 for all four titles. There is no minimum number of books to buy and I may cancel my subscription at any time, plus there is no additional charge for postage and handling. No matter what I decide to do, my first 4 books are mine to keep, absolutely FREE!

KF0496

Name _____

Address _____ Apt._____

City _____ State_____ Zip_____

Telephone (____) _____

Signature _____

(If under 18, parent or guardian must sign)

Subscription subject to acceptance. Terms and prices subject to change.

as plastic as his smile, like off the cover of a magazine. His smile was too quick, the charm to it far too practiced.

"I've heard so much about you, from so many sources. It's a pleasure to meet you."

"And not a surprise, since Jacques knew you were coming," Mama Lili Mae said.

"Mama Lili Mae is, remarkably enough, my great-great-great-aunt. As she was Gina's."

"Quite remarkable," Ann agreed. Indeed. This was like an Arabian mare being the ancestress of a cobra.

"It's been a rough day for Mama Lili Mae. A very long day. With the funeral. She will try to make you welcome, but you must realize it has been difficult . . ."

"Indeed," Ann murmured.

"I've endured many a year, you know," Mama Lili Mae said. Her tone was sharp. She still seemed to be as uneasy as Ann was with the man's appearance.

"You need to leave, Mrs. Marcel," Moret said bluntly.

"Jacques!" Mama Lili Mae said. "It is my home—"

Jacques Moret didn't seem to hear her. "You are a lovely woman, Mrs. Marcel. Petite, delicate. With a lovely neck. These are dangerous times. You should not be here."

"She's my guest," Mama Lili Mae said.

"You're tired, worn!" Jacques told her.

"I'm well!"

Ann looked at her, trying to keep up a facade

of courage. The old woman did look tired—and worn. Ann thought of her very great age.

Mama Lili Mae had told Ann what she could.

And Ann didn't like Jacques Moret.

She wanted the safety of Cindy and Gregory being near her. In fact, she wanted to run past him.

And hope that he didn't slither over to touch her. Stop her.

"Well," she said with forced and stern courage and determination. "Mama Lili Mae, you're wonderful, and I do look forward to painting you. It's probably time for me to go," Ann said, approaching Mama Lili Mae. "Even if I am actually *your* guest." She embraced the woman in a warm hug—unhappy that the hug forced her to put her back to Jacques Moret once again.

Had he killed Gina? Had he been his distant cousin's lover, a man who refused to accept that she would no longer see him because she had fallen in love with someone else?

The idea seemed entirely feasible. Ann could well imagine him rising to a murderous rage, attacking Gina. Right when she was to meet Jon. And Jon would have seen what was happening, and he would have tried to help her. And in turn, he would have been attacked . . .

And the murder weapon would have disappeared because the actual murderer would have disappeared as well.

Perhaps coming here had not been a good idea. Perhaps she should have told the police.

Perhaps she could have said something to Mark, and he . . .

He would have yelled at her and told her to keep her nose out of police business.

And of course, he would have infuriated her. And things would have been worse.

Because she would have kept on wanting him, even if she had been angry. Even though he had dropped her like a leper, swearing at her, after he had suddenly kissed her.

Oh, God. It had all been a tremendous mistake. She needed him now. Wanted him now.

She was afraid. Damned afraid.

She wanted his strength. She wanted to cling to him. She wanted to feel the touch of his piercing gray eyes sliding over her, angry.

But protective.

Exit quickly . . .

Get the hell out of here. . . .

Now!

"I know you've got to go now. You'll be fine. Gregory and Cindy will be right outside. Don't you worry none. And you come back," Mama Lili Mae whispered.

Ann gave her another gentle squeeze. "I will. You know that I will."

Mama Lili Mae squeezed her back. A strong squeeze. The woman wasn't nearly as fragile as she appeared.

She wasn't afraid of Jacques Moret, Ann thought. Not for herself.

Yet . . .

She was afraid. For Ann.

Ann rose from Mama Lili Mae's embrace. She faced the man in the doorway.

Blocking the doorway.

She squared her shoulders. "Well, nice meeting you, Mr. Moret," she said.

And started to walk past him.

Mama Lili Mae's bayou cottage was still some distance down the trail. Mark was through the muddy area that rose from the water, walking on more solid ground. His pace quickened as he mentally cursed her.

Little fool.

She shouldn't have come here. Or if she'd wanted so desperately to come here, she should have talked to him.

She was okay with Gregory.

Wasn't she?

He pictured her eyes, so very green. So wide. Filled with integrity, passion. Determination to save Jon Marcel at all costs.

At all costs.

He pictured her eyes . . .

Then Gina's, as she had lain dead.

He started running.

He was almost there.

Almost.

But not quite.

The house was not yet within his sight when Mark heard the first ear-piercing scream.

And the rain began to fall.

Twelve

"Cindy!"

Gregory heard the scream, but the rain had begun. It was an instant and complete deluge, battering down upon him in giant, stinging droplets. The sound of it against the earth and foliage was deafening.

It brought the darkness.

Complete darkness.

"Cindy!" he cried out. "Cindy, damn you, where the hell are you, Cindy, answer me!"

His voice became blended with the violence of the storm. He cursed himself; he should have seen the rain.

"Cindy!"

He tried to shout. Already he had become hoarse.

"Cindy!"

His voice was fading.

So were his hopes.

He shouted once again.

Then he started trudging through the mud, cursing himself.

He stopped. Was it Cindy who had screamed? He knew the bayou; he thought he knew the bayou. Yet he didn't know where he was, and he didn't know now from which direction the scream had come.

"Cindy? Ann?"

He tried to rub the rain from his eyes, tried to see through the darkness.

There was someone . . . something . . . ahead of him. No, the figure was gone.

He had the uneasy feeling of a man being stalked. He turned in the rain. Turned again. "Cindy? Ann? Where the hell are you two girls? Sweet Jesus, ladies, answer me!"

The rain was his answer. And the wind, rising now, whipping around in the foliage.

No one was answering him, yet he knew . . .

Someone had heard him. Someone was . . .

Behind him.

He knew it for certain in the few seconds before the searing pain from the crack upon his head sent him sinking down into a pit of blackness . . .

And oblivion.

Mark cursed and swore. The scream had come long moments ago now, and he was nowhere near the house; he was, in fact, being pressed farther away by the rising winds and the flooding. He was beginning to feel as if he were out in the middle of the water itself for all the progress he was suddenly making.

The rain caused the lowland areas of the bayou to flood almost instantly. The cottages, like Mama Lili Mae's, survived because they were built up on stilts. But the trail was now washed away, and the scope of the storm had settled over them like a giant black miasma.

He heard a sucking sound. Someone else moving through the mud, someone who had just all but passed him in the rain and mire. Someone he might have reached out and touched.

Instinctively, he changed direction, making his way to where the boats had been.

The rain was bad. The flooding was wiping away paths and trails and landmarks.

But he knew, staring at what had been the water's edge, that he was in the right place.

And the boats were gone.

Moret . . .

Ugh! Ann shivered, running over the bridge and down the trail. He made her skin crawl. She had been certain that he'd been about to reach out for her. That he would stop her from leaving.

But he hadn't touched her. She'd managed to walk past him in a fairly sedate and dignified manner—one with applaudable bravado. But at Mama Lili Mae's door, she had begun to run. And she was certain that she heard his laughter following her.

"Gregory, Cindy?" she called, across the bridge and onto what she thought was the trail. No one was anywhere around. Was she even on the trail? Had it been so overgrown before?

"Gregory? Cindy?" She spoke the names more softly, rather than shouting them.

Where were the two?

She looked up. It was almost as if the sky were squatting down on the land. The billowing darkness was sinking down upon her.

She heard footsteps.

Behind her.

She whirled around. Nothing. No one. She felt eyes—night eyes—staring at her from within the brush.

She was losing her mind. "There are lots of little creatures in the woods!" she said aloud. And they were allowed to look at her, right.

That creature was out here. Old Billy. That old alligator. What had Cindy said? He was nearly fifteen feet long.

Ann didn't know a lot about alligators, but surely, fifteen feet was big.

"No problem," she muttered to the wind. "If I find the sucker, I'll just talk to him. I'll talk fast. Please don't eat me, Old Billy, please, please, please, don't eat me. Nice weather, eh? Maybe you like this kind of stuff."

Footsteps!

She heard footsteps, running, she was certain. Near her.

"Gregory, Cindy!"

Her blood seemed to freeze as she heard the scream. She didn't know where it came from. It seemed a part of the wind, of the air, of the angry gnash of the foliage as the weather whipped air and earth into a frenzy.

"Cindy?" she cried.

The first big splash of rain fell into her left eye with such force that she staggered back from it, blinking. Then the heavens let loose, and in a matter of seconds she was drenched beneath the deluge.

Which way to go? Where had the scream come from? Should she be trying to follow the sound of that scream, or should she be running as far from it as she possibly could?

With her arms huddled closer around herself, her teeth chattering, Ann started to move in what she thought was the direction of the house.

But there was no more trail. The rain had already risen high enough to make mush out of the ground. The water was going to keep on rising, she realized.

And pretty soon it would be just as if she were attempting to navigate a shallow channel of the bayou itself. "Oh, hell!" she whispered aloud.

She couldn't just stand there.

"Cindy, damn you, where are you, are you all right? Where the hell are you?"

There was no answer; she hadn't expected one. She couldn't possibly have heard one.

Except . . .

She was hearing something.

She swirled around. There was movement in the brush to her left. Wasn't there?

A sucking sound to her right when she looked nervously to her left. Which was the storm? Which was real?

Which was the danger . . . stalking her?

She didn't know from which direction the menace was coming, but instinct, intuition, every fiber in her being warned her that she wasn't alone.

And it wasn't a friend trying to find her. Panic seized her. She tried to breathe in deeply; she inhaled rain. She gritted her teeth together hard, trying to weigh her chances in either direction. Where was the house? Where were the boats?

Where was there something that most resembled a trail?

She started to move, cautiously at first. There, to her right. The brush was moving. There might be something in it. An animal. A bayou creature.

A snake.

That thought didn't help any. This country surely offered a good home for moccasins, maybe more.

This must be one big snake.

Snakes came in human form.

She turned blindly then, certain that she was in terrible danger, and that the danger was close. It didn't matter in what direction she ran anymore, as long as she ran.

She reached out blindly, trying to part the rich green foliage that slapped back at her. She could hear it . . . yes, even above the storm. A pounding, a thudding, a sucking of sound against the earth behind her, coming closer and closer. Someone was after her. Closer, closer.

She veered course.

Along with the wind, she could hear her

breathing. Against the cold of the storm, her lungs burned.

She burst into something of a clearing. The water was ahead of her. Not just a flooded trail; the water, the bayou. She spun around, feeling as if she were at the edge of a precipice, about to go tumbling over. Did she hear it anymore? The pounding? Anything?

Something . . . cracked, nearby. She strained to hear against the driving wind. She backed toward the water.

She shrieked as she came against flesh. Hard, unyielding flesh and muscle. A hand clamped down over her mouth. Strong, ruthless arms swept her back from the trail.

Mama Lili Mae stood on her porch, heedless of the wind ripping around her, of the rain that the wind lifted and slashed against her, despite the porch's overhang.

She should have forced the girl to stay with her. The rain was coming. Anyone could have seen that.

Maybe not the violence of this storm, though. She hadn't seen a storm like this one, rising in this kind of tempest, in years.

She shook her head; she couldn't see a thing. They had to be all right out there. In spite of that scream she'd heard. They all knew this place well enough. That little Cindy had probably just had a little brush with a tree snake and sent chills down everybody's spine because of it. They all had to be okay.

Jacques would find them. He'd gone after Ann Marcel when the rain had started. He'd been directly told by her to do so, so he'd come back with her, if the three of them hadn't managed to get to the boats and take off already. Foolish. They should have come back. Cindy and Gregory should have known to do so. They should have.

They'd come back.

She shook her old head worriedly.

Maybe they wouldn't.

She walked back into her house, through the living room, to her bedroom. At a corner altar, she lit purple candles. She knelt down, and began to sway.

And chant.

She took out of her pocket the little doll she had gotten from Ann Marcel.

One by one, she removed the tiny pins that had been stuck into it . . .

Chanting all the while.

The man who grabbed her wasn't going to have to kill her. Her heart was racing a million miles an hour; it was going to arrest on her any second. She couldn't breathe, couldn't think; she was going to pass out.

No, no, she wasn't going to die without a fight!

"Hey, shush!"

He was talking to her. He'd stalked her, he

was going to kill her, and he wanted her to shush up while he was doing it. She kicked him as hard as she could manage in her backward position. She hit a shin. He swore, falling down into the mud.

Dragging her with him.

His bloody remained over her mouth as he struggled to find a position splayed over her. She looked up at the face hovering over hers, rain slaking off it, hair so sodden it was almost like a hose above her.

"Shut up, will you, sweet Jesus. I come to save your damned life and you kick me. Women."

Mark. Mark LaCrosse. He was here in the swamp with her. On top of her in the mud.

He moved his hand from her mouth.

"Mark?"

"Yes."

She was so shaken that she took a swing at him. "Bloody hell!" he muttered, catching her flailing limb.

"You scared me to death. You stalked me through the woods and the rain—"

"Don't be an idiot. I wasn't stalking you—I was trying to find out who the hell it was." He jumped to his feet, reached down for her, and dragged her up. They were both covered in mud. They must resemble two brown-colored Swamp Creatures.

"Damn you—" Ann began.

"Shush!"

Shaking, she went silent. They both stood dead still in the rain, listening. There was nothing but the continual downpour coming at them.

"Come on," he told her.

His hand closed over hers. He started walking.

"Where are we going."

"Back to Mama Lili Mae's."

"Cindy and Gregory are here somewhere."

"Maybe."

"What do you mean, maybe?"

"The boats are all gone. They might have left already."

"Would they leave without me?"

"Have you seen them anywhere?"

She shook her head. "But I heard a scream."

He stopped abruptly. "You didn't scream?"

"No. It had to have been Cindy."

He nodded. "All right. We'll keep looking. But Cindy was with Gregory, right?"

"Yes. I—I went to talk to Mama Lili Mae. She wanted to talk to me alone, so Cindy and Gregory went for a walk together."

"If they're together, Cindy's got to be okay. Gregory would never leave her. But we'll keep looking as long as we can." He turned and started walking again. She followed, keeping her head down against the pounding of the rain. He could lead now.

Oh, God. He could lead now. What a relief. They'd be out of this hell soon. He'd yell, he'd be miserable, but they'd be out of the swamp soon. She couldn't wait to shower. In the hottest water she could stand. For as long as she could bear. She'd scrub her hair until there wasn't a single vestige of this mud left in it.

He stopped suddenly, swearing. She rammed into his back, it was so abrupt a movement.

"What—"

"Son of a bitch. We're not going that way."

"Why?"

He drew her around him. Giant trees had uprooted. It would take a machete to cut a way through the tangle of bark, root and foliage that had ensued.

"Well, we're not getting back to Mama Lili Mae's," he said.

"Will she be all right?"

"Mama Lili Mae? She'd be in better shape than me in almost any given combat situation," Mark said dryly. "Maybe Gregory and Cindy did make their way back to the house. We'll keep looking, but at least they're together, whether they're in the house or the rain and the muck."

"Should we just leave and go back?"

"We can't go back."

"Why?"

"You didn't see that there were no boats?"

"I—are you sure? Maybe it was the wrong place—"

"It was the right place. There were no boats."

"My God, then what—"

"We'll have to head my way."

"To where?"

"To a shelter."

"A shelter! We've got to get out of the swamp."

"I know. For now . . ."

He pulled something from his pocket. Ann realized that it was a cellular phone.

"Oh, thank God! Someone will come for us."

"I don't know if I can get through. And I don't know if anyone can get out."

The tree at Ann's side suddenly began to move. A branch—moved. And it suddenly dropped right from the tree and onto her.

She let out a shriek of terror, jumping back.

Slamming into Mark.

Mark swore.

The tree branch slithered away.

The cellular phone went flying out of his hand. Into the darkness. Into the mud and muck.

"Son of a bitch!" he yelled.

"It was a snake!"

"It was a harmless little tree snake."

"Quit shouting at me and find the phone."

"Excuse me! I wasn't the one having a heart attack over a pathetic little tree snake."

"It wasn't little."

"It was tiny."

"The hell it was."

"Get the phone!"

Swearing away, he started looking for the phone. Ann fell down on her knees beside him. All she could feel was mud and muck. The rain continued to pelt down upon them. She rose. She had the uncomfortable feeling that she was beginning to sink.

His arms were on her, wresting her away from

the spot where she had stood. The mud let out a horrible, sucking sound.

"Idiot!" he railed in the darkness and cold, blinding rain.

"What?"

"Quicksand."

"Quicksand?"

"Swamp hazard. Use some God-given sense when you feel yourself being pulled down."

Tears of fear and anger stung her eyes. She blinked them away furiously.

"I feel as if I'm being sucked down with every step I take."

"Well, the phone is gone. Gone, have you got that!"

"I'm sorry! Sorrier than you'll ever know!"

He stared at her. They were both being pelted. "Damned thing probably wouldn't have worked anyway."

"Maybe not."

"Just follow me. And quit giving me a hard time."

"I'm not giving you a hard time!"

He started walking again, retracing the steps he had already taken. They came back to the water's edge, and he kept walking, into water that came nearly to Ann's waist.

"Mark!"

He didn't respond at first.

"Mark, damn you, where do you think we're going? What are we doing?"

"We can't go back the other way!"

"We can't walk through the damned water."

"We have to!"

"Let's try going back. Come on, you're a cop; you can do something."

"Damn it, Ann, I can't shoot my way through fallen trees!"

He started moving again. She dragged back on him, frightened. Tree branches fell along the water's edge like giant, skeletal fingers. Roots tripped her with every step she tried to take.

More of the branches, she was certain, moved upon occasion.

Her teeth chattered. She couldn't do this. She couldn't keep going.

Ann caught hold of his shoulders, drawing herself up enough to shout against the back of his ear. "I know—there are no poisonous snakes out here, right?"

He turned to her. "Don't be ridiculous. It's a bayou. There are poisonous snakes."

"Shit!"

"Don't bother them, they won't bother you."

"Right! I can see what I'm stepping on!"

He stopped, swirling around on her. "You got a better idea what we should do?"

She stared at him blankly, clothes completely plastered to her body, shivering, hair glued to her face in clumps, water dripping from her nose. "Piggyback," he told her suddenly. "It will get your feet out of the mud at least."

She smiled, shaking her head. "No, I'm all right. Lead on."

He did so. It seemed to Ann that they walked forever. It might have been only a few minutes.

Suddenly, they hit an area where the mud was so soft beneath the water that she tripped into it, falling beneath the water's surface.

Before she could right herself, he had pulled her up, placing his arms beneath her body. She instinctively slipped her arms around his neck. His eyes on hers, he started walking again.

"You—you don't have to carry me. You won't get very far that way."

"You're not that heavy."

"Heavy enough in the rain and the muck."

"It's not that much farther."

"What's not that much farther?"

"You'll see. We're almost there."

She bit into her lower lip. She was miserable, naturally. She was saturated in rain and mud, and worried about her new friends. But he was right; Cindy and Gregory were together. Mama Lili Mae was in her element in the swamp.

And she wasn't alone anymore. She was in his arms. He even looked good soaked. In mud. She felt the silver-gray of his eyes touching hers through that mud, and though she was drenched and cold, that touch warmed. Burned. Sizzled through her.

"Ahead," he said suddenly, gruffly.

He let her slip to her feet. The darkness was so complete that for a moment, she didn't know what he was talking about. Then she saw the structure looming before her, up on a high mound. The water was rising all around it, but the cabin sat very high above it all.

"Come on." He tugged on her hand. He was

running as he led her, up something that might have been a walkway to a huge cypress overhang. Beneath it, he released her hand, leaning against a wall of the log cabin, inhaling vigorously. Ann gasped for breath as well, watching the rain as it continued to fall beyond the overhang.

"A drink," Mark muttered.

"A drink?"

He turned then, pressing open the door to the cabin. Ann entered behind him, moving precariously. Inside the cabin, it was as dark as India ink.

"Let me just get my shoes off . . ."

She heard a thumping, then suddenly, the flare of a match. A second later, the cabin was filled with a soft glowing light as Mark used the long match he had struck to ignite the wick of a large oil lamp.

Incredulously, Ann looked around. It was a one-room cabin, kind of like Mama Lili Mae's living room, except that this combined sitting room with bedroom and kitchen. There was a double bed covered in an old-fashioned quilt to one side of the cabin, a desk and chair in the middle, a round table with four chairs near the kitchen, and a counter and cabinets and a gas stove and sink to make up the kitchen itself. Like Mama Lili Mae's, the sink was old fashioned, the pump kind. To the rear of the room was a large fireplace with kindling and logs set.

"I'll just start a fire," Mark said.

Ann stayed near the doorway, unsure.

"Whose—whose is this?"

He turned around and stared at her, a brow arched. "Mine."

"Yours?"

He watched her. "Mine. Is that so surprising."

"I—I just didn't know—"

"That I hailed from the swamp? Why, Mrs. Marcel, you are talking to an original coon."

"Cajun."

He didn't reply. He turned back to the fire, though it seemed little effort to ignite. Everything had been left in readiness in the cabin for the arrival of its owner. Kindling was already set on logs. He had only to poke the fire a few times to get it started on its way to a steady blaze. He rose, staring at her.

"You can do what you want. The shower's outside. I'm not wearing mud all night."

"Shower's—outside."

"Yep."

He opened a door that led to a half bath. There was a toilet and a sink—manned by a pump once again. But there was a small closet in it as well. He dug around until he found a couple of functional white towels, then dug some more. He tossed her something. It was a huge flannel shirt.

"I think it's probably the best I can do. You're welcome to dig around in here."

He crossed the room with his towel and exited the cabin. Ann stared after him, numb. She shook out the shirt he had given her.

She wasn't taking a shower. She couldn't. She had wanted him, did want him, but this . . .

This was unbelievable. And he was still yelling at her. And worse, he was here.

What was he doing out here? He had a cabin out here. But he had just happened to crash into her out in the swamp. She set the flannel shirt down on the bed, then turned in sudden fury, ready to demand answers. She went on outside and saw that the shower was indeed outside the cabin, connected to the wall, drawing water from a well. To pump it, Mark was pulling on a cord that sent new waves of fresh water crashing down on him time and time again.

He was naked.

He was all that she had imagined. Broad shoulders, taut body, extremely well toned. Water and mud sluiced from his chest. His arm and shoulder muscles rippled and stretched as he worked the pull pump with one hand and scrubbed the mud from himself with the other.

The hair on his chest was very wet and very dark, swirling down to a thin line at his waist, then swirling down again below his waist to form a thick dark nest for his sex. She stared at him, forgetting what she had come to say.

Oh, God, yes. He was all that she had imagined.

And more.

But, oh, God. She was pointedly *staring* at him. He returned her stare.

She turned on her heels and headed quickly back into the cabin.

She'd talk to him when he was dressed.

A few minutes later, he came through the cabin door again, wrapped in a terry robe, drying his hair with his towel. "Shower's all yours," he said.

She was about to tell him that she simply wasn't going to shower.

And what would that prove?

She was dying for a shower, even if it was icy cold. He looked so good, so comfortable, no longer clad in inches of black mud. The stuff itched. She felt as if things crawled in it. She had to take a shower.

"Thanks," she muttered curtly, moving for the door with her towel and shirt.

"Aren't you forgetting something?"

"Like what?"

"Soap appeal to you?"

He tossed the bar over. She caught it reflexively. "Thanks. Thanks so much," she muttered, and quickly stepped outside.

Once on the porch, she hesitated. She looked around nervously as she shed her clothing. Who was she expecting to come peeping at her during this storm in this wilderness. No one.

But there was Mark.

He didn't come out. He wouldn't come out, she determined. He was the one who had pulled away last night, cussing at her. Oh, God, it felt so good to be out of her clothes. Had there been leeches in them? Were there leeches in the swamp? Probably. Anything at all could be in her clothing.

Suddenly, she could not be completely stripped quickly enough. Then she couldn't man the pull pump quickly enough. She brought cascade after cascade of water tumbling down over her hair. She ran her free fingers through it again and again, until she was convinced that she had rinsed it all to the very best of her ability. She closed her eyes. The water was cold; viciously cold. It didn't matter. Shivering, shaking, she brought more and more of it down upon herself, sluicing it over her breasts and belly, her legs. She closed her eyes again while she splashed her face. She opened her eyes.

Mark.

He was standing there. Next to her.

She had been wrong. He had come out.

There was shadow and light around them on the porch now, with the glow from the oil lamp radiating from the windows that lined the cabin. His eyes seemed to be pure silver; his face was angled and planed in such a way that he seemed incredibly tense . . .

Masculine. Threateningly masculine . . .

In a way that sent heat streaking through her with the pure power of lightning.

Her throat went dry.

Her heart fluttered.

Her breathing came in rasps.

"I thought you might need help with your hair," he shouted over the wind and the rain that pummeled on beyond the overhang of the porch and the shower beneath it.

His eyes sizzled into hers. But then they fell

from her face, to her breasts, to her belly. To the juncture of her thighs. The burning seemed to run rampant within her.

Her hair . . .

His eyes rose to hers again.

"My hair?"

"Yeah. Your hair."

"You're staring at me," Ann said.

He shrugged. A slight smile curved his lip. "You came out and stared at me."

"I did not."

"You sure as hell did. But I really came out about your hair. You're too stubborn to ask for help, and it's hard to clean it and pump the water at the same time."

"I managed."

"Sorry, then. I didn't mean—" he began.

But then he broke off.

"You are staring at me!" she insisted.

"Right. And you stared at me! We've established that we've both stared."

"I didn't stare that long."

"You stared first."

"By accident."

"Like hell."

"Well, you've stared long enough now."

"I told you that I didn't mean . . ."

His voice trailed away. "Oh, fuck what I meant! You're damned right. I've stared long enough!" he agreed suddenly, vehemently. And he reached for her, drawing her from the shower and into his arms.

Thirteen

He didn't say a word to her, just kicked the door into the cabin wide with a foot, and slammed it shut the same way. He walked to the quilt-covered bed and fell upon it with her, kissing her again, mouth devouring hers, tongue thrusting, invading; hungry, evoking all manner of wild searings within her. His hand was on her cheek, stroking, then her throat. Then moving again, molding over her breast, sliding down the length of her ribs to her hips, moving, more. His hand was cradling her breast again, thumb padding over her nipple, rubbing, eliciting wild, sweet, raw, violent responses within her body.

Oh, God, she felt . . .

Everything. Everywhere. His passion and urgency swept her into a raw, dizzying desire that broke all the barriers she might have imagined the first time making love with a different man. The length of his body against hers was evocative. Where his body was bare, touching her own nakedness, she felt a burning. Where his robe still hung about him there was intrigue. Where his hands moved. . . .

She was made erotically aware of his tongue

again, tasting her lips, ravaging deep in her mouth, entering, withdrawing, stroking . . .

Then suddenly he was over her, balanced upon his palms as he stared down at her.

"Any protests?" he demanded huskily. He was breathing heavily; the pulse at his throat pounded. His eyes were silver against the taut constriction of his handsome face, made golden in the lamp glow. "Sweet Jesus, Ann, if you've got any, send me back out to the rain now."

A slight smile curved her lips. She should have had a half dozen protests.

She couldn't think of a single one of them.

She simply couldn't think of anything to say. Nothing at all. She shook her head.

"Sure?"

She nodded.

He groaned softly.

His mouth lowered to hers once more; then he was straddled atop her, quickly shedding his robe, and his flesh was all bare, touching her nakedness everywhere with that burning. . . .

He shifted, coming lengthwise against her again, pulling her into his embrace. The stroke of his fingers moved down her back, over her buttocks. He was kissing her again. Touching her lips, moving on. His mouth covered her breast, laved it, his tongue rubbing her nipple as his fingers stroked her spine. She arched against him, gasping, fingers splaying into his hair. His touch moved over her with rapid-fire awakening, the texture of his fingertips rough, the brush of them mercurial, stroking her limbs, sliding to create a part between them, dusting, stroking, probing again . . .

Inside her. Creating a rhythm.

She cried out, fingers digging into his shoulders now, nails raking lightly over the bronzed flesh there. God, oh, God, she hadn't known what a lifetime it had been since she had felt this way, so desperate . . . so good, so damned desperate again, wanting, feeling. . . .

His mouth fastened over her breast once more, tongue encircling, lathing, while the stroke of his thumb rubbed at an exquisitely unbearable, intimate spot deep within the dampness of her sex. Then suddenly, so suddenly, he kneeled before her, catching her knees, lifting them, parting them. And she was staring again at him, flushed with the fever of seeing, of wanting, of feeling . . .

Newness. God, he was new to her; he aroused her to the depths of her passion, his eyes on her then as he demanded every intimacy. She thought that he meant to rise, to thrust into her. He was so aroused himself, tensed, wire-taut; so urgent, so demanding. But he didn't thrust into her, not with his sex. He leaned forward. The roughness of his cheeks rasped against the soft flesh of her abdomen as his lips left soft kisses there.

Then . . .

Oh, God, then . . .

He ravished her. More intimately than she had ever been seduced in all her life, more passionately. The rain plummeted outside, mercifully

muffling the shrieks that ripped from her throat
as wave after wave of sensation filled and burst
within her. She protested; she begged. She demanded he leave off . . . she forgot the words she
said as sweet satiation soaked her once again. She
thought she had died; then she thought that she
had never so lived. The world blackened, and
burst again into pale gold light. Then . . .

Then he suddenly rose over her. And he was
in her at last. And it was beginning again. Oh,
Lord, she couldn't bear anymore . . .

She couldn't bear not to feel him. Her eyes
were so tightly clenched. Then opened. And his
were on hers. Silver. Watching her still with a
sweet, hungry passion that made everything
within her soar as she felt the hotness of his body
thrusting and stroking with her own.

It would never end, this agony, ecstasy. Yet it
would never be enough. The rain pounded the
wooden walls, the wind began to rip at the cabin,
lightning tore at the swamp . . . it all seemed to
happen right within her. Yet when at last his
body contorted over hers in a massive knot of
trembling tension and his climax erupted, the
new wave of searing heat that swept into her
brought her to a last violent climax herself. She
drifted down from it in a cocoon of comfort and
bewilderment. Oh, she just hadn't remembered,
no, she had never known anything quite like
this. Jon had been a good lover, but never, never,
quite like this. . . .

The rain had stopped at last, she realized,
sucking in breath as she lay beside him on her

back, her heart still hammering a wild beat within her chest. He, too, had fallen to his back. His elbow shielded his eyes. She found herself turning to watch him, staring once again.

His body was . . .

Beautiful. And, oh, God, what he could do with it. . . .

He turned to look at her. A deep smile creased his features. He pulled her warmly into his embrace. "Wow," he said simply, his lips then nuzzling her forehead.

There was something about the way he said it that made it . . .

One of the nicest things she had ever heard.

He lay in a very dark world, a world of emptiness; living in a void.

Yet there were strange moments . . .

Nightmares sizzled through his sleep in this void. He walked contorted streets in which the blackness was occasionally lifted. He could hear her calling his name. Again and again. He knew where she was; he saw her face. Saw the pain, saw the terror. She tried to warn him. Because she was in the shadows.

And she was not alone there.

He cried out her name, trying to reach her. The faster he ran, the slower it became. His voice was distorted as if he spoke through an audio tape that had stretched and failed. His limbs failed him, as if he were under the whim of a cruel motion picture director, demanding that they go to slow motion. He heard music; the beloved music of his beloved city that now drowned out her desperate cries for help.

"Gina!"

He was running and running . . .

He reached her. Oh, God, there was the sudden pain.

And the blood, oh, God, the blood . . .

And the face. The face in the shadows. For one split second he saw that face. But then it was gone. And even in his dreams . . .

He wasn't sure if he would ever be able to draw it from the shadows again.

Compact. He'd called her compact.

What a totally inadequate term in every way, shape and form.

She was magnificent. Her legs were beautifully shaped. Her breasts were exquisite, just the right size; her waist was slim, her length supple—her damned elbows were perfect, he told himself. Her eyes were like clouded gems when she stared at him. Her smile made his heart catapult; her passion made him feel more alive than he had ever imagined he could be again.

He shouldn't have done it. Too bad. This was a hell of lot better than walking away.

His chin now rested on her head as he held her close. Not even including the fact that he'd just climaxed like a bulldozer, she was remarkable. Her loyalty to Jon Marcel was a rare quality, down to her own determination to risk everything to prove a man innocent. On blind faith. He'd come to have contempt himself for blind faith—job hazard. But she had the ability to make him believe.

"Hungry?" he asked her.

"Meaning?" she asked suspiciously.

"Meaning, would you like some food?"

"You have food?"

He laughed, rising, padding lightly across the wooden floor to the kitchen area. "The menu isn't extensive, but I've usually got a couple of bottles of decent wine . . . and I try to keep some sealed tins of crackers, soup and the like. And then there's always . . . hmm. Wrap up. We're going outside."

"Outside?"

"Come on."

She didn't respond instantly; she just stared at him as if he'd lost his mind, green eyes very wide, blond hair a tangle about her face. He tossed her the robe, slipped into a long shirt himself, caught her hand, and tugged her from the bed. "We'll raid nets," he said.

"We're going to raid nets?"

"Yep."

He drew her outside on the porch, then around to the back of the cabin where it actually sat over the water.

The cabin was his. The land it sat on was his— for what that piece of bayou was worth! The nets belonged to cousins, who also made use of the cabin if they needed to, and everyone silently kept it all up.

"Give me a hand here," he told Ann. She was still staring at him in bewilderment, having no idea of what he was doing, but she was going to help him.

Blind faith.

She was going to offer it to him, too.

Shit. He was falling in love.

"Right there, grab that length of rope."

Between them, they dragged up the net that had stretched from one post to another of the dock that composed the back part of the porch. It came up filled with crawfish, bringing a gasp from her.

"They're really good." He pulled one out, caught it firmly by the head and sucked out the meat of the tail. She stared at him, her face a shade pale. "Don't worry," he assured her. "The oven is gas—I can cook them. I mean, if you want."

"I've had crawfish," she said indignantly. "After all, I've lived here awhile now." She hesitated. "I've just never had them raw."

"They're not so awful. Especially when you're starving."

"Are you starving."

"Sex builds an appetite."

She flushed suddenly.

He found himself reaching out to touch her cheek and jaw. "I—I make wonderful Crawfish Diablo a la Mark LaCrosse."

"I make a wonderful kitchen slave. Let's go for it."

They did. His cabinets were filled with hot

sauces and spices. The crawfish were quickly simmering away in a frying pan, wine was uncorked, and crackers were unsealed to accompany the crawfish. They soon had something of a meal set before them at the table, and they sat down to it. For several seconds, they ate exchanging few words.

"Very good," she assured him.

"Thanks. It's better with fresh ingredients, of course."

"The crawfish couldn't be any fresher."

"The assistant chef was a wonder," he applauded.

"Of course, we're both starving."

"That's true. Maybe most famous chefs get their reputations by feeding starving people."

"Hmm, could be." She wiped her fingers, looking at him. "I'm eating stolen crawfish with a cop."

He grinned. "It's unlikely I'll arrest myself. Besides, they're not exactly stolen."

"We can hardly return them."

He lifted his wineglass, swallowed, grinned. "I'm from these parts. I have family here. I told you, I'm a coon hound."

"What a term!"

"It's all right—only if we're using it on ourselves."

"I like Cajun."

He smiled, reaching out, drawing his fingers idly over her hand. "You would."

"What does that mean?"

"Only the best. You don't harbor a single

prejudism in your soul." He swallowed more wine, then sighed. "New Orleans is a great place; we're a great mix of everything, a tolerant city. But historically, the Creole aristocrats looked down their noses at the Cajuns who descended from the Acadians who had to flee Nova Scotia. When I was a child, I lived out here full time. My father harvested crawfish. He had clients who called us Cajun children 'swamp nits.' So there you have it."

"Well, you've had your revenge," she said.

"Really?"

She nodded. "Cajun cooking, I mean. Surely, Cajun food is the most popular food in the country today."

He grinned.

"You can't really have a chip on your shoulder, can you?" she asked him.

"Not really. I like what I am."

"I like it, too," she said. Then she blushed, bit into another crawfish, and waved a hand in front of her mouth. "Good, really, good. Just hot."

He lifted her wineglass to her. She swallowed down a sip, then studied her glass.

"Good Cajun food is supposed to be hot," he told her.

She glanced up at him with a wry smile. She was breathtaking, hair still tousled, eyes so green against the fragile sculpture of her face. She wasn't a kid; he still hadn't determined her age. But she was everything beautiful about the natural maturity and sophistication that came with living life at peace with one's self. Her smile was mellow, almost wistful. She captured his heart, and his loins. He might be falling in love, but he had yet to fall out of lust. The situation was damned good. How often was a guy going to have the object of his lust imprisoned with him in a remote cabin where they couldn't possibly be reached for hours to come?

"Good Cajun cooking is supposed to be hot," she repeated. "And good Cajun men?" she queried.

He took a long swallow of his own wine. Actually, this was almost as good as a rag-mag fantasy. She was still in his robe; he was in nothing but a shirt.

"Is that . . . an invitation?" he asked huskily. "I mean, are you inviting me . . . ?"

"I guess so."

He stood so abruptly, his chair fell backward. He reached a hand to her; she hesitated just briefly. "I mean, unless you'd like some more crawfish?"

"No, I'm, er, fine . . ."

She took his hand.

They made love.

Slept.

Made love. That third time, she didn't just invite; she became the aggressor. Oh, Lord.

The things she did.

Her hair, sweeping down the bare flesh of his chest. Her kisses, the tip of her tongue, snaking down the length of him, over his chest, belly, teasing, taking . . . until it was all unbearable, until something of the male beast roared within him and he had to seize her, hold her, sink into her, *thirst* into her. He was on fire, taking her, all of her, rhythm like a rabbit until they exploded, falling together, slaked and sated again for the time being.

He stroked her hair, exhausted, yet awake, keyed. He wanted to sleep with her, but didn't actually want to spend his time sleeping with her—sleeping.

"You're amazing," he told her quietly.

She rolled over to prop herself on his chest and look down at him.

"Am I really . . . okay?"

He grinned, startled by the question. "Okay?" He cradled her face with his hand. "You're beautiful. Perfect lines. I'm no artist, but even I can see that."

She accepted the compliment, commenting, "But things . . . well, they change, you know."

"Meaning?"

"Well the skin isn't precisely on the bones where it was twenty years ago."

He laughed, angling his head to study her. "Change is good, too; it's something that seeps into the soul, you know."

"Umm." She arched a wry brow to him. "It seeps into the breasts and sags them as well."

He shook his head, laughing again. "Personally, I like yours right where they are. On the chest. They're actually great boobs. Even my partner said so."

"Did he?"

He nodded, fondling one of the mounds in

question. "He pointed out the assets of your butt as well."

"Very professional."

Mark shrugged. "At least he only commented. His was an artistic appreciation. I admit to having been blinded; I saw you as rather tiny at first."

"I'm still tiny."

"God, but great things do come in small packages."

"You really think that?"

"I do." He studied her more intently, touched by her uncertainty. "Just how old are you, Ann Marcel?"

"Forty-five."

"Ah."

"Does it matter?"

He shook his head. "I wouldn't have given a damn if you were any age at all. Well, that's not true; I wouldn't want you to be too young."

"That's a relief."

"I'm not a spring chicken myself."

"I don't know. You're one hell of a rooster."

"Red-hot Cajun?" he teased.

She nodded solemnly.

He took her face between both hands. "I love the way you look; you're a beautiful woman now, you were probably beautiful twenty years ago, and you'll be beautiful twenty years from now. Your heart is beautiful; it shows in the way you care about people. It shows in your passion and care for others, in your simple courtesy, in your art, in your movement. I haven't felt as good as I feel at this moment just holding you since . . ."

She moistened her lips. "Since your wife died?"

"Since before," he admitted. "She was sick, you see, for a while. I knew that she was going to die. The last days were precious; they were also agony."

"I'm so sorry."

"The agony was worth it; I loved her."

She nodded, understanding what he had said, not needing to say anything further on the matter.

He laced his fingers behind his head, the better to study her.

"I've been with a number of women since," he told her.

"Men are like that."

"Like what?"

She grinned. "I saw it on a television talk show. Men just need to be near women to want them; women need emotion to want men."

He grunted. "I'm not so sure that's always true."

"Does that mean that this was more than sex?"

She was teasing him, he thought. Yet perhaps it went a little deeper than that.

"What was it to you, Ann Marcel?"

She straddled him, watching his face, thinking over the question. She drew a line over his chest.

"You are quite an appealing male. Devastatingly handsome in all the right, mature ways. Broad, muscular chest, wonderful spattering of silver in the rich, masculine growth of hair upon it."

"Oh?"

"You've got great eyes. Just like a pair of knives."

"Umm. Somehow, that didn't sound terribly romantic."

"You're right. It didn't come out quite as it should have. You have the ability to look at someone and . . . and see into them. And kind of strip them in a way. It can be extremely annoying, of course. And then again, well, it can be terribly sexy."

"Yeah?"

She nodded solemnly.

"Go on. Keep talking."

"You've a great voice. Husky, deep, rich. Gets beneath the skin. It can cause hot, shivery sensations inside the bloodstream."

"Great."

"Then there's the way you kiss."

"Yeah?"

"Woah."

"Woah?"

"Sooo . . . intimate," she explained.

"That's good, I hope?"

She nodded again. "And by the way . . ."

"Yes?"

"You've actually got a great butt yourself."

"God, am I glad you approve."

She smiled.

"So, tell me," he demanded. "Is it just sex with you?"

She leaned against him. "You are trying to fry a very good friend of mine."

"Ah, the old ex-husband."

She nodded. "It shouldn't even be sex," she told him primly.

"But desire was overwhelming?"

"Something like that," she admitted dryly.

"My butt was just too damned good."

"Yes, well, then you got into it . . . and there was a lot that was just too damned good."

Her voice was low, honest, husky, sincere. It caused some of those hot shivers she'd been talking about to leap into his bloodstream and more.

"I think I'd like to test a little more gravity," he told her suddenly.

She was tiny.

Compact.

But so damned perfectly tiny and compact. She was easy to flip. She was on her back in seconds, and he was on top of her. And the words he used to describe just how fine he found her breasts to be were muffled by the fact that he lathed them again with his lips, teeth, and tongue as he spoke, feeling his own arousal grow as her nipples puckered and hardened to the play of his mouth. The sweet, natural scent of her was mingled with soap from the shower and the musk of their previous lovemaking, awakening his primal senses once again. He moved against her body, bathing her with his tongue, kissing, licking, caressing, giving, demanding. . . .

This time, when it was over, he lay on his back, staring at the ceiling, amazed that he could feel it only got better and better.

He pulled her against him once again.

"So is it only sex?"

"The sex is awfully good."

"Is it only sex?"

"Did I just tell you that women needed the emotion?"

"You told me that a television show said that women needed the emotion."

She laughed. Then she spoke seriously. "You're quite incredible, Mark LaCrosse. Half the time, I wish that I were really huge, a prize-fighter, and that I could beat you to shreds."

"Hmm. That doesn't sound very good."

"But maybe not quite so bad. You arouse incredible emotion—be it anger, or something else. And I admire you, I like you. I like your honesty, and even your persistence." She grinned. "I like your personal struggles; I like your outlook on life."

"I'm glad."

"So, I've poured half my heart out. What about you?"

"It's just the sex."

"What?" she demanded indignantly.

"Just the sex."

He laughed. She moved to strike him; he caught her hand. He drew her to him, kissing her lips, then whispering against them. "I wish it was just the damned sex. I wish you weren't beneath my skin; I wish I wasn't worried sick about you."

She smiled, easing against him. "There's no reason to worry about me."

"Yeah, I find you running around in the worst storm in years in the middle of the swamp, and I shouldn't worry about you."

"What were you doing in the swamp?"

"I came to find you."

"Why?"

"I was worried."

"Why?"

"I don't know, intuition." He hesitated, realizing that he still hadn't told her about Jane Doe. "You know that another woman was found dead, right?"

She nodded, frowning. "Strangled?"

"With a nylon stocking."

"So, could the two killings be related? I thought that serial killers had to have some kind of a pattern, that they kill because their twisted needs were fulfilled in some way by the very method of their killing?"

"This wouldn't necessarily fall into serial killings," he told her. He rolled over. "Way back when I just started in police work, the killings we investigated were usually personal. Jealousy was a motive, greed was a motive. The world has changed; we do have more and more crime that is carried out by bizarre people against total strangers to fulfill those warped needs you're talking about. But I'm convinced that Gina's killing was personal."

"You're back to Jon—"

He lifted a hand. "I'm not."

"You've decided he's innocent—"

"No. I'm just not as convinced of his guilt as I was."

"Why?"

"Jane Doe," he told her.

"You've found out about her?"

"We know that she was in the club the night that she died."

"Oh, my God! She was another of the dancers?" Ann said with horror.

"No, she didn't work at the club. She was just there, in Annabella's that night. Several of the staff saw her. The only problem is, no one knows who she came with, if she came alone, or who she left with."

"That doesn't help a lot."

"We'll have her identity soon; in this day and age of computers, there are certain things the police can do quickly."

"The cases could still be unrelated," Ann mused.

"They could be. Jon Marcel could have stabbed Gina; a nut case in the club could have followed Jane Doe."

"Maybe Jon will come out of his coma soon."

"Maybe. And when he does, we'll have to pray that he can help us—without convicting himself."

"He has to know something."

"We can only hope," Mark agreed.

She laid her head down against him, shivering. He tightened his arms around her.

"Mark?"

"Yes?"

She hesitated. "Mark, when I was with Jon in the hospital the night Gina was murdered, he did actually say something to me before he became unconscious."

"I know."

"You know?"

"You're a terrible liar. I knew that he had said something the minute you said that he hadn't."

"Really."

"Yes." He was quiet a minute. "Well, did you bring that up because you're willing to share now?" he queried.

"Yes."

"Well? What did he say?"

"I thought that he recognized me. That he was clinging to me, that he was trying to say my name."

"But that's not what he was saying."

He felt her shaking her head no against his chest. "He said, 'Annabella's.' As I did tell you, when he fell into my doorway, he kept saying that he hadn't done it. And then, in the hospital room, he said the name of the club."

"So that's why you went to the club?"

"The murderer is connected with the club."

Mark hesitated. It hadn't been a shocking revelation. But if Marcel was innocent . . .

And all right, so maybe it was starting to look a little bit as if the guy didn't do it.

Annabella's.

He pulled her more tightly against him. "You get your nose out of everything going on with this, do you understand?"

She didn't reply.

He tugged on her hair, drawing her head back so that she was forced to meet his eyes.

"I want you to keep your nose out of this case."

"Fine."

She was lying. She had no intention of listening to him.

"This really could get very dangerous."

"Yes, I can see that."

"You don't see anything. You were running around out here in the swamp—"

"I came to see an old woman just to ask her a few questions. I didn't come alone—"

"But you wound up alone."

She sighed.

"Ann, I mean it. You stay out of this case."

"I said, fine!"

"Damn it!" She was making him angry again. Hell. And getting angry again did something to him. Physically. He wanted her again.

Two things could happen: They could leave this cabin and, in the days to come, form a real relationship.

Then again, they could leave this cabin, and the world could fall apart on them.

"One more time, Ann. I mean it! Stay out of this case!"

She opened her mouth to protest. He kissed

her, determined that she wasn't going to tell him another lie. It was going to be dawn soon.

And he was going to make love to her one more time before the light of day came to start the world rolling on them once again.

Mark could feel the growing light and warmth of the sun as some sense of danger woke him. His eyes flew open. There was someone . . .

Someone outside the cabin.

He rose, carefully, silently, reached for the flannel shirt he had pulled from the closet last night, and slipped it on. He backed to the closet, listening, found a pair of jeans, and slipped into them.

Footsteps. Furtive. Slow.

Foliage rustled, just slightly.

He had set his service revolver in the closet before heading out for the shower. He reached for it, still listening, weighing every quiet footfall.

Every rustle of each little leaf. . . .

He walked across the cabin floor on his bare feet.

Silent . . .

He waited.

The door burst open.

He jumped forward, his gun at the ready in both hands. "Freeze!" he cried. Then, "Son of a bitch! You!"

Fourteen

It was early. April didn't know why she was coming into the club so early herself, except that Marty, who choreographed many of the numbers done by two or more of the dancers, needed to come in to work out a few steps in his mind on the stage. Normally, she would have stayed home being a mom; today, her sister was available, and she felt the need to stay close to Marty.

She sat at the bar, drinking coffee. She hadn't said anything to Marty about the awful feeling she'd had coming home the other night, when she'd been so certain she was being followed. When she'd felt eyes . . .

Watching her.

But she was unnerved, and her husband knew it. Now, of course, he was unnerved, too.

Because that woman had been here, in the club, before she'd been murdered.

Gina had been murdered.

And now a stranger had been murdered.

Life had gotten so scary. And the newspapers didn't help. There had been a few articles hinting that women who frequented clubs deserved to be murdered. That made her feel so indig-

nant she was tempted to write and demand to
know if poor innocent college girls deserved to
be murdered for being young and wearing biki-
nis to beaches. Maybe she would write a letter
to the editor. Soon.

Not now.

She was too unnerved.

With her life; with everyone in it. She had
thought Harry Duval okay as a boss. Now, she
didn't know. She hadn't been close to him, but
others had. He'd treated her decently, he didn't
beat anybody, but still. . . .

She had thought that their customers were,
for the most part, okay. Now, she didn't know.

April was startled when Cindy suddenly
crawled up on the stool next to hers, reaching
over for the coffeepot.

"Cindy!"

Cindy was ghastly pale, exhausted-looking.
"What are you doing here at this hour?"

"Worrying," Cindy said.

"What happened?"

Cindy shook her head. "I—rain. A lot of it."
She drank down some of her coffee, then
looked at April, huge tears forming in her eyes.
"I went out to the bayou yesterday with Gregory
and Jon Marcel's ex-wife."

"For what?"

"Ann Marcel wanted to meet Mama Lili
Mae."

April shook her head. "I think we should
watch out for that woman. She's his ex-wife, after
all."

Cindy shook her head. "April, she's as nice as can be. She's just trying to find out what happened."

"Yeah, well, maybe her trying to find out what happened could get somebody else killed."

"April, if Jon didn't kill Gina, then—"

"Then someone else did. Somebody maybe who just wanted to kill Gina. Damn, Marcel is half-dead anyway, a vegetable, right? Gina is dead; he's dying. Maybe we should really, truly, just leave it alone. Maybe that's the only way any of us can be safe!" April realized what she had said. She shivered. "I do want justice—just not at the risk of my own neck!" she admitted. "Cindy, I'm scared. Oh, God, I didn't let you finish—what happened?"

"Ann Marcel was in with Mama Lili Mae. Gregory and I were outside sitting by the water. You know me. I grew restless, and started wandering around. I was standing under a tree when one of the limbs broke. It scared me to death. I screamed like crazy, and started running wildly into the swamp right when the rain started. I got lost. I probably scared everyone else to death by screaming, and they all got lost coming after me. I don't know. I never found anybody. I made it down to the boats and decided to set out to take a look and see if I could find anybody running through the trees by the embankment. I looked and looked. I tried to go back to Mama Lili Mae's; but a whole tree had come down, so I had to back track again. I figured then that Gregory and Ann Marcel must have made it back to Mama Lili Mae's to weather out the storm. I can't tell you how bad the storm was; I'm so lucky I wasn't drowned. I made it back to the road, though, and a fisherman picked me up and brought me into the city. I tried to get hold of Mark LaCrosse, but he didn't answer. I finally got his partner. Jimmy headed out to the bayou as soon as I talked to him, so I'm just waiting to hear back."

"I'm sure Gregory and the woman are both okay," April said. "Sometimes I think that the bayou is the safest place to be these days."

"Yeah. With the real gators and snakes," Cindy agreed dryly.

April hesitated, then said, "Cindy, you know the night they said that woman who had been here in the club was strangled?"

"Yes?"

"Marty worked later than I did that night. Gregory was going to walk me home, but he had to come back in for some reason or another and I wasn't scared yet, so I went out walking on my own."

"Oh, April!"

"None of us should be alone anymore!" April said determinedly.

"What happened?"

"Well, nothing happened. Really. Except that I became convinced that I was being watched. Then I was certain that I was being followed. I ran half the way home, certain that a dark figure was following me. Then . . ."

"Then?"

"Then, when I got home, there was no one behind me at all. I went right up to my apartment. Locked myself in. That was it. I felt like a paranoid fool suffering delusions."

Cindy grimaced. She looked up at the one-way window to the office. "Well, let's look at this intelligently. Gina had been murdered—you had every right in the world to be paranoid. You'd be foolish not to be careful. And when you think about it, we all know that Harry Duval is watching us most of the time; so naturally, we're going to walk around with that feeling of eyes knifing into our backs."

"I guess," April said. She glanced up at the windows and shivered. She looked at Cindy. "You ever make it with Duval?"

Cindy flushed.

"Did you?"

"Yeah," Cindy admitted.

April shivered. "Thank God for Marty. No one ever expects anything out of either of us, just so long as we dance our little hearts out. Pretty soon, we'll make the money to get out of here. God, I only wish it was now . . ." She, too, stared up at the window. "What was Duval like?"

"April!"

"Oh, come on, Cindy! I know about half the three-way tricks you've turned and some of the other kinky stuff."

"April, you're a married mom—"

"That's right. Content in my own life, living vicariously through you and some of the other girls."

"But Duval—"

"Duval can be frightening sometimes. I'm just so jumpy lately. Is he scary?"

Cindy pondered the question. "He's hung like a horse. He loves to walk around naked looking at himself, and—"

"And what?"

"I don't know. There's something maybe just a little Satanish about him. A touch that he wants to go beyond, but actually . . . it's what's sexy about him. He takes what he wants. There's nothing hesitant. He can be exciting. He likes two women. He gets really excited watching others. Gina. He just loved to watch Gina when . . ."

"When what?" April demanded.

"When she did anything," Cindy said. "He— he likes women. In general. He likes sex. With lots of women. Singly, in pairs, in trios. He gets off on watching, but he has a strange power as well. He compels lovers. I don't know, what do you want me to say?"

April hesitated. "Does he get off on causing pain?"

Cindy paused, thinking again. "I—"

"Hey, you two!" Marty called.

They both started.

"Since you're here, come work with me. Let me see if I've got the moves for this down right, huh?" He grinned affectionately at his wife. April smiled back. They were both scared. He wasn't going to let her out of his sight. She was lucky. Marty was tall and built like an ebony Adonis. He was talented, and one of the nicest, most intelligent guys she'd met in her whole life. She loved him so much.

Maybe they should just quit now. Get away from here before something did happen to someone.

Between them, they made so much money. Soon they'd be able to really build a new life somewhere else. They'd have more kids.

And their children could have the entire world.

"Let's see what this is!" called another male voice.

Again, both women started.

Harry Duval was down, striding toward Marty, waiting to see the new dance. He looked back to the girls, hazel eyes glittering against the sharp contours of his face. "Ladies?" he said.

They both moved.

April walked past him.

She felt *eyes*.

She felt a hot, quivering sensation streak down her spine.

She glanced back at him. Copper-planed face, gold glittering eyes, dark hair, white flashing smile, full, sensual lips. He watched her. As if he knew something about her; knew more, maybe, than she knew herself. . . .

The man was Satan.

"Marty, where am I supposed to be?" she demanded, hurrying toward her husband.

* * *

Ann woke up with a start. She'd heard a commotion.

"Mark!" she whispered, running her hand over the bed.

But Mark wasn't in it.

She was in the bayou, in a cabin—alone. Completely alone.

Old Billy was out there somewhere. Who else? What else?

Where the hell was Mark, and what had she heard?

She crawled out of the bed, half afraid that any second the door was going to burst open.

The killer would have tracked her down.

And if not the killer . . .

Well, then, Mark's Cajun cousins would come across a naked woman in the woods. Naturally, it would be better if his relatives arrived, but she was definitely uncomfortable wondering about what was going on either way.

She found the shirt he had given her on the floor, and she quickly slipped into it. It was huge—thankfully. On her small form, his shirt was almost as good as a dress. She buttoned it up and rolled up the sleeves, then moved cautiously to the window.

The rain was gone. The day was beautiful.

There was movement outside the cabin. She heard footsteps, approaching the door.

She shrank back against the wall, then decided that she'd just be a sitting duck all lined up for a shot if she stayed where she was.

She grabbed hold of a pot from the kitchen, then dived beneath the bed.

The door opened. She saw a pair of bare feet and jean-encased calves.

Did she recognize them? Were they Mark's?

Had she just made love with a man a half dozen times in so many hours and failed to notice his feet? It wasn't that—she just couldn't see clearly enough.

The man swore, moving through the cabin. The footsteps paused.

He'd seen her.

She shrieked as hands grabbed her feet, yanking at her hard, dragging her out from her hiding place. She fought frantically, wielding her pan as a weapon the first chance she got.

She struck home, catching the man in the temple.

The door burst open again.

"What the hell?"

Mark's voice.

"You tell me, what the hell?"

Ann inhaled on a gasp; it was basset hound Jimmy, Mark's partner. She'd just creamed him with a sauce pan. And Mark was back, staring at his wounded partner and his half-clad lover.

She jumped to her feet, trying to pull the flannel shirt down around her.

"I'm sorry." She glanced from Mark to Jimmy. "Well, you weren't here and I heard footsteps and suddenly the door was bursting open . . . oh, now, Officer Deveaux, I didn't hit you that hard; it can't be that bad."

"It hurts like hell!" Jimmy said.

Mark, hands on his hips, watched the two. He sighed with exasperation.

"Well, why were you dragging me out from beneath the bed like that?" Ann demanded.

"Because it looked like a derelict thief had broken into a friend's cabin!" he said sternly.

"You knew she was out here," Mark said.

"I didn't expect her to be hiding under your bed," Jimmy shot back. "Where the hell were you?"

"Jacques Moret was out here, over at Mama Lili Mae's. We've got some serious trouble."

"You were the serious trouble," Jimmy told Mark. "Cindy McKenna called this morning in a tither because she'd lost Gregory Hanson and Mrs. Marcel out here last night. She couldn't get a hold of you. I knew where *you* were, but I thought you might like some help."

"Jimmy, your timing was perfect. We definitely need help. I hope you've got your phone. We've just dug Gregory up from beneath a fallen tree. He's hurt badly. Besides what is surely a major concussion, he's been terribly exposed to the elements. I think he's in shock. Mama Lili Mae and Jacques had warmed him up the best they could when they came for me, but we've got to get him to a hospital fast."

Ann stared in horror as Jimmy pulled out a small cellular phone and punched in the few numbers necessary to reach police emergency services. He spoke quickly and concisely, repeating the conditions Mark had just given him. He folded his phone and replaced it in his jacket pocket. "Let's get on it."

They turned and hurried out. Ann looked at the pile where her mud-packed clothing lay from the night before. There was no help for it. She couldn't worry about her clothing or her current, ridiculous state of dress.

Gregory could be dying.

Jimmy had come with a fairly large motorboat. Gregory was already in it, wrapped in several blankets, supported by Jacques Moret. He nodded gravely to Ann as she stepped into the boat, his gaze quickly assessing her mode of dress. She tucked the flannel carefully beneath her as she took her seat, reaching out to touch Gregory's face gently. He felt cold. So cold.

His eyes were open, she realized. Open, and staring.

"My, God!" she whispered. "He's . . ."

"Shock," Mark said.

She was startled when Jacques spoke to her. "His heart is beating strongly, Mrs. Marcel. He is a strong man. A very strong man."

She nodded, biting her lip. "He is a good man, too. Where did you find him?"

"Not a hundred feet from the house," Jacques said. "He might have been calling out, but the storm was so loud . . . we didn't hear him. This morning, Mama Lili Mae had one of her psychic intuitions. We found him, but couldn't get the tree up by ourselves. She told me she thought that Mark might be out here—if he had known you were coming, he would follow." He shrugged with a half smile. "She was right. We got the tree up, and carried him here." He grinned. "Mark said that Jimmy would come this morning. Cop's intuition."

She nodded, still watching Gregory. His coloring was ashen.

She wished she'd taken nursing instead of so much art.

The motor roared with a fury; Mark was at the helm. Ann gripped her seat, praying that they wouldn't shoot right into a root and all perish in an explosion.

But Mark knew the bayou.

Of course, it was his home.

They made unbelievable speed and progress across the water. When they reached the embankment, a helicopter was waiting in the field just across the road. Waiting paramedics raced for Gregory, and he was quickly taken away.

Ann, Mark, Jimmy, and Jacques watched the helicopter whirr away.

Mark turned to Ann. "Get in your car. Go home. I'll follow you. I have my own car here."

She nodded, feeling numb. She turned to walk to her car. *It was her fault. If she hadn't wanted to come out to see Mama Lili Mae. . . .*

He'd been struck down by a tree. An act of God. Wasn't it?

Or was it?

She crawled in behind her steering wheel. She stared at it. Mark came to stand beside her at the driver's side window. "What's the matter?"

"Keys," she said simply.

He swore. "Scoot over."

She crawled into the passenger's seat. He played beneath the dash.

It was alarming to see how quickly he hot-wired her car. She stared at him, her amazement probably pretty obvious.

"Hey, you hang around crooks, you can't help but learn a few things." He brushed her cheek. "He's going to make it, Ann."

She nodded, swallowing. "Right. Gregory's got a prayer of making it. So does Jon. And two women are already dead."

"Go home."

She nodded.

He crawled out of her car. "I'll be behind you until I see that you're up in the apartment."

She nodded again.

She pulled out, lifting a hand to wave to the others. "Go home," Mark reminded her. He still stood on the roadway, barefoot, jeans hugging his muscled thighs, handsome in his red plaid shirt.

Going home was going to be easy right now. She needed a shower.

She needed clothing.

Shoes.

Coffee. Oh, God, did she need coffee.

"And stay there!" Mark called more firmly to her.

Stay there. . . .

In lieu of everything that had happened, that might be harder to do.

Fifteen

Ann showered, drank three cups of coffee, and prowled her apartment, aware that the three cups of coffee had added to her restlessness.

She stretched, she sat in a chair, curled up, and relived the night.

It had ended so abruptly. Maybe that's all that there could be right now.

She ached for more.

She didn't want to let the tension of her feelings overwhelm her, and she prowled the apartment again, then decided that she was a fool—she needed to be working. She set a pad upon an easel and managed to sketch for a while. She needed to take a few pictures, she thought; when she wasn't able to sketch her subject in person, she liked pictures. To do the painting of Cindy she wanted to do, she was going to need some Polaroids. She wondered if Cindy would mind; she doubted it.

Though her work kept her totally absorbed for nearly two hours, it wasn't enough.

At twelve, she decided to go to the hospital. She tried to find out about Gregory. She was told that his condition remained critical, but that he was stable.

She wandered to the chapel, and sat there awhile. She tried to pray; she stared at the flowers on the altar. She felt numb, and helpless.

She left the chapel and found her way to Jon's room in intensive care. She sat with him, talking to him.

The nurses told her again that his vital signs and color were really excellent. The nurses left her.

She didn't just talk to Jon. She yelled at him. He needed to think about what he was doing; he needed to be careful. He had a daughter, for God's sake, and it wouldn't be long before Katie did phone home. And, oh, God, then what was Ann going to say? "Don't worry, sweetheart, if Dad should come out of his coma, he's going to be arrested for murder"? *Oh, Jon, you've just got to get well and solve this damned thing.*

Even in the hospital, she grew restless. She phoned her house to check her messages, but Mark hadn't tried to reach her.

Finally, she knew that she couldn't hold back any longer. She went outside and hailed a taxi, and went to the club.

It was early afternoon; things were very quiet. A disc jockey was playing records.

Cindy was on the stage.

The slim girl behind the bar recognized Ann and offered her a pleasant smile. Ann ordered a glass of wine, and watched Cindy as she sipped it.

Cindy was, quite simply, really beautiful. She was probably at least five-foot-nine, and every inch of her length was well composed. "Delilah Delite," the persona on stage, wore rose-colored lipstick, dusky eye makeup—and very little else. She swirled, twirled, dipped, ducked and undulated against one of the phallic-looking poles. Her very, very blond hair swirled around her face until she was joined by one of the male dancers, a handsome man with muscles like corded steel. The movements they made together were exquisite; Cindy so fair, the man so dark, the two of them so extremely supple. The dance was absolutely erotic. Ann realized that she was finding the pair more titillating now than she had found any of the dancers before.

Because, she admitted to herself, she'd suddenly discovered a sex life again.

A young black woman suddenly slid into the seat beside her. "You're Ann Marcel."

Ann nodded, studying the woman. She was very pretty. Again, she recognized her as one of the women she had seen on stage.

"I'm April Jagger. That's my husband, Marty, with Cindy."

"Oh!" Ann said, trying to smile, taken by surprise.

April laughed. "Don't worry. They're quite harmless together."

Ann blushed. "It's just so . . ."

"Right."

"But beautiful. Really."

"I hope so. Marty is really a good choreographer. He's done some music videos, and naturally, some of us get jobs in them."

"You're all very talented."

April laughed. "It's not so difficult really. We can teach you to dance. Anyway, they're almost finished. Cindy will be really glad to see you; she was worried sick about you this morning."

"I knew she was back; I should have tried to call her."

"It's okay; the police got hold of us. We knew that you were okay. And we know, of course, that Gregory's hanging in."

"I just came from the hospital. They told me that he was still critical but stable. He must have taken one awful whack on the head."

"That storm was fierce. Worse than a few hurricanes. Amazing how quickly they can come up and then comes the morning, and the wind and rain are just gone as if they'd never been. Anyway, they both should have seen how bad the weather was getting. The middle of one of those storms is no time to be running around in a bayou. Anyway, come on backstage. See what the other half is like. Bring your wine."

Ann took her wineglass and followed April through the darkened center of the club around to the left side of the stage. They entered into a large hallway with numerous doors leading off it. "Lots of us share this one," April said, opening the door to one of the rooms. She stretched out an arm, indicating that Ann should precede her. Ann did so.

The room had one occupant, a very buxomy

brunette with a feathered headdress that surely swept the ceiling. A few feathers made up the rest of her costume, carefully placed. Some would stay, Ann assumed, when she was done with her appearance. Some would not.

She was standing, just finishing an application of lipstick.

"Jennifer, this is Ann Marcel. Jon's husband."

"Hi, nice to meet you, he was a dear, is a dear, he's still alive, right? Oh, sorry, that sounds so terrible. I'm late as usual. It's really nice to meet you; I hear you're as nice as he was. Is."

"Thanks," Ann said. "It's a pleasure to meet you."

"You takin' a job here, honey? I thought you were an artist as well?"

"I am. I'm not taking a job."

April laughed. "We're waiting for Cindy. Then Cindy and I are going to give her a few pelvic gyration lessons and see if we can't tempt her."

"Go to it, girls. See you in a sec."

Jennifer flew out, her feathers waving away.

"Have a seat," April offered. "I've got to get dressed myself."

She indicated a comfortable sofa near a rack of costumes. The sofa faced a long makeup counter with five individual mirrors. To the far right of the room was a dressing screen. April selected a skimpy tigress costume and strode behind the screen.

"I heard that the strangled woman the police

found had been in the club that night," Ann said.

"Yep. I saw her myself," April said, "right before I left for the night."

"You did."

April, her head appearing above the screen, nodded. "She was right up at the bar."

"Maybe she came alone."

"There was a drink in place next to her."

"Well, someone must have ordered the drink."

"Not from the bartender."

"Then how—"

"Somebody must have ordered the drink I saw from one of the waitresses—which would mean it could have belonged to a hundred people. It is amazing. There isn't a soul in this place who could begin to describe who she was with."

"Scary, isn't it?"

"Terrifying."

Cindy, a terry robe wrapped around what remained on her of her costume, burst into the room. "Ann!" She walked right to the sofa and offered Ann a warm hug. "God, I'm so glad that you're all right, at least. I was so worried. I'm off for a bit now. I think I'm going to head over to the hospital and see about Gregory. I'm just sick; it was all my fault."

"How can a tree falling be your fault?" Ann demanded.

"Because I was restless, because I walked away, and Gregory, being Gregory, was going to make certain nothing bad happened to me. We were all so dangerously stupid—not you, you don't know the swamp. But once we were out there and that storm started, we should have all just stayed with Mama Lili Mae. Big slumber party. We'd have been fine. And Gregory—" She paused, her eyes filling with tears. "Gregory wouldn't be in the hospital."

"But thank God that Ann was all right," April reminded her.

"Well, the detective of the year went after Ann." She smiled, then sighed. "But that didn't help Gina any."

"Gina and he weren't an exclusive thing," April said.

Cindy stared at Ann. "I didn't know that you and Mark were an exclusive thing. Actually, I didn't know that you were a 'thing' at all. I mean, Jimmy Deveaux told me that he'd gone out to the bayou, but . . ."

"He came out to the bayou and found me, and we're not an exclusive thing," Ann said, impatient to ask questions rather than answer them. An incredible uneasiness was sweeping over her. "I didn't realize that he and Gina . . . were a thing."

"Well, they weren't a thing. They were upon occasion. Or had been upon occasion."

"Well, you know, they kind of grew up together," April offered.

Cindy sighed. "You didn't know? Mark and she saw each other. Mark is a descendant of an aunt of Mama Lili Mae who married a LaCrosse. So they were distantly related. Which makes him distantly related to Jacques as well. But as to Gina, well . . ."

"They had a relationship awhile after Mark's wife died. Then they cooled off. Then they had a relationship again. Then they were friends, then . . ."

"So, he might have been sleeping with her when—when she died?"

"She really was in love with Jon, I think, at least," April said.

"Yeah," Cindy muttered. "Well, she might have been in love with him, but that didn't stop her from keeping some other people dangling at the same time."

"She did spend a fair amount of time up in Duval's office the Monday before she was killed."

"And what about Jacques Moret?" Ann asked.

"Oh, well, I never did know what his hold over her was. She saw him," April said. "It was never love. Maybe they got together now and then when one of them was lonely."

"I don't know," Cindy murmured. "It seemed to me that they got together when Jacques felt like it."

"Well, it didn't matter. Jon was the one she cared about. I think it could have worked," April said. She stepped out from behind the screen dressed in her costume.

"Go get 'em, tiger," Cindy teased.

"I think I still have a few minutes," April said. "Ann, come on, get up. We'll teach you how easy these movements really are."

"Oh, God, no, I really can't. I'm forty-five years old, I'm not—"

"Anyone can be!" April laughed.

"Be what?" Cindy asked.

"Whatever it is. Come on, Ann, get between us. Think of it as an anatomy lesson. It will help if you get into painting *Red Light Ladies.*"

"It will, it's easy," Cindy insisted.

She wasn't sure that she would have had the physical power to resist the two if she had decided to struggle. They actually had her laughing, even though she was seething inside—but determined not to let either of them know it. Before she knew it, she found herself being "costumed." The girls—not at all shy themselves—had her street clothing. She was prodded into an exotic, flaming fuchsia, daring harem-type outfit, complete with outrageous headdress.

Something in her felt shattered. Her world was a mess, but her night had been beautiful. She'd been falling for him, living him, breathing him, falling in love with him . . .

And he'd not only been trying to fry Jon, but he'd been trying to fry him while *he'd been sleeping with Gina at the same time.*

"Undulate, undulate!" April commanded. "Think where all the parts of the body are!"

"I am undulating!" Ann laughed.

"Loosen your body," Cindy said. "Let the hips follow the knees, think like a snake. That's it. Very sexy. Very nice. That's it, that's it . . ."

"She's damned good!" April applauded.

Jennifer came back into the room. "April,

you're up, better get moving—you two are teaching the artist how to dance? Cool. Show her some of the arm movements. Actually, though, half of us did take dance lessons the whole time we were kids. Did your mom stick you in ballet?"

"Ten years of it," Ann laughed.

"No wonder. See, it all comes back. The body learns, and the body remembers," April said.

"April, get going," Cindy warned.

"I'm out of here. Ann, that was fun. If you take off before I get back, please come see us again."

"I will, thanks."

Ann inched backward toward the doorway. She didn't think she could remain calm much longer when she wished she could go back to the morning and crack Mark LaCrosse on the head with the sauce pan instead of his sad-eyed partner.

She changed back into her own clothing as she spoke. "Cindy, I wanted to make sure you were okay. I think I'm going home for some sit-coms and a good night's sleep. If you hear anything, give me a call. If I find out anything, I'll get with you."

"Thanks, Ann."

"Oh, Cindy! Can I take some pictures of you tomorrow? I like to work from photographs."

"You're going to paint me?" Cindy seemed pleased.

"If you don't mind."

"No. I'm an egotist. I'll love it."

"Great."

"Yeah, it's great; we'll see you tomorrow. We'll get you out on that stage after all."

Never, Ann thought.

But she smiled. "The lesson was fun. Bye, now."

Ann walked out of the dressing room, through the back, around the audience in the darkened center, past the bar area and dais, and to the door.

Odd.

She felt . . .

Watched.

Everyone watched her, she reminded herself wearily. They all watched her, because she didn't belong. She was Jon Marcel's ex-wife. And Jon Marcel . . .

Well, they all seemed to feel almost the same way about Jon.

They all liked him.

Yet some people seemed to think him guilty.

And others seemed to know damned well that he wasn't.

Damned well.

Mark sat with Lee Minh in his office, reading Jane Doe's autopsy report.

"Cause of death . . . strangulation." He set the report down. "She was found in the water—"

"With a nylon stocking ligature around her neck," Lee finished. "That's the obvious, the easy."

"Okay, so—"

"No water in her lungs. She was dead before she was thrown in."

"Naked."

"Right."

"And she'd had sex with a man whose basic blood type is O positive—"

"The same as half the world's male population."

"So, sex, then strangulation. Our murderer is male."

"Unless she had sex, then found someone else who was angry with her."

"Someone strong?"

Lee shrugged. "Well, it wasn't a weak child. But if you were to get behind someone so with a noose already slipped into the ligature . . ."

"I see. You wouldn't have to be strong."

"You could be."

Mark sighed with exasperation. "So we're nowhere."

"Maybe not. I'm still working on the contents of her stomach. We know where she drank her Bloody Marys—but not with whom she drank. Maybe we'll find out where she ate dinner."

"And if she ate with company," Mark agreed. "I've already sent her picture and the artist's conception of her appearance before death around to the local restaurants. Hopefully, we'll have something soon."

"We will," Lee assured him.

"I just hope it's soon enough," Mark said.

He thanked Lee, then called the hospital and

asked about both Gregory's condition, and Jon Marcel's. Both men were slightly improved. Gregory had gone from "critical" to "serious." Mark was relieved. Gregory had always been a friend to everyone around him; he deserved the very best. If God was paying any attention at all, he'd look after Gregory.

Marcel was beginning to look really good, but no, he hadn't actually come out of the coma; he certainly hadn't spoken. Still, the doctors were optimistic.

He left Lee Minh's office.

And headed for Ann Marcel's house.

She was curled up on her couch, drinking hot chocolate, trying to convince herself that she didn't need to find a shady doctor who would put her on tranquilizers until this was over, when she heard the knocking at the door. She tensed, staring at it.

"Ann!"

She didn't reply. Maybe he would think that she wasn't there, and go away.

"Ann!" He kept pounding.

She set her hot chocolate down, feeling as if its heat now brewed in her blood. She walked silently to the door, listening.

He kept pounding. How the hell did he know that she was in there.

"Ann, damn you, what's the matter with you; open the door! It's Mark."

She leaned against the door. "I know who the hell it is!" she assured him.

There was silence for a moment. "So . . . why aren't you letting me in?"

She was ready. "Because you're a self-serving bastard, worse than all the rest of them."

"What?"

"All but boxing and gift wrapping an innocent man to hand him over to the courts—*when you're every bit as likely a suspect as he is!*"

"What the hell—"

"Oh, yeah, what the hell! You were sleeping with her, too, you wretched bastard!"

"So what?"

"So you're a suspect."

"I wasn't wearing her blood!"

"And you weren't stabbed, and you're not in a coma!"

"Ann, let me in—"

"Go the hell away."

"This isn't any way to solve this—"

"Solve what? You're a cop. I'm Jon's ex-wife. If he lives, I'll see you in court."

"Damn it, Ann—"

"Go to hell, go away."

"No."

"Son of a bitch! I'll call the cops."

"I am a cop."

"There are other cops, you know."

"Ann, damn it, let me in."

"Why the hell didn't you tell me?"

"You never asked."

"And you didn't think that it mattered?"

"We weren't the affair of the century, and we weren't sleeping together when she died."

"Oh. Was she just sex?"

"Ann, I don't want to keep talking to you through a goddamned door!" he exploded.

"Then go away!"

She spun away from the door, furious. Let him rant and rave. She strode over to her easel, where she'd been working on the sketch of Cindy. She picked up her pencil, shading in the eyes.

He didn't pound on the door again. He didn't say anything else at all.

She paused, gnawing on her lip. Then she walked back to the door and leaned her head against it, listening.

Nothing.

She turned away from the door and gasped.

He was standing in her living room, a brow arched as he watched her at the door.

"Damn you!" she cried, racing for her bedroom. He came after her.

"Ann!"

She tried to slam the door on him.

He stopped it with his shoulder. The door shuddered on its hinges. And swung open.

And for the life of her, as she backed away staring at him, she didn't know if she was more furious than ever . . .

Or just glad that he was damned persistent.

Sixteen

Maybe it was something he should have discussed with her, Mark thought, seeing the indignation in her eyes. He'd never meant to avoid telling her the truth; it had just never come up between them.

And now . . .

She was in a soft velour robe, as dark a green as her eyes. Her hair was freshly washed, fluffing around her face. He was itching to go to her, sweep her up, find what he had found last night, drown everything else out in the feelings he had found for her.

"You know, I think this could be considered police brutality," she informed him.

"I haven't touched you."

"You've done unbelievable damage to my bedroom door."

"Why the hell won't you talk to me?"

"You had a relationship with her."

"Yes. Why are you so furious about that? I didn't know you then—"

"Close enough. Were you sleeping with her when she died?"

He grated his teeth together hard. "To the

very best of my knowledge, no one was actually sleeping with her when she died."

"You know what I mean."

"No."

She was silent. He crossed his arms over his chest. "Does that mean you think that I'm lying?"

"I don't know. Why didn't you tell me about her?"

"Well, let's see. When I first met you, it was really none of your business."

"When you first met me, you were after my husband."

"Your ex-husband."

"It was a cut-and-dried case. He'd been sleeping with her. He had to be guilty."

"He was covered in her blood. How do you keep missing that minor fact?"

"I don't! But there's an explanation for it."

"What's that?"

"He was trying to help her."

"Oh? Maybe he thought she was better off dead?"

"Get out!" she snapped at him.

Mark inhaled deeply, fighting the war that waged within him. He wanted more than anything in the world to just walk over to her, take her into his arms. But that wasn't the way to end this fight.

Not to mention the fact that his pride was deeply injured that he could be so easily cast aside for what she considered a past digression.

He settled back on his heels, watching her

with a growing irritation and fury as he realized her *sudden* knowledge. Gained today.

"When I left you this morning, I told you to go home."

"Well, Lieutenant, I did come home this morning. Not that you have the right to tell me to do anything. I am a grown woman."

"I told you to go home and stay home."

"You have no right to tell me to do anything—"

"I should arrest you."

"For?"

"Reckless endangerment."

"Of . . . ?"

"Of everyone around you. The club is dangerous; haven't you figured that out yet?"

"The club is only dangerous if Jon is innocent."

He couldn't help himself—he strode over to her. He balled his hands into fists and crossed his wrists at his back, determined not to touch her.

He saw her pulse racing.

She moistened her lips with the tip of her tongue.

But she stood her ground.

God, her throat looked good, leading to cleavage exposed by her velour robe. Nearness, she had told him, made a man want a woman.

Emotions made a woman want a man.

And want to kill him, so it seemed.

"I granted you the fact that your precious Jon might be innocent—bloodbath and all. That being the case, you're an idiot to hang around the club. Another woman—*last seen alive in that club*—was murdered. With Jon Marcel in a coma. So whether Jon did or didn't kill Gina, someone else killed our Jane Doe. Are you trying to get yourself killed?"

"No!" She pointed a finger at him, then poked it against his chest. "I'm trying to get you out of my house."

"You did go to the club."

"Will you go home."

"And someone at the club told you about Gina and me."

"You do have a home, don't you?"

"She was there when I was really in pain, can you understand that? And I got to know her, like your ex-husband did—"

"Yes, that's the point, isn't it?"

"She was a special woman."

"So I have heard."

"She became a friend. A good friend. She was looking for something solid and permanent. I had just been struggling for help. We stayed friends, she fell in love with Jon, and he fell in love with her. Damn you, what is it that you're so unwilling to forgive?"

"You kept the truth from me."

"I never did so intentionally."

"You came after Jon like a bulldog! You'd have hanged him on the spot if you could have done so."

"I'm not judge and jury. I've never tried to be judge and jury. You—"

"I just want to be alone tonight. Now!" she told him angrily.

She was still too close. She slammed her palm against his chest, trying to force him from the room.

He lifted both hands, backing away from her. "You want to be alone. You little fool. Does it ever occur to you that you might be in danger."

"I'm safe in my home. What can happen to me here?" she demanded, green eyes glittering like emeralds, chin high.

He arched a brow to her. "I'm in here, aren't I?"

"Because I left the balcony open—"

"I'm in here, aren't I?"

"I would have closed up before I went to bed—"

"Yeah, and if I had been a murderer, what were you going to fend me off with, your paint brush?"

"Would you get out of here?"

Yes, he would. He was completely exasperated.

He wanted a cold shower. He wished he was back in the damned swamp after the rain storm so that he could just dunk himself in the cold water and stay there until the heat that fused his body cooled completely.

But . . . could he leave her? Safely?

"All right, listen, you're really angry, right?"

Her eyes widened as she stared at him. "Lieutenant, you are some detective. Your powers of observation are simply beyond human belief."

"I'll sleep on your sofa."

"What?"

"Police protection."

She pressed against his chest, pushing him out of the way.

He struggled with himself as she tried to brush by him.

Struggled, fought.

Won.

Lost.

He grabbed her elbow, swinging her back around to face him. "Damn you, you're just throwing everything right away!"

His arms curved around her, drawing her up tight against him, forcing her thighs, her sex, her belly, flush to his body as he found her lips. She held stiff . . .

For seconds.

Just seconds. Her hands pressed against his chest, fighting him, her lips primly clamped . . .

Then opened.

Her body softened. He drew the caress of his fingers up over her derriere, along her spinal column, down again. Her mouth parted more and more freely to his . . . she tasted of chocolate, of warmth. Her mouth was so sweet, so sensual as she slowly gave in to the assault, as her tongue stroked his in return, as the softness of her body melded to the movement of his hands. . . .

He drew away, staring down at her. She was trembling; he could feel it.

"Damn you, Mark—"

"Fine! Have it your way."

He released her, and spun around to stride back out to the living room. He slipped off his jacket, then removed his gun and shoulder holster, placing them both on the coffee table. He sat down, slipping off his shoes.

She had come to stand in the bedroom doorway; stunned perhaps, the back of her hand against her damp, swollen lips. "You're—you're not staying! I'm safe."

"The hell you are. Go to bed. I won't touch you. You are a big girl. You get to make up your mind on what you want."

A cry of exasperation escaped her. She slammed her way into her bedroom—or tried to slam her shattered door. It didn't actually close; she seemed to pretend that it did.

She didn't come out.

At first, the night was endless. He tossed, turned, swore she had the most uncomfortable sofa in the universe.

At midnight, just when he had begun to doze, a sound awakened him. He opened his eyes, waited. Yes, there was something outside.

He rose quickly, his socks making his steps silent as he made his way through the darkness to the balcony doors he had never closed.

Clouds covered the moon in sporadic bursts, spun past it, covered it again. There were shadows everywhere, cast by the street lamps, as well as the moon.

There was a shadow . . .

Coming over the balcony railing.

The shadow paused, as if it sensed Mark in the darkness. It turned, and leapt back down to the street.

Mark swore, leaping after it.

Maybe the shadow was a little bit younger than he was; it made the fall to the pavement more easily than Mark. He landed hard, but came to his feet and started to run.

But the shadow was gone, and Mark knew that he wouldn't find it. Too many of the clubs remained opened; there were too many nooks and crannies in the various alleys into which the figure might have run.

He trudged back to Ann's house, made a weary reentry through the balcony, and tapped on her bedroom door.

She didn't answer.

He opened the door. She was sitting up in bed, staring at him.

"Intruder," he told her. "I just wanted to let you know that I'm calling it in."

"Intruder?"

"Someone on your balcony."

"A thief?"

"Or a murderer," he said dryly.

He closed her door, and called it in. There wasn't much that could be done, but Mark told the guys in fingerprinting to give it a try.

Ann had slipped into a cool summer halter dress. She watched the proceedings in her apartment silently, then offered to make coffee. The cops thanked her; she did so. Ralph Fellows, on fingerprints that night, shook his head. "We've pulled up some prints, but they're going to prove to belong to you and Mrs. Marcel. Your shadow wore gloves." He hesitated and spoke softly. "You're not just spooked, Lieutenant, are you? You really did see a shadow?"

"I'm not spooked; when the hell have you ever seen me spooked?" he replied angrily.

"Sorry, sorry, sir! Must have been a practiced thief—New Orleans is full of them. Guy who wears gloves knows what he's doing. We'll file everything; maybe Mrs. Marcel can get some sleep now. Do we leave a man on the door?"

"No, it's all right. I'll be here."

"Sure. Well . . ."

The boys drank their coffee, thanked Ann for it, and left. Ann studied him.

"Did you just invent an intruder to prove to me that I was an idiot leaving the balcony doors open and I'd be in big trouble if it weren't for you?" she demanded.

He stared back at her and swore. "You know, there is a fair bit of crime in New Orleans. I do my best not to drag officers away from doing their best to stop crime when they can."

He settled back on the sofa, turning his back to her.

Yet . . .

He was certain she stayed where she was, watching him for a while.

Maybe she even wanted to speak.

Maybe he should speak.

Right. He'd already tried that. Hadn't his pride taken a big enough blow for the night?

Instinctively, he knew when she turned away and returned to her room.

He slept late. The sun was pouring in through the glass of the now locked balcony doors.

He still felt so groggy. He wondered what had awakened him. The phone. The phone was ringing.

Ann came bursting out of her bedroom. Then she noticed him. She paused, staring at the phone, and then at him.

"It's your phone," he said.

"How good of you to notice."

"Well?"

"The machine is on."

She frowned suddenly. He could almost see her mind working. Yes, the machine was on. If she didn't answer the phone, he'd hear whatever her caller had to say.

She made a sudden, awkward dive to reach the phone at the kitchen counter.

Too late. The machine had already picked up.

"Hi, this is Ann. I can't get to the phone right now. Please leave your name, phone number, and message and I'll get back with you as soon as possible. Thanks."

Ann opened her mouth to speak when the message finished.

But the caller began speaking first.

"Mrs. Marcel, this is Roana Jenkins; I'm one

of Jon Marcel's nurses in the I.C.U. I just wanted to let you know that Jon has come out of his coma. Naturally, the doctor informed the police right away, but I wanted to reach you as soon as possible; perhaps you can get here first, I mean, naturally, I know how you feel about the man, and you've been so loyal and dedicated to his recovery—"

Naturally! Mark thought irritably. Thank God the good doctor had called the police in first. And if this had been a couple nights ago—before she'd made him toss his cellular into the mud—he'd have been informed already.

He strode to where Ann stood, jerking the receiver from her hands before she could speak. She glared at him furiously. He ignored her. "This is Lieutenant LaCrosse, Ms. Jenkins. Mrs. Marcel and I are on our way." He smiled grimly at Ann as he spoke to Nurse Jenkins. "Together."

The phone on Jacques Moret's desk rang, and he picked it up absently. "Hello?"

"Hello, oh, I did catch you in your office!" the woman on the other end said anxiously. "I tried your home, but Ms. Trainor always did say that you were a tireless worker, coming in very early! This is Sherie, Ms. Trainor's secretary. We're growing a little anxious in the office here. Ms. Trainor was due back to work; yet she didn't come in yesterday morning, and we haven't been able to reach her at her home so far this morning. We're hoping that maybe she stayed on in New Orleans and you might know where she is." Sherie cleared her throat awkwardly. "We're simply concerned, you know."

"Of course."

He stared at the receiver. *Oh, hell. Oh, hell.*

He spoke pleasantly. "I don't think that you need to be too concerned. I can't really help you because we parted company as planned, but she did say that she was very anxious, now that she'd been in New Orleans, to take a few extra days to do the plantation-route tourist thing, you know?"

"Oh! She's so efficient, though, she usually calls in."

"She is the boss, right?"

"Yes, yes, of course."

"Maybe she just got carried away with her vacation. I understand that she plans them for other people all the time, but rarely gives herself much vacation at all."

"That's true. I'm certainly not saying that she shouldn't take all the time that she wants and deserves . . . like I said, we were just concerned."

"I'm sure things will prove to be all right."

"Sure. And I'm sure she'll call in soon. Thank you so much for all your help."

"I'll see if there's anything I can find out."

"Thank you so very much."

"Of course."

The receiver went dead in his hand. He stared at it, horrified.

And very slowly hung it up.

He was sweating bullets.

Ann felt as if she and Mark were a pair of children, playing a game in which one kept trying to walk faster than the other.

It didn't matter. When they reached the hospital, he took the lead—he was simply bigger, and his hold on her arm was quite restraining.

"I'm the relative," Ann grated.

"You're an ex-wife."

"That counts."

"Yeah. Tell that to a man paying alimony to more than one."

As they neared Jon's I.C.U. room, a young, dark-haired doctor appeared, beaming. "Lieutenant! Good to see you."

"You too, Michael. How is the patient."

"He's going to pull through."

"How is he now?" Ann asked anxiously.

"Gaining strength. I think you'll be pleased when you see him. He's bathed, he's had some food orally—are you the ex-wife?"

"Yes," Ann said, glaring at Mark.

"No one has talked to him yet, Lieutenant. If you want time alone . . ."

"Isn't the family supposed to get time alone first?" Ann demanded.

"You are the *ex*-wife, right?"

"I'm the one who got him here!"

Mark's hand clamped down on her arm again. "We'll see him together."

"Fifteen minutes. Tomorrow, he'll be stronger."

"Thanks," Mark said.

They started down the remaining short distance of corridor together.

"So you know Doctor Michael, eh?" Ann grated.

"He was an intern when my wife was sick. And he's friends with my younger son. Who is in medical school now."

"He would be," Ann muttered.

At Jon's door, she took the lead. She hurried in, then paused at the foot of the bed, scarcely believing what she saw.

He was sitting up. His eyes were open. Big and blue. He still looked thin, weak. But so good. He saw her, and smiled.

He saw Mark behind her, and frowned.

"Jon!"

She raced to him, ignoring Mark to reach the bed, to start to throw her arms around him, to awkwardly pause as she reminded herself how weak he still must be.

"A hug from you, I can take!" he whispered to her, holding her tightly. She drew away from him, studying his face as he studied her.

"Oh, God, Jon, you made it!"

"Katie?" he asked anxiously.

"She doesn't know anything yet. I had the school tell her to get a hold of me, but I didn't want to worry her and say it was an emergency. You—you were in a coma."

"You handled it just right. When she does

reach you now, I'll be able to talk." He stared past her to Mark. "From my jail cell, I imagine. Hello, Lieutenant."

Ann jerked her gaze from one man to the other. "You know each other?"

"We've seen each other," Jon said.

Mark stared at Ann. "At the club."

"Am I being arrested?" Jon asked.

"I don't know yet. Do you remember what happened?"

"Jon, do you know the seriousness—" Ann asked.

"Gina is dead, yes. But I didn't do it."

"You told me that, Jon," Ann said. "The night that it happened. I know that you didn't do it. But we're all praying that you can help give the police some lead on what really did happen. You must have seen something."

He shook his head, wincing.

"Are you in pain, are you all right?" Ann asked anxiously.

"Marcel, if you know something—" Mark began.

"Shadows."

"What?" Mark said sharply. His eyes, the gray tinged silver sharp, riveted on Ann, then returned to Jon. "Shadows?"

"I don't know exactly what I saw. There was something, yes. When I was coming to, I must have been dreaming. I saw that night over and over, replaying it in my head. There was something . . . I might have seen the shadow's face, a hint of the face, something . . . for just a split second. Then I lost it. And all I saw was shadows."

"You don't know who attacked you?" Ann said with alarm.

He shook his head, and looked at Mark. "LaCrosse, I know what it looks like. I knew at the time. I was probably dying, but it seemed that I had to get to Ann's because I knew that she would believe that I was innocent. I was supposed to meet Gina just down the street from Ann's at the Swiss bakery, by the long alley."

"Where Gina was found," Mark said.

"Yes. When I got there, I heard her screaming. I charged into the alley. Someone, a shadow, someone dressed in black, was on top of her. I tried to wrench the figure away. It turned on me. I was reaching for Gina . . . I knew . . ." He shook his head and started over. "I reached for Gina, trying to get her behind me. She fell into my arms. I knew she was dead. I threw up my arms to try to ward off more blows, but the knife was coming into me. I saw . . ."

"Saw what?" Ann pleaded.

"Something I lost. A fleeting, split second of—something. Someone." He stared at Mark. "So—am I going to be charged?"

"The D.A.'s office has a fair amount of evidence against you. You were wearing her blood."

"You can bring me in on suspicion, then have the D.A.'s office come up with their charges."

"I can only hold you so long—though I say

again, the D.A.'s office has a strong evidence file."

"Are you arresting me now?" Jon asked.

Mark let out an impatient tcking sound. "You just came out of a coma; there's a police guard on you. No, I'm not charging you right now."

"I didn't do it," Jon said. He glanced at Ann. "I—I loved her. I was bringing her to meet you that night. I wanted to marry her, but I didn't want to take you or Katie by surprise; so I thought that I'd bring her to meet you, and we'd all go together to the gallery opening of my *Red Light Ladies*. Ann, my God, you and I had our ups and downs; did you ever know me to be violent?"

"No," Ann assured him, holding his hand, glaring at Mark.

"I loved her," Jon repeated. He looked lost. As if it might not really matter if he was charged with her murder or not—one way or the other, she was dead. And nothing was going to bring her back.

Mark took a seat at the foot of his bed. "There's been another murder as well."

Jon's eyes widened. "Not—one of the other girls?"

Mark shook his head. "We don't know the woman's name yet. She was strangled to death with a stocking."

Jon looked puzzled, not understanding the connection.

"She was *in* the club the night she was killed.

Lots of people saw her. They just don't know who they saw her with."

"So another woman is dead," Jon said bitterly. "But it helps my case."

"Yes. It's unfortunate that another death is what it takes," Mark said.

"But . . if someone out there is killing women from the club, wouldn't they kill in the same way?"

"Serial killers tend to use the same method, yes. I don't think that these will fall into the category of serial killings."

Jon suddenly smiled. "You actually do doubt that I'm your man, don't you?"

"You have a lot of friends, apparently," Mark said. "They've all insisted that you couldn't have done it."

"So you think I'm innocent—"

"No, I don't think you're innocent." He glanced hard at Ann. "My mind is simply open to the possibility."

Jon kept staring at Mark strangely. "You know, LaCrosse, Gina always said that you were a straight shooter. I'm telling you the truth. I didn't kill her. Someone else did."

Ann was startled when she heard a throat being cleared behind her. The doctor had returned.

"He needs to regain his strength," he reminded them. "Time's up."

"I'm going to want to send someone in for a deposition from him tomorrow," Mark said.

"That will be fine. We'll have him out of the I.C.U. by tomorrow."

"Can I just sit here with him, if I promise not to talk?" Ann asked. She was loath to leave Jon right now. She was afraid that if she walked away, he might fall back into a coma again. She needed to be with him for a while to assure herself that he was really on the mend.

Mark glared at her.

"It's really not advisable," the doctor said.

"Ann is my closest relative," Jon said. "I'd like her here. That is—if the police have no objection."

"I thought she was your *ex*-wife," handsome young Doctor Michael said. "I don't think she's technically related to you at all anymore."

"I'm the closest thing to family he's got left," Ann said. "Well, here, anyway. Our daughter is out of the country. I am his family."

"Lieutenant?" Jon asked Mark.

Mark suddenly glared at Ann. "You stay here with him."

"Yes," she murmured vaguely.

"I mean it. You stay here."

"Jon has just come out of a coma. I'll be here," Ann promised quietly. She couldn't quite manage to bring her eyes up to meet his.

"There will be an officer on the door," Mark told her.

"There's been an officer on the door since the night Jon came in," Ann said steadily.

"Is that house arrest—or protective custody?" Jon asked.

"Consider it both," Mark said.

He turned around and left. The doctor followed him out. Ann looked back to Jon to discover that he was staring at her pointedly. "What the hell was that all about? What's going on?"

"Nothing, really."

"He wasn't worried about me trying to walk out of here. He was worried about you."

"I think he was worried about both of us. Jon, you and I both know that you're innocent. That means that there is a killer out there who would love to see you dead before you did get to prove your innocence."

"He was worried about *you.*"

Shadows, Ann thought.

She didn't want to tell him that a *shadow* had nearly crawled into her apartment via the balcony. That she had been saved from the shadow because Mark LaCrosse had been sleeping on her couch.

Sleeping on the couch, because she'd been so disconcerted to discover that he'd slept with Gina that she'd been damned determined to keep him out of her bed.

"Ann?" he sounded both worn and worried.

"Jon, I promised I wouldn't talk if they let me stay in here. It's funny, they told me to keep talking to you all the other times I was in here; now they want me to behave. Because you have to rest. And you do have to rest. You've got to get well, and you've got to get out of here."

"She's dead, Ann," he said quietly. She heard the despair in his voice.

"Jon, you've got a daughter; don't you dare give up on life on me. You've got your daughter, your art, and me."

"Life's amazing, isn't it? That blasted show was so important to me . . . and now it doesn't matter at all. Did you ever see it?"

She shook her head. She smiled. "I've been here a lot. And . . ."

"And?"

"Well, otherwise occupied. We'll talk about it later. Jon, you've got to rest. You need your strength. If not for me, for Katie. If not for either of us, for Gina. Don't let her killer walk free."

"No," he agreed. His eyes closed. She thought he was sleeping, but his hand suddenly squeezed hers.

"Annie . . . I'll prove it somehow. I'll find who did kill her, I swear it."

"I know, Jon, I know," Ann said.

He slept at last. She kept holding his hand. She thought about the things he had said, over and over.

Shadows . . .

But he had seen a face, or part of a face, and lost it.

She didn't think that Jon would have to wander very far to find the killer.

The killer was locked within his mind.

The important thing was for Jon to realize that he already knew what he wanted to learn.

Then . . .

Then they all had to hope that the truth was

discovered before the killer realized that Jon had seen . . .

A face.

The face of death.

"You'll be with me," Jon murmured suddenly.

Umm, she thought.

If he only knew just how far she'd been with him already!

But he wasn't strong enough for the truth yet. Soon enough, he'd know everything that was going on.

Seventeen

Mark gave the uniformed officer watching Jon's door strict instructions that he was to be informed if Ann Marcel so much as stepped outside the hospital door; then he started out himself. He wanted to get a hold of Jimmy, then get by to talk to the chief, Charlie Harris, who kept threatening to retire and force Mark to take his job. He wanted to discuss his growing convictions with both Jimmy and Charlie; then he wanted to take a trip by the D.A.'s office. Oddly enough, he was going to change his recommendation.

Now that Jon Marcel was conscious, Mark, as a policeman, could arrest him and hold him twenty-four hours on suspicion of murder while the D.A.'s office finished preparing the charges—which wouldn't take long.

But Mark didn't think that Jon Marcel should be arrested for the murder—though he did think that Marcel should be followed every step that he took once he left the hospital.

Before Mark could leave the hospital, he was hailed by another officer in uniform.

"Lieutenant. Lieutenant!"

It was Billings, Mark saw. The earnest rookie came puffing up to him.

"Did something happen with Marcel?" he asked anxiously.

Billings shook his head. "It's Gregory Hanson, sir."

"Gregory, my God—"

"No, no, nothing bad, sir. His condition has improved. He heard you were here and wants to see you."

Mark smiled with relief. "Thank God. Gregory is alive and ticking! Thanks, Billings!"

He knew Gregory's room number; he'd called in for the trumpet player's condition often enough. He strode there quickly, then paused briefly in the doorway, studying the man.

His head was bandaged as if he were a damned mummy. His color was still more gray than black. A nurse was at his side, checking his blood pressure.

But he was propped up on a pillow, and he was watching Mark with sharp, clear eyes.

"Hey, my friend!" Mark said, stepping into the room. "You're looking fine! You gave us one hell of a scare the other morning."

"I thought I was done for," Gregory agreed. He glanced at the nurse, and Mark realized that he was waiting for her to leave before saying what he really wanted to say.

"Hell of a storm," Mark said.

"And you wound up out in it."

"I came after Ann," he said honestly.

Gregory arched a brow.

"Well, you know. She's—trouble."

Gregory grinned. "Mama Lili Mae liked her right off."

Mark lowered his eyes and nodded. "Yeah, well, she's one good judge of character. But you, sir—what were you thinking, taking her out into the swamp?"

He shrugged. "She's the inquisitive type. It seemed safer for her to be inquisitive with me. Of course, great help I turned out to be!"

"Hey—none of us can combat an act of God."

"Keep my patient calm and in bed," the nurse said, rolling her blood-pressure machine away from the bed.

"I'll do that," Mark promised.

The nurse left, closing the door behind her.

"Act of God, my ass!" Gregory swore the second they were alone.

"What?"

Gregory shook his head. "I don't know what's going on anymore. Cindy and I are sitting together, and she gets restless, and can't sit still anymore. You know Cindy. She ups and wanders off on me. She couldn't have been too far from me. I heard her scream, I thought she was in trouble, I hurried off after her. I started to look around; the storm was beginning to whip into real action—and then someone came and hit me on the head."

"Who?"

"Damned if I know!" Gregory swore. "But it was someone."

"You're sure. You were under a whole damned tree when we found you."

"I'm sure, I'm sure, I'm sure. Mark, you've known me a long time, and you know I'm not any idiot. Someone came up quick behind me, and pelted me good and hard on the damned head. I went out like a baby long before that blasted tree came down."

Mark sighed. "Shit."

"Yeah, I know."

"And you didn't see anything."

Gregory miserably shook his bandaged head. "Fleeting movement. A damned shadow. Nothing more."

A damned shadow.

Now he was chasing a shadow.

A shadow who had killed twice, and attempted to murder Gregory. It was beginning to feel like a game of *Clue*: Gina in the alley with a knife, Jane Doe by the water with a nylon, Gregory in the bayou with a slam against the head.

A shadow . . .

The same damned shadow that had nearly been in Ann Marcel's house.

"What the hell is going on here?" he said aloud.

"I haven't said a word to anyone else. When I came to here in the hospital, I knew right off that everyone thought I'd been downed by the tree. I just kept the truth to myself. I figured I'd keep it. 'Til I got my chance to see you. But, hey, I heard that Marcel came out of his coma. Amazing. Great. But did he see anything."

"Yeah."

"What?"

"A frigging shadow," Mark told him. "A damned, frigging shadow!"

Ann spent most of the day in the hospital, just sitting by Jon's side. The nurses were wonderfully kind, bringing her coffee and magazines so that she could keep herself occupied while Jon dozed on and off, regaining his strength. He was still connected to an I.V. which kept him hydrated and supplied glucose and minerals, but at noon, he ate solid food again, soup and crackers and Jell-O.

After he ate, Jon fell back asleep again, and Ann decided to go out for a sandwich herself and perhaps to a local store for a sketch pad.

When she started out of the room, she was stopped by the quiet young officer on duty.

"Mrs. Marcel!"

"Yes?"

"Where are you going?"

Ann arched a brow. "To get some lunch."

"In the hospital?"

She frowned. "Maybe, maybe not. Why?"

"Well, I'm . . ."

"I'm not under arrest—or suspicion—am I?"

"No, no, of course not."

"Then, sir, please don't worry about me, or where I'm going," she told him, smiling to make her words as pleasant as possible.

Mark.

He wasn't going to get into telling her where she could and couldn't go.

She hurried down the corridor, reminding herself that Mark was trying to keep her alive and well. The only problem was that Mark didn't share her positive conviction that Jon was innocent.

She ate in the hospital cafeteria, and found a small writing pad in the gift shop, which she determined would do for the afternoon.

She was a little bit spooked—and she had said that she wasn't going to leave Jon. She went on back up to Jon's room and was startled when she saw that Mark's partner, Jimmy Deveaux, was standing quietly at the back of the room, just watching Jon as he slept. She felt a wave of acute uneasiness sweep over her at sight of the man.

"Officer Deveaux," she said quietly. "What are you doing here? The police aren't supposed to be questioning Jon any more today. Mark was already in here—"

"I know."

"Jon's supposed to give a deposition tomorrow."

"I know." Jimmy Deveaux offered her one of his sad, blood-hound smiles. "I just came to check that everything was going all right. You need anything, you doing okay?"

"I'm—fine," she said.

He nodded. "Well, you know, you're really not fine."

"I beg your pardon?"

"There was some excitement at your house in the middle of the night."

"Someone—came up on the balcony."

"Yeah. Thank God Mark was there to stop whoever it was."

"Yes, of course."

"You need to stay away from the club, Mrs. Marcel. You're going to wind up putting yourself into more and more dangerous positions."

"So . . . ," she murmured. "You agree with me, then, that Jon is innocent?"

"Not on your life," he admitted.

"Then I'm not in any danger. And I thank you for your concern; but the doctor has said that Jon is not to be questioned any more today, and I will appreciate it if you will leave him alone."

"Sure. I just came by to help if I could. In lieu of Mark." His smile was strange, Ann thought. Again, she felt uneasy.

"I'm fine."

"I'll be seeing you, Mrs. Marcel," he said.

And left her.

Ann sat back down by Jon's bedside, staring after Jimmy Deveaux. She looked down at Jon. He appeared to be sleeping peacefully.

She leaned her ear against his chest to make sure that he was breathing, and that his heart was beating.

He was definitely still alive. Deveaux hadn't come in here to smother him in his sleep or anything.

So why had he come?

* * *

Mark sat with Chief Charlie Harris at a small table at one of the unique little cafes right off Bourbon Street. They'd ordered the crawfish and linguini, and though the mild tomato sauce that tenderly enwrapped the little shellfish was far different from his own hot sauce—which he had so recently enjoyed—the meal kept reminding him of the cabin. Of Ann. Of Ann in the cabin. Naked.

He set his fork down. She had told him that a man just needed the proximity of a woman to become aroused while a woman needed emotion. She was wrong.

He didn't need the proximity. Just the memory.

He didn't need to be thinking about Ann now. He heard himself grinding down on his teeth. Marcel was conscious. Clinging to her. And she was with him. His best friend. His buddy. His next of kin.

Marcel who had been in love with Gina. But Gina was dead now. So Marcel had only his ex-wife to cling to. His ex-wife—who was willing to risk her own life to save his ass.

"The evidence, as I see it, still weighs against Marcel," Charlie Harris was saying. Charlie should have been the governor. He was large, with snow-white hair, a ruddy face, fine blue eyes, and a quick smile. He was a reassuring individual—which was a bit deceptive, since Charlie could be hard as nails.

"Well, if we consider the fact that the man was covered in the victim's blood, yes," Mark said.

"That does seem to be an important fact," Charlie agreed dryly. He sat back, sipping a cup of piping hot coffee. "But you're telling me you don't want to bring him in once he's released?"

"Another murder took place while he was in the hospital."

"Different type of murder."

"It's associated somehow—I know it."

Charlie shrugged, wagging a finger at Mark. "The D.A.'s office has the evidence against Marcel. If they decide to press charges now, the police officers of the Parish of New Orleans are not going to stand in the way. However . . . did we I.D. our Jane Doe yet?"

"No, but Lee Minh is convinced that something will come in during the next twenty-four hours. The computers are scanning missing persons reports right now. The problem is, you know, if a visitor was killed, friends and family may not know for days that the person is missing."

"I'm aware of that. I'm still not sure that these killings can be connected just because one girl worked at the club and another was seen at the club."

"It's all we've got to go on."

"Mark, I wish it wasn't so, but we do get our fair share of murders here in the Big Easy."

"I know that."

"What does Jimmy say?"

"Don't know. Haven't had a chance to talk with him yet today. He was taking Jane Doe's picture around to a few places himself."

Harris hesitated, drumming his fingers on the table. "You're a good detective, Mark."

"Thanks. I hope so. I've worked hard at it."

"You know how to study and weigh evidence. You know how to make sure that it's all collected properly—we've never had a case thrown out of court because you failed to follow the proper procedure."

"What good is catching them if you can't convict them?" Mark asked.

"Good point, but your procedure isn't what makes you a good detective."

"No? What is?"

"Those gut reactions of yours. They aren't whims—they come from years on the streets, from knowing people. From seeing through them. I'm leaving this one up to you."

Mark exhaled. Life was damned strange. He could bring in Jon Marcel far easier than he could many a perp he had managed to hold—and then have charged.

Not long ago, he would have sworn on his own life that there was no way in hell Jon Marcel could be innocent. He still wasn't convinced of it.

But he was convinced that the only way the truth was going to come out regarding Gina's death was to let Marcel out—and make sure that everyone else who had been involved with her had to do a little sweating as well.

"The call is yours," Charlie Harris repeated firmly. "You know, I could retire if you'd just take my job."

Mark smiled. "I'm not ready to leave the streets yet. I like to think that I can still make some differences out here. But then again . . ."

"Yeah?"

"I don't know. I've also become . . ."

"Become what?"

"Well, fonder of living lately. Don't go planning any exotic excursions down the Nile or anything yet."

"Make up your mind before I get too much older, huh?"

Mark grinned and nodded. "I'll try to do that." He quickly grew serious. "Once Marcel is out on the streets, I want him followed."

"You've got yourself and Jimmy."

"I need more than that. I'm telling you, someone was trying to break into the ex-wife's home—"

"But you were there."

Mark sat back, hesitating. Charlie Harris was regarding him bluntly.

"I can't be everywhere."

Harris arched a brow. "I'm not going to ask you what you're doing, Mark. You're a grown, intelligent man. Just don't let your lines get crossed. Murders have taken place. No one is innocent until the truth is known."

"I know that."

"Don't start thinking with your dick."

"You know me better than that."

Harris studied him steadily for several seconds. "I'll give you Latham and Hinkey, late shift. I can't spare you any more than that. Like I said—we've got our share of crime here."

"Latham and Hinkey. That'll do, then. Thanks."

There were no phones in the intensive care units, but there was a plug-in kept at the nurses stand that could be brought around. At around six, a pretty, little dark-haired nurse brought the phone into Jon's room, telling Ann she had a call.

It was Mark.

"How's he doing?"

"Good. He's slept most of the day."

"I'll come get you for dinner."

Ann hesitated, staring at the phone, biting into her lower lip. Just the damned sound of his voice made her want to forget anything evil she might have heard about him. A rush of fire swept instantly into her limbs.

Breathing became immediately more difficult.

"I should stay here—"

"There's a cop on the door to watch him."

"Umm. Cops are everywhere."

"What do you mean by that?"

"Your partner was in here this afternoon."

"Jimmy?"

"You've got another partner?"

"No. I just hadn't known that he'd been by."

"I don't think I should leave."

"Ann, Jimmy wasn't at the hospital to do any harm to your wonderful ex."

"How can you be so sure?"

Mark sighed. "We're the cops. The good guys."

"There have been dirty cops."

"That doesn't make criminals out of entire police forces."

"It doesn't help that some cops are liars."

"I never lied to you."

"You never mentioned to me that you'd slept with her."

She heard his sigh of impatience at the other end.

"Nor did it occur to you to tell me that you are *related* to Jacques Moret. And Mama Lili Mae."

"Since I didn't know you were planning on making the acquaintance of Mama Lili Mae, it wouldn't have occurred to me to tell you that she was my distant relative!"

Was he telling the truth?

"There's Jacques—"

"Jacques is a slime bucket. Did anyone ever tell you that you can't pick your distant kin?"

The bit about Jacques really didn't bother her so much—it was the sleeping with Gina, she had to admit. Good God, was she jealous of a poor dead woman? *Jon had been in love with Gina; she had been beautiful. Mark had been involved with her as well. . . .*

"I'm coming to get you," he said.

"Don't—" Ann began.

Too late; he had already hung up. She stared at the receiver. Fine. Dinner. But she was still going to *think* about what their relationship was going to be.

Think about it long and hard. Discuss it, make him understand her feelings and position in all this!

Ann started to hang up, preparing to pull the plug out of the phone and return it to the nurse's station. She hesitated, and dialed the club, asking if she could speak with Cindy.

Cindy wasn't in. But when the girl who answered the phone would have hung up, someone else took hold of the receiver.

"Ann? Is it you? How's Jon? I hear he's out of his coma and doing well."

"Jon is doing remarkably well."

"I'm so glad. Everyone will be."

"I hope. Well . . . I was just calling . . . to see if everything was all right there."

"Fine. All is status quo at the club, but did you hear? Gregory is awake and aware."

"No! I'm so glad. I'll have to sneak in quickly and see him while I'm here."

"Things are starting to look a little bit better, don't you think? Except, of course, I guess they might arrest Jon any time now."

"Maybe. I don't know."

"For your benefit, and Jon's, I hope they don't. But it makes things scarier, doesn't it?"

"How so?"

"If Jon is on the loose, he might well be in danger himself. Just like the rest of us."

"Maybe."

April hesitated. "I don't know if I should tell you or not, but . . ."

"Oh, God, great, April! Don't do that! Either tell me something, or don't, but don't tease like that!"

"I can't talk on the phone anyway. Get by here tomorrow, and I'll talk to you then."

The phone went dead. Ann stared at it and swore. She glanced over at Jon.

Still peacefully sleeping.

She stepped out of his room. The officer on the door was new. She smiled at the man. "I'm going to go and see another friend who's in the hospital. LaCrosse is on his way here, so just tell him that."

She didn't wait for a reply. She took a few seconds to return the phone and tell the nurses she was leaving, and ask for Gregory's room number. They gave it to her, and she hurried down the corridor.

Cindy was sitting at the foot of Gregory's bed. She offered Ann a huge smile, leapt up, and gave her a hug. Ann accepted the hug, looking past her to Gregory.

"You're starting to look pretty good!" she told him, escaping Cindy to walk to his side.

"For a mummy," Gregory said with a wince.

Ann kissed his cheek. "It's just wonderful to see you alive," she told him. "That storm was so awful!"

He nodded, watching her gravely. "Yeah, the storm was bad." He shook his head. "Something about life is just bad right now. I was just telling Cindy and I'm telling you the same—watch it!"

"I promise."

"Jon doesn't know anything at all?" Cindy asked anxiously. "I wanted to see him, too, but they wouldn't let me come in. Not to the I.C.U."

"Jon didn't see anything," Ann said.

Gregory shook his head in frustration, then winced. "Ladies, I am telling you both, please be very, very careful!"

"We will be," Cindy promised.

"Everyone keeps warning me away from the club," Ann murmured.

"I can't afford to stay away from the club," Cindy said. "But nothing can actually happen in the club—it's coming to and leaving the club that can apparently be dangerous."

"You've a point there," Ann said. She hesitated, not wanting to worry Gregory more. She drew her hand down his cheek. "I'm so grateful that you're okay! I'm not going to stay in here; you, like Jon, need your rest." She kissed his cheek carefully, to avoid his bandaged head. "Cindy?"

"Oh—sure. You need your rest. I need to go to work."

Cindy rose and followed Ann out of the room. "Cindy, April was about to tell me something on the phone; then she told me to come to the club. Do you know anything about what she wants to tell me?"

"Not off hand. I'm really sorry."

"Well, I guess you're right about the club. There are usually at least a dozen people in it— it can't be dangerous to be there; it's the coming and going that's dangerous. Tell April that . . ."

"Yeah?"

"Tell her that I will see her tomorrow."

Cindy nodded. She cleared her throat in warning then, her eyes indicating that Ann should be careful of the person now coming up behind her.

She spun around to see Mark.

Cindy smiled at him. "Hey, there. Isn't it wonderful? Gregory is doing great . . . and Jon Marcel is out of his coma!"

"It's looking good," Mark answered pleasantly. "You were visiting with Gregory?"

Cindy nodded. "Ann thinks he needs more rest now."

"He probably does."

"And I need to get to work."

"Let me take a quick peek in on Gregory myself now, and I'll give you a ride."

"Great," Cindy said, relieved.

Mark stepped past them and into Gregory's room. "I know he's the one who has a fit about you being at the club!" Cindy whispered. "Are you sure you should—"

"Cindy, I'm not under arrest or anything myself. He can't really tell me what I can and can't do."

"Right. I guess. I—"

She broke off. Mark was already out of the room. "Shall we go, ladies?"

He headed out of the hospital. They walked along the antiseptic corridors behind him.

At his car, he opened the doors for them. Ann crawled into the front seat; Cindy into the back. They drove to the club, exchanging views on how Gregory looked, and how Jon was doing. At the club, Mark parked his car right in front of the door.

"Cindy, go on in. I won't leave until you open the door and wave at us, huh?"

"Yeah, thanks, Mark."

"Sure thing. Get in there."

Cindy walked to the door, opened it, looked in, looked back and waved with a jaunty smile. She disappeared into the club.

Mark instantly turned to Ann, wagging a finger at her. "You stay out of there."

She pushed the finger away.

"You quit acting like the gestapo."

"What, are you walking around with a death wish?"

"I didn't say that I was coming here."

"You didn't say that you weren't."

"I said that you had no right to tell me what I could or couldn't do."

"I'm trying to keep you from being stabbed or strangled or—"

"Or what?"

He let out a furious oath, driving into traffic. Ann had no idea where they were going until they pulled into what looked like an old carriage house. He slammed out of the car, came around and jerked open the passenger's seat. While she got out, he opened his trunk and took out some bags. A tantalizing aroma made it's way to Ann. She was famished, she realized.

"What is it?" she asked him.

"Cajun-Chinese."

She started to laugh.

"I swear."

It was Cajun-Chinese, and in a matter of minutes, they had walked from the old carriage-house-turned-garage through a walled and wrought-ironed garden, past a fountain and to a broad porch. They entered a handsomely appointed old house, probably one that was nearly two hundred years old. The living room was lined with bookshelves. Handsome leather sofas faced a fireplace and entertainment center.

It was both a beautiful place, and a comfortable one. As Ann strolled through the living room or parlor to the dining room, she heard Mark in the kitchen. When she joined him there—a large space with an island work area, copper pots hanging from rafters, and a breakfast nook—Mark was pouring iced tea from a pitcher into glasses and setting plates on the table in the breakfast nook.

"This is your home, I take it."

"It is. Sit down."

"Is that an order?"

"It's an invitation."

She sat. He opened cartons. There was chicken in a hot sauce, rice, red beans, lo mein, orange beef, mung beans, and broccoli. A feast—of different flavors. The name of the restaurant from which the food came was on the bag—*Wong Sartes Cajun-Chinese.*

"Wong is a friend," Mark said. "He's a great cook—you'll see for yourself. His dad is bayou country Cajun; his mom is Chinese."

Ann found she had to smile. "Do you know every restauranteur in New Orleans?"

"I know a lot of them."

He seemed to be starving himself. He piled his plate high and ate, watching her as she more carefully tested each dish, then began to eat with a greater fervor herself.

She was here, she decided. She might as well make the best of it. Wong Sartes' intriguing cuisine was definitely better than hospital fare.

"So what are your plans?" he asked her.

"For what?"

"For the evening."

"You mean—I'm allowed to leave? I thought I might be a hostage here—since we did come to your home, and you are prone to tell me where I can and can't go."

"If I told you that you had to stay here, would you do it?"

"I—I really don't think that this is the right time for me to be getting involved in a relationship with you."

"Really? So if I *asked* you to stay, it wouldn't make any difference."

"I just said—"

"What if I was trying to stay with you for your

own good? I didn't tell you, but Gregory wasn't knocked unconscious by a tree in the bayou.''

"This whole thing is still in the air. You could be arresting Jon at any minute now."

He set his fork down, drained his tea. Then he stood, and reached for her, drawing her up to her feet and against him. "So don't get involved with me," he told her.

"You're holding me . . ."

Oh, God, yes, he was holding her. So flush against him that the fabric of her clothing seemed to melt. The full force of his body heat infused her; the extent of his arousal fit against her. His fingers were in her hair, drawing her head back. His lips were just inches from her own.

"Don't get involved. Just have sex," he told her.

"I don't want—"

His mouth. On top of hers. Open, forceful, his tongue inside her deeply, moving, his hands. . . .

She was suddenly off her feet. Moving through the house. It was a blur. She was hiked up around his hips; then she was falling backward into a nest of comfort. His bed. Her limbs seemed to have turned to liquid. She was staring at him, not saying a word. Her dress was shoved up to her waist; she was dimly aware of the sound of his belt being removed.

Then he was swearing, his fingers on the silk panties she wore.

She felt them rip.

She opened her mouth to protest.

But it didn't matter.

She couldn't bear waiting. Something hot and molten rushed throughout her limbs and centered between her thighs. Burning, throbbing.

She gasped as he touched her, rubbing her with thumb and forefinger before suddenly thrusting into her. The feeling was so sweetly erotic that she shrieked out then, grasping his shoulders, digging into them, shaking as she fought to catch each fevered pitch of his body as he plunged within her again and again, tempo increasing wildly. Her hunger was as deep as his, the fire that filled her as violent, as passionate. She arched against him, unable to do anything at all but cling to him, feeling nothing except that one spot where he filled her and filled her, where she throbbed so sweetly for release.

She climaxed, crying out with the volatility of the sensation that claimed her, trembling with the force of it, only aware then that they were basically still dressed, that he had seized her up and basically seduced her in less than a handful of seconds.

So much for *thinking about* what their relationship was going to be.

And discussing it—and her position.

Her position was . . .

Vulnerable.

Oh, God. So vulnerable.

He had just made the earth shake. She was still drifting downward from her high. It didn't deter him. His lips were on her. His hands. His lips. His kiss. On flesh that was so attuned to every breath . . . damp. Open. . . .

He rose above her, whispering against her lips.

"Don't leave. You don't have to want a relationship. Just sex. Damned good sex."

"Damn you!" she whispered.

"Don't leave."

She refused to answer the demand.

But neither did she manage to rise.

Or depart his house that night.

Eighteen

Ann awoke very slowly.

Oddly enough, when she had finally slept, she had slept like a log, completely comfortable, secure, at ease.

He was beside her. She had been certain that no ill could come to her.

She slept so deeply that awakening was hard. Yet she sensed that she should awaken. She opened her eyes.

And nearly screamed aloud.

Someone was watching her.

Someone small.

Oh, God.

She drew the sheets around herself, trying to reconcile herself to the little creature staring at her. A little girl, a very little girl, perhaps four years old, holding a teddy bear, and studying her intently. "You definitely need the *Eye Opener*," she said gravely.

Ann swallowed, pulling the sheets more tightly about herself and trying to sit up with some kind of dignity.

"Brit!"

Mark suddenly charged back into the room,

shirtless, barefoot, but decently clad in a pair of jeans. He came to a halt five feet from the bed, staring from the child to Ann. He ran his fingers distractedly through his hair, obviously and acutely disturbed by the situation.

"Brit!" he repeated, dismayed.

The little girl's face crumpled. She was aware that she had done something very wrong bursting into the room; she just wasn't sure what.

"Hi, Brit," Ann said, trying to give Mark a menacing stare.

"Honey," Mark said evenly, "can you come out of my room and let Mrs. Marcel wake up on her own."

Brit nodded gravely but returned her stare to Ann. She hesitantly smiled, then said to Mark, "Who is she?"

"A very nice lady who needed to stay here because she might have been in danger at her own home."

"Oh," Brit said, as if his words made entire sense. "Hi," she said back now, less hesitant.

Ann smiled.

"Grandpa keeps the *Eye Opener* in the shower, you know. You'll be okay."

"Thank you," Ann said gravely. "I can certainly use—the *Eye Opener.*"

"Coast—soap," Mark informed her quickly, setting his hands on Brit's shoulders to lead her out of the room. The door closed behind the two of them.

Ann showered—with Coast.

The child was adorable. Mark didn't look at

all what she had imagined a "Grandpa" to look like; yet he seemed to enjoy the role, and Brit obviously adored him.

Ann grated her teeth in the shower. Being a grandparent—with a grandchild quite at home in his house—seemed to make him more likeable.

She didn't want to like Mark this morning.

She had wanted him too badly last night.

She had no choice but to slip back into her clothing of the previous day—minus panties—before daring to stick her nose out of the bedroom. She could see through the parlor to the kitchen. Mark's back and dark head were to her; facing her, she could see a striking young dark-haired, light-eyed man in a knit shirt and jeans sitting across from Mark, and little Brit was up on her knees next to the man who must have been Mark's son. He resembled his father a great deal.

Brit was happily munching on a glazed donut and telling her father and Mark, "The poor lady! I hope she knows that she's safe with you, Grandpa, except . . ."

"Except what, Munchkin?" Mark demanded, tousling her hair.

"Except, we should do something nice for her. We should go out and buy her a nightgown so that she doesn't have to sleep like that without any clothes on."

In the whole of her life, Ann had never felt her entire body flush to such a vibrant shade of red. Right at that moment, naturally, Mark's son looked up, and saw her staring—crimson and frozen—into the kitchen. He stood instantly, drawing Mark to his feet as well.

"Ann," Mark said. He looked extremely awkward and uncomfortable; then he grinned and threw up his hands. "Ann, please, come in here. I'd like you to meet my son, Michael, and my granddaughter, Brit—you've already met."

"I'm sorry I was so rude," Brit said. She'd been coached; but she was a sweet little girl, and she was trying hard to say her words just right. "I didn't know that anybody was sleeping in Grandpa's room."

"It's okay," Ann said.

"I woke you up."

"I needed to wake up anyway."

"Coffee?" Mark asked.

"Sure." She slid into the seat he had vacated, and smiled at Brit. "Although I did use the *Eye Opener,* and it worked tremendously well."

Brit smiled happily. "Oh, I knew it would help!"

"How do you do," Michael LaCrosse said politely. He had a killer smile, a lot like his father's. "I'm in advertising, and I'm afraid Brit takes it all rather seriously. It's a pleasure to meet you. I understand you're embroiled in one of the hottest murder cases to hit New Orleans in quite some time."

His honesty was disarming; it seemed that he, too, had decided that there was no way out of an awkward situation except to plunge right into it.

"So it seems," Ann said. "It's nice to meet you, too. And your daughter is adorable. And Coast is certainly a fine, eye-opening soap."

"You know," Michael said bluntly, "you're really gorgeous. Even prettier than you appeared in that picture in the paper."

"Thank you," Ann told him.

Mark groaned, handing Ann a cup of coffee. "Just swell her head all to pieces there, son, make her more difficult than ever to manage."

"Manage?" A wicked grin teased Michael's face, and he smiled at Ann. "You're managing Mrs. Marcel, Dad?"

"Let me rephrase that," Mark said. "I'm trying very hard to keep Mrs. Marcel alive, and out of danger."

"Ah . . . ," Michael said.

"And by the way, son," Mark added, "don't you have a busy day ahead of you?"

"Pretty much so," Michael agreed pleasantly. "Mrs. Marcel, I've been following this closely—through the papers, that is. But you really believe that your ex-husband is innocent, despite all the damning evidence."

"I know that he's innocent," Ann said.

"Michael—" Mark began.

"Then, you know," Michael said, sitting back comfortably, "my dad is right. You think that Jon Marcel is innocent. So someone else is guilty. To the guilty person, you are a danger because you're supporting Marcel. You need to be very careful. You most definitely are in a *very* dangerous position."

"Michael, would you like more coffee?" Mark asked.

Ann grinned, staring down into her coffee. She met Michael's sparkling eyes and thought that she liked him very much.

And she felt an even greater warmth where Mark was concerned, and a tremendous sympathy for him. Theirs must have been a very warm family; he and his wife had raised a charming and intelligent son. Something special remained in the relationship between father and son now, and he spoke very well for them both.

"I do know that I need to be very careful," Ann assured him.

"Good," Michael said. "Yeah, Dad, a little more coffee, then Brit and I have to get going. We've got to pick up Mommy at the dentist's, and head for camp."

"Swimming camp," Brit said happily.

"That's wonderful," Ann assured her.

"Do you like to swim?"

"I love to."

"Maybe we'd better get her a bathing suit, too," Brit said worriedly.

Ann felt color rush to her face again. "I—I have a bathing suit, Brit, but thank you very much, anyway." She swallowed down her coffee and stood. "Actually, I've got to get going myself."

"Give me a minute," Mark said.

"I can call a cab—"

"Give me a minute," he insisted firmly.

"All right," she agreed. Michael and Brit

stood. Mark left the kitchen for the bedroom to finish dressing. "He is trying to keep you alive," Michael said.

"I think he still believes that Jon is guilty," Ann told him.

"Well, he must have some faith in your judgment because he is very worried where you're concerned. It's hard to be a cop and go against the evidence, you know. He's trying. They're not going to charge Marcel yet, you know."

Ann arched a brow. "It's a definite decision?"

Michael nodded. "For now." He hesitated. "You've got to be really careful if you're right. And you've got to convince Jon Marcel of the same."

"I will. Thank you very much."

He smiled, then raised his voice. "Dad, bye— Brit and I are out of here!"

But as Michael called out, Mark appeared, a short-sleeved, cotton tailored shirt tucked into his jeans, sneakers on his feet. "I get a hug from my girl first," he said, sweeping Brit into his arms. The little girl giggled delightedly, hugging her grandfather fiercely in return. He set her down. "Give your mom a hug for me, too. Tell her that we're on for dinner next week."

"I will, Grandpa." She hesitated just a second, then slipped her arms around Ann, hugging her. Ann instinctively hugged her back, crouching down to the balls of her feet to be on Brit's level.

"It was lovely to meet you, Miss Brit La-Crosse."

"And we will go swimming?"

"Sure."

"When?"

"When?" Ann repeated. Brit's eyes were huge and very blue and worried as they gazed into hers. Ann had forgotten how persistent and exacting young children could be.

"Brit—" her dad began.

"No, no, it's all right," Ann said quickly. "Brit, I'm not quite sure yet. But soon, I hope."

"You won't forget?"

"I won't forget. I promise. It's a date. A real date, honest to God."

Brit seemed quite happy with that. Ann rose. They all walked out together, Mark locking up the house as they went. Michael and Brit took off in a sturdy silver Volvo; Mark ushered Ann into his car and turned the key in the ignition. "Where to?" he asked her.

"I've really got to get home," she told him.

He drove to her house. She was surprised when he stopped the car, but kept the motor humming.

"You're not coming up?"

He shook his head. "I've got a court reporter meeting me at the hospital to get a deposition from Jon. I'll wait here until you've gotten in. Come out on the balcony and wave down to me that you're all right, that the closets are empty of thugs. Then lock up the balcony and don't let anyone in unless you know who it is for sure, and that it's someone you trust completely."

"Don't let anyone in but you?" she teased.

He nodded, somewhat amused. "Exactly," he informed her.

"I'll probably be coming to the hospital this afternoon," she said. "And I'm going to have to get by the car place to pick up a new key."

"Take taxis for now—I'll send someone out to my place to collect your things from the cabin today. You'll have your key back then. By the way, how did you get into your house when we came back from the bayou?"

"Key under the mat," she admitted.

He groaned. "Make sure you keep your bolts locked when you're in the house, huh?"

"I will."

"I'll put new locks in for you as soon as possible."

"But no one bothered with the key—"

"How do you know that? How do you know that your key was exactly as you had left it under the mat?"

"How do you know that anyone would have looked under my mat? What would make anyone want to break into my apartment? Nothing was touched, nothing was stolen."

"How can you be sure? Someone did try to break in the night before last."

Ann sighed with exasperation.

"Maybe no one looked because it is so incredibly stupid and ridiculously obvious to leave a key under the mat."

"Incredibly stupid?"

"Well?"

Ann started to slam her way out of the car. He reached over and caught her arm.

"Well? Isn't it?"

"You really do have a way with words, La-Crosse," she told him.

"Check the closets and everywhere else, Ann. I mean it."

"All right!"

Ann went on up. She dutifully checked all the rooms and closets, then came out on the balcony and waved to him. He waved back, and swerved his car out onto the road.

Ann started to step back into the house, then noted a man leaning against one of the columns of the cafe across the street, reading a newspaper. He had a baseball hat pulled low over his forehead.

But she recognized him. Mark's partner. Jimmy Deveaux. Had Mark asked him to watch her place? Why hadn't he told her? Or was Deveaux there all on his own—for his own reasons.

Ann shivered, stepped back inside, and locked the balcony doors. She hurried to the phone and put a call into the I.C.U. at the hospital, planning to have one of the nurses bring the phone to Jon in his room.

She found out he'd been transferred late during the night into a regular room. She finally got put through to the right room.

"It's Ann, Jon. Mark LaCrosse is on his way over there to take a deposition from you—do you want me there? Should I come down quickly and—"

"And guard me?" Jon asked. "No, I'm okay on this, Annie. Do me a favor, sit tight right where you are until you hear from me again, will you?"

"All right. If you're sure you don't need me—"

"Not for this. I intend to tell the truth, the whole truth, and nothing but the truth. I want to cooperate with the police in every conceivable way. Ann, you were so right. I've got to prove the truth on this for everyone. For Gina, for Katie. For you—for me. I'll be okay. But things here may be changing a little. Hang tight like I asked you, okay?"

"Sure."

She hung up the phone, changed clothes, and began prowling around her apartment. She turned to an easel, starting to work on her sketch of Cindy again.

She set it aside. She hadn't had the chance to take any pictures yet. She wasn't ready for the way that she wanted to work on Cindy.

She set up a new sketch pad, then set it aside as well, going for a canvas. She started to sketch directly on the canvas. Her mind and fingers worked with astonishing ease. The time began to pass quickly. Hours slipped by; she didn't even pause for a coffee, soda, sip of water, or bathroom break.

When the phone began to ring, she was stunned to realize that it was late afternoon. She'd barely noticed how she had been losing the sun in her skylight.

"Annie."

It was Jon.

"Hey! How did things go?"

"Great. Listen, I'm on my way over. I've been released."

"What?" she gasped, stunned. "Jon, they did surgery on you! You can't—"

"Ann," he said with a sigh of impatience, "you're not thinking of the modern world, HMOs, sky-rocketing health costs. I've been sewed up good enough, I've got my instructions, and I've been released."

"You just came out of a coma!"

"Right—I came out of it."

"I don't believe this—"

"Ann, I'm on my way. I've got to see you, we've got to talk, we've got to figure this out."

Jimmy Deveaux was probably still watching her from below. Her bedroom door was still broken; Mark could show up here at any time.

And she'd nearly forgotten that April had told her that she had something to say to her.

"Jon, don't come here."

"Why not?"

"I can't explain now. Meet me at the club."

"Annabella's?" he said, puzzled.

"Yes. Meet me there in thirty minutes."

"All right. I'll be there."

Ann hung up. She noticed that her message light was blinking, and she realized only then that she hadn't bothered to check on her calls since she'd left for the hospital when the call had come regarding Jon.

She pressed the play button. Message number one was nothing more than some breathing.

Message number two was louder breathing.

Someone playing games. Someone trying to frighten her, she thought, when message number three turned out to be very heavy breathing.

She was about to turn the machine off without even listening to the fourth message. She hesitated just long enough to hear her daughter's voice.

"Mom? It's Katie? I got a message to call home, are you there?" There was some fumbling with the phone and a mumbled swear. "Mom? Okay, Mom, they said you said it wasn't an emergency, but to please call as quickly as possible. Mom—I'm back out at the camp tonight, please, please, please, pick up the phone. Are you okay? Is Dad okay? Mom? All right, Mom, I'll try back tomorrow night, ten o'clock your time. Please be home; you're making me frantic. Love you. Tell Dad I send my love, too. Be there, Mom, please? It's just terrible when you don't know where your parents are!"

Ann sank into the chair by the phone. "Oh, Katie!" she murmured out loud. She checked the date and time by the message; Katie had called this morning about ten minutes before she'd come back into the house. Well, the good thing was that it had taken Katie long enough to reach her that she would no longer have to tell Katie that her father was in the hospital.

Now she'd only have to tell Katie that if something wasn't discovered soon, Jon would probably eventually be charged with murder.

Ann groaned aloud, then remembered that she had to meet Jon. She stood, then remembered that basset hound Jimmy was watching her from the street below.

She hesitated, working on a way to slip out of her house without Jimmy Deveaux seeing her go.

Cindy thought that she had danced exceptionally well that afternoon.

She'd added a dimension to her costume—a delicate little white purse that attached to a slender white string that dipped very low around her waist. With the right sways, dips, and gyrations, thrown kisses, pouts, and smiles, she'd managed to get the purse very nicely filled.

Leaving the stage, she congratulated herself as she headed toward the dressing room. Halfway there, she was stopped by one of the bouncers, a big, burly redhead called One-Eye-Jack—his name was Jack, and he'd lost an eye in a rumble when he'd still been in high school. He was actually a nice enough guy, which made him a good bouncer. He liked people until they got rowdy or out of line. Then he was sorry about it, but he was really capable of kicking them out of the place by the seat of their pants.

"Cindy!"

"Yeah?"

"The boss wants to see you."

"What?"

"He sent you this." Jack lifted his hand; two crisp hundred dollar bills stood between his fingers.

She snatched the money from him.

"Are you that good or is he that desperate?" Jack asked, grinning.

"Why don't you ask him that question?" Cindy said.

" 'Cause I like my job," Jack said.

Cindy shook her head and walked past him. "It would serve you right if I told him what you said!"

"You won't do that," Jack said, " 'cause you're a good kid, Cindy."

"Yeah, yeah, yeah," Cindy muttered. She started for the stairs that led up to the office, feeling sick inside.

She didn't want to see Duval. Her own fault. She'd gotten greedy today. He'd been watching her from up there while she'd done her number with the purse. Something new . . . it had given him the hots for her all over again.

He paid well, she reminded herself.

Still, her palms felt clammy. She didn't want to go up to him.

She tapped on the door to the office.

"Who is it?"

"Cindy."

"Come in; I'm waiting."

He was waiting. When she opened the door, he was standing in front of the window, naked, staring down now at April, who was dancing with

Marty. He was tall, powerfully built. Her eyes skirted over him.

Well hung.

Her stomach crawled.

He turned. Saw her face. Smiled slowly, then started to laugh.

"Cindy . . . Cindy, you just looked so damned good down there today . . . well, it's not going to be quite the same, is it? Gina's gone, and the real thing's all for you."

"Yeah, Gina's gone," Cindy repeated. It was hard to swallow. He'd sent her two hundred dollars. She wasn't giving back the money.

No matter what he wanted.

"Well, come on, sweet thing. You've been paid. Get on over here." He paused and looked her over, his gaze lingering on her. "And do it right, babe. Do it with enthusiasm. With or without Gina, I want it good. In fact, I want it better."

The guy with the patch was on the door. He grinned when he saw Ann—he'd gotten used to seeing her come to the club.

When she stepped inside, she saw that April and Marty were on the stage together. She'd have to wait a few minutes to get to talk to April.

She started for the bar, then realized that Jon was already there.

Surrounded.

Jennifer was there, along with several of the girls Ann hadn't really had a chance to meet.

They were fawning over Jon, delighted to see him, supporting him.

"Sugar, we know you're an innocent man," Jennifer assured him.

"I'm going to prove it, but ladies, I'm grateful for the votes of confidence you're giving me. If you all trust me, then the police will have to see the light."

"Yeah, just so long as no one else turns up dead now that you're out of the hospital!" a tall, leggy, blond girl said.

Ann cleared her throat.

"Ann, you're here!" It was Jennifer who spoke. "Look, it's Jon!"

"Yes, it's Jon," Ann said, smiling her amusement as she met her ex's eyes. He flushed. She shook her head, still smiling.

"Annie!" Jon said, standing, giving her a long, tight hug. She felt him flinch as she returned the gesture, and quickly let him loose.

"I think they need to talk," Jennifer murmured.

"If you don't mind?" Jon said.

The girls moved away.

"Sorry," Jon said, flushing again.

"Hey, you can't help the fatal charm, huh, kid?"

"They're just friends."

"I know. You really were in love with Gina— but those were the lovelies you painted."

He nodded.

"When I came here, and watched them, I understood."

"How many times have you been here?" Jon demanded sternly.

"A few."

"You shouldn't have been here."

She arched a brow. "You came here. Besides, I thought you were going to give me this marvelous thank-you for saving your life by whispering my name when you came out of surgery. But you weren't whispering my name—you said 'Annabella's.' "

"Did I really?"

"Yes, you did."

"I had to have meant something by it."

"So I assumed."

"But you haven't learned anything here?"

"You already heard—the Jane Doe who was strangled had come here before she was killed."

"Yes, I heard. We both know that. But, I mean, you didn't learn anything that would help find the murderer?"

She shook her head.

"There's something I should remember," Jon said, irritated with himself, "something I had, something I saw, something that should be in my hands right now . . . but I lost it! I can't see beyond the shadows. I'm so damned frustrated."

"Jon, it may just come to you."

"But when?"

"I don't know. I—" Ann broke off. Harry Duval was approaching them. He was handsomely decked out in a silk shirt and chinos. Smiling broadly, he offered a hand to Jon. "Marcel! It's great to see you. Last I heard, you were out like a light, a damned veggie. At the best, they'd be hauling you in to the clink. You're looking fine, alive and well—and free as a bird."

"Yeah, well, luck was with me."

Duval slid onto the bar stool by Jon's, flashing Ann a smile as he did so. "It's been a tough time for us here, Jon. Without Gina. A lot of people hurting. The police crawling all over. That's kind of bad for business. But a lot of people here believe in you. And we're glad to have you here."

"Thanks," Jon told him. "I'm pretty sure I gave the police the slip when I came."

"Someone was following you?" Ann asked.

He nodded gravely. "I'm sure of it."

"Mark?"

He shook his head. "LaCrosse got called out right after the deposition. I managed to get myself released about an hour after that—and I sort of managed to depart by way of a back cafeteria door."

"You know," Duval said, "we're glad to have you back; the girls are all crazy about you. But—you know, you're not half as pretty as your ex-wife."

"You watch it with Annie," Jon warned. "She's . . . she's the mother of a college student, you know."

Jon was so indignant. Ann didn't know whether to feel flattered by his determination to be protective—or indignant in return that he might think it so impossible that she could be found attractive here among so many other women.

"I've been trying to give her a job," Duval said. He winked at Ann.

She was startled as she felt a tinge of warm unease. Duval aroused strange sensations. He made her very uncomfortable. At the same time, he definitely had a sensuality about him.

"Ann doesn't need a job. She's an artist!" Jon said. "She's—she's . . ."

"She'd be perfect in my book," Duval said.

Jon was staring at her strangely, Ann thought. "Well, she's perfect in her way, yes . . . ," Jon was saying. "She's my ex-*wife*, Duval. Not a dancer."

"Ex-wife, and very, very sexy!" Duval teased.

"Now—" Jon began.

Ann jumped up suddenly. April was off stage. She'd been standing in the darkened area to the left of it, beckoning to Ann, and Ann had just now finally seen her.

"Excuse me," she told the men. She smiled as they both stared at her. "Got to hug a friend," she explained, slipping away from the men.

April had already disappeared. Ann made her way through the tables in the darkened area, around to the side of the stage. She was sure that April had gone back to the dressing room. Ann moved along the corridor backstage, and hurried on to the dressing room where she'd talked to Cindy, Jennifer and April the other day.

She tapped on the door, then pushed it open.

The lights were off in the room. It was filled with shadows.

"April?"

She stepped into the room.

Suddenly, the door closed behind her.

And the room was plunged into complete darkness.

She started to cry out, but a hand descended firmly upon her mouth.

And a hissed warning sounded in the blackness . . .

"Shhhhh . . ."

Nineteen

Mark sat in Lee Minh's office, reading the report on Jane Doe—now presumed to be Ms. Ellie Trainor of Los Angeles, California, thirty-eight years old, president and chairman of the board of Time Travel, Inc., a tour company specializing in preparing itineraries for people with very little time. She lived alone, lived for her work, made a small fortune, no children, no exes, parents deceased, greatly admired by employees and associates.

"The match just came in on the computer," Lee told Mark. "We'll verify, of course, but it looks like we've got the right identity now. She was due back from a scouting trip out here in New Orleans. She didn't show. The statistics match—a five-foot-seven, one-hundred-and-thirty-pound blonde. We're waiting for a reply from dental now, but I'd stake my reputation that we've got the right name on the right body."

Mark nodded, glancing at the picture they had of the woman when she'd been alive. Very pretty, sleek, sophisticated.

"She had fish for dinner," Lee said.

Mark stared over at him.

"Done up in a way only two places prepare it, that I know of, at any rate."

"I knew you'd come through. Where?"

"Divinity's, on Chartes Street, and Abelone, right off of Bourbon."

"I'll be right on it. Can I use your phone?"

"Be my guest."

"Ms. Trainor's place of business has been informed, right?"

Lee nodded.

Mark stared down at the report, punching in numbers. He glanced at his watch. "It's afternoon in L.A. now, right?"

"Yeah."

The phone was answered by a girl with a breathy voice. Mark identified himself, told the girl how sorry he was, and then asked for her help.

"Can you tell me anything about what she was doing in New Orleans, who she was seeing?"

"Well, there was one gentleman in particular. In fact, he was so charming. He told me not to worry when Ellie first . . . when we first realized that Ellie had disappeared."

"Who?"

"The company has done a bit of long distance business with him before, but this time Ellie was planning on sending a lot of people in his direction."

"Can you tell me his name?"

"Jacques Moret."

Mark stared at Lee, thanked the girl, and hung up the phone.

* * *

Harry Duval and Jon Marcel studied one another in silence for several seconds.

"Don't look at me like that. I didn't do it!" Harry insisted.

"Well, I didn't do it either," Jon said firmly. "I was in love with her. You know that."

"She made a fortune for me," Harry Duval said.

"That would have ended if she'd married me."

"I'm telling you, I didn't do it," Harry repeated. "The case is still far stronger against you. She had one hell of a past. She was seeing other people right up until the end. You weren't naive enough to think that she'd given up all the others the moment you met?"

"I wasn't naive in the least—I fell in love with her despite her life, and I'm willing to bet that Gina was killed simply because she almost had a real life with me. Someone wasn't willing to let her have it."

Harry Duval shook his head, staring down into a glass of Campari he'd had his bartender pour. He picked up the glass and swallowed the liquid, wincing as he watched the stage. Jon looked to the stage as well. Jennifer was on. She wasn't as perfect as some of the other girls, but the guys at the front tables didn't seem to care.

"I didn't kill her. You didn't kill her. Jacques?" Harry shook his head again. "I don't see Jacques as a killer. He's too much of a user. He would have tried to blackmail her, yes, but kill her . . . ?

I think that Gina was seeing someone else as well. Someone none of us really knew about."

"The cop?" Jon grated. "Mark LaCrosse?"

Harry glanced at Jon, a curious smile curved into his features. "She liked the cop. Liked him a lot. She told me once he was the best she'd had, and she'd had a lot of men."

Duval was irritating him for his own amusement, Jon realized. He determined to keep control of his temper. Duval sighed. "But I don't know. Once . . ."

"Once, she left here with the other cop," Duval revealed.

"What other cop?"

"LaCrosse's partner. Deveaux. Jimmy Deveaux."

"How many people knew about that?"

Duval shrugged. "I knew. I think she went with him because he had discovered that . . ."

"Discovered what?"

Duval stared at Jon and smiled slowly. "Silly play. Gina wanted more than the spiritual advice Mama Lili Mae gave her. She liked the spells and incantations. Some ritual was performed in the cemetery, and apparently Deveaux was planning on taking her in on some kind of destruction of public property charges."

Jon stood. "What cemetery?" he demanded.

"It's me, it's me, it's me!" came a whisper.

The hand was gone. Ann inhaled deeply. "April! Dammit! You scared me half to death!"

"I'm just trying to be really careful."

"My heart nearly stopped beating!"

"I'm sorry, I'm sorry. I just didn't want anybody to see me talking to you. I'm getting really spooked around here. Duval called Cindy up to his office today, and she hasn't reappeared since then. I'm just so uneasy! We heard that Jon was out, and ever since then everyone here has been staring at everyone else. But there is something that I never told you; I don't know whether it will help or hurt, but I think that I know something not many other people do."

"What, tell me, April!"

They still stood in the dark. April opened the door to the dressing room, looking out into the hallway. She half closed the door, watching the hallway as she spoke in a tense whisper. "Gina had some kind of a secret correspondence going on. With someone practicing an illegal form of voodoo. She was involved with a cult. They performed rituals at the cemetery." She lowered her voice even further. "This cult slips in and out of there fairly frequently without getting caught. Gina loved that damned cemetery. She'd do a lot to protect it—and the cultists who met there. She told me once to look for 'Manning' if I ever needed help and couldn't get it."

"Why didn't you tell me this before? Why didn't you tell the police?"

April shook her head. "I don't know. I didn't think that it mattered, that it could mean anything. I thought it was just so silly at first. I mean, who would take people killing chickens in a cemetery seriously in this day and age? I didn't want to hurt Gina's friends. Maybe I wanted Jon to be the killer so that everything would be safe."

Suddenly, out of the darkness, they heard a groan.

Both women froze, then looked into the darkness of the dressing room.

Ann hit the lights.

Cindy was lying on the sofa, curled into a fetal ball. She looked so very small—like a wounded sparrow.

"Cindy!" Ann cried. She hurried over to the young woman and knelt down beside her.

She was dressed in dark jeans and a denim shirt. Most of her body was covered; but the sleeves of her shirt were rolled up, and it appeared that she had bruises on her arm.

"Cindy!" Ann cried again.

"Ohh . . ." Cindy sat up, blinked, and stared at the two of them.

"Oh, my God, what did he do to you?" April demanded.

Ann stared at April in horror. "Duval?" she queried sharply.

"No, no . . . ," Cindy protested. She tried to smile. "Harry had nothing to do with this."

"Who did?"

"A shrimp."

"What?"

"I think I ate bad shellfish."

"And got a bruise on your arm?" Ann demanded.

"I got sick and fell. Really. I just need to lie down awhile longer. I took something for it. I'm feeling better. I swear. I was sleeping until I started hearing your voices."

"Oh, Cindy," April said.

"Cindy, you've got to tell me the truth! Someone else could wind up dead."

"I'm telling the truth!" Cindy insisted. "Please believe me, Ann. You've got to believe me."

Ann hesitated. "I'm going to go give that man a piece of my mind."

"Wait, please!" Cindy said. "You could just make matters much worse—"

But Ann had already left the dressing room in a hurry. She skirted the tables in the darkened area, and came back around to the bar. Jon was standing, as if he was ready to leave.

Ann set her small form in front of her ex-husband, facing Duval furiously. "Did you hurt that girl?"

"What?"

"Cindy!"

"What's the matter with Cindy?"

His manner was both sincere and annoyed; Ann began to doubt her own conviction that Cindy had been lying about her condition to cover up for Duval.

"She's—sick," Ann said.

"I told her not to eat the damned shrimp. She reacts to them every damned time. I hope she can work tonight. I haven't talked you into taking a job yet, have I?"

"No, no, Ann and I have to go," Jon said. He

glanced at her anxiously. "Actually, we need to go really quickly and get a few things done before the friendly police of our Parish of New Orleans find me and follow me again. We'll be seeing you, Duval."

"Yep, we'll be seeing you," Ann agreed as Jon propelled her out of the club. The guy with the patch on his eye was still watching the door. He smiled broadly and waved goodbye to them.

"We need a taxi," Jon said. "Quickly. The cops will definitely have figured out that I've left the hospital by now. And they'll come here." He glanced sharply at Ann. "Were you followed?"

She shook her head.

"I can't believe they don't have somebody watching you."

"They do. I think."

"You think?"

"It was Mark's partner today."

"Mark's partner?"

"Deveaux."

"I don't trust him—and I'm not even sure I trust LaCrosse. At least I knew LaCrosse had slept with Gina—I just found out that she had an evening out with his partner as well."

"Really?" Ann shivered. "He was the one watching my house, but I went out through the back of the shop on the ground floor."

"Good for you. Still, we've got to get moving."

"Wait! I know something. We've got to go—"

"Duval was just telling about—"

"You don't understand! April said Gina was leaving messages—"

"There were voodoo practices going on—"

"At the cemetery." They finished in unison. Jon stared at Ann blankly.

"You shouldn't come there," Jon said.

"I'll be with you. We'll be all right. For God's sake, Jon, I'm not letting you go alone. There's a cab, flag it down, quickly!"

She shoved Jon. He jumped into action in just the nick of time to flag down the cab.

The driver didn't believe their destination. "Full moon tonight, folks. More crazies than ever going to be out."

"Yes, well, that's all right," Jon assured him.

"The cemeteries are closed up at night!" the cabbie said firmly.

"We just want to walk around," Ann told him.

"Somebody will shoot you in the head, you walk around too much."

"We'll be careful," Jon said.

"You want me to wait for you?" the cabbie asked.

"No!" Ann said. She glanced at Jon. "We—we have friends picking us up."

The cabbie let them off; Jon tipped him well. He kept muttering anyway.

"Dead friends. That's what you're going to have. Dead friends." Then he laughed. "Hell, it's a cemetery, a full moon, and I just dropped the whackos off with the dead folks. It's a hell of a world, a hell of a world!"

At last, he drove off.

They stared at the walls, and the fences. "I'll give you a boost up," Jon said.

"You've got stitches! I'll give you the boost."

"I'm the man."

"But I'm in the best shape."

"Ann—"

"Sh!" she cried suddenly. "Listen!"

They could hear something.

Chanting.

"Give me a boost!" Jon said. He leapt for the wall; Ann gave him a firm push. He was quickly atop it, reaching down for her. She accepted his hand and crawled up. They both dropped silently to the earth on the other side of the wall. Once there, they remained very still again, listening.

"It's coming from the rear of the cemetery."

"Jon, this is really scary. Maybe we should wait for the police to follow us."

"We'll never find anything out if we do. The first second these guys hear the police, they'll break, and they'll be out of here."

His fingers curled around hers. "Come on. We've just got to stick together."

They moved through the cemetery.

It was a frightening place by night. Time and weather had eroded a number of the tombs. Cherubs, dancing above a vault, had been chipped, and they now seemed to stare down at Ann with evil leers upon their chubby faces. The full moon shining down upon effigies and tombs caught them in a strange reflection.

The chanting began to become louder. It was sing-song, all in patois.

"We're getting closer," Jon whispered.

Ann suddenly tripped. She nearly cried out;

Jon clamped his hand over her mouth. She sank down on the broken stone beneath her, rubbing her shin.

"I almost fell over that broken cross!" she hissed.

Jon wasn't really paying attention to her. He was looking toward the far end of the cemetery.

"They're back there!" he whispered. He stood straight, staring in that direction, ambling just a few feet from her. "Can you walk, Annie?"

She didn't answer him at first, but rubbed her shin. As she looked up, she suddenly noted a family vault. The surname was chiselled out cleanly at the top of it.

MANNING.

She inhaled sharply and rose, automatically walking toward the tomb. She came onto an overgrown stone path leading to it, and kept going.

There was no longer a closed gate on the tomb; the wrought-iron closure hung on its broken hinges and wedged into the earth. Outside the tomb, Ann hesitated.

Once she walked in, the moonlight would be gone.

"Jon?" she said, and turned. She immediately cursed herself.

She'd walked off. She'd forgotten Jon.

And now . . .

She was alone.

"Jon, damn you, where the hell are you?" she whispered furiously aloud.

There was no reply.

MANNING.

Some kind of an answer might lie in that open vault. She hesitated, then took a step closer. And closer. She tried to look in.

"Like I'd be sensible enough to have a flashlight with me, right?" she muttered to herself. "But then again, I didn't leave the house knowing that I'd be prowling around in a cemetery tonight. I didn't used to prowl around in cemeteries at night. And then again, I didn't used to frequent strip joints either. Then again, what's an ex-husband for, if not to provide a little emotional turmoil here and there? Then again, of course, I didn't used to have a sex life either . . . hmm, is a sex life an even exchange for the terror of prowling through a cemetery in the middle of the night?

"I'm talking to myself." She was silent for a moment, just at the threshold of the vault.

"I need to talk to myself. That way, I can be certain that I won't hear it if the people in the tombs start talking," she murmured.

A thin strand of moonlight was filtering into the tomb. It was perhaps ten feet by ten feet, with ledges indicating different rows of deceased Mannings.

Many of the vault drawers were broken. She could see the coffins within them. Here and there, the coffins appeared to be smashed.

On the bottom level, there seemed to be a large gap where both wall and coffin had been smashed. The moonlight was reflecting on something.

Paper? Was this where Gina had left her messages? To a secret lover?

Ann took a step into the vault. Suddenly, the paper, or the slip of reflecting-white whatever, disappeared. Ann moved forward.

Only to feel something, someone, moving behind her. She swirled; something crashed down heavily against the tomb, just an inch from her head. She shrieked, ducking as she heard and felt the rush of air as a bludgeon was lifted and lowered.

She spun around, racing out the doorway of the tomb, tearing down the path.

The moon slipped behind clouds.

An awful darkness filled the night.

She kept running, crying out. She tripped, and fell. She'd fallen on a low tomb. A broken tomb. Something was beneath her chin. She touched it, and a well of pure panic rose within her.

Bone. Human bone. A thigh bone?

She rose to her feet, heedless of what injury she might have done her body. She ran down another path, completely disoriented. The clouds began to shift; the moon was coming out again.

She drew to a sudden dead halt. Right in front of her was a figure in a black cape and hood. She couldn't make out its features at first, because the figure's head was lowered.

It raised.

She was staring at Jacques Moret.

She let out a terrified scream.

"No, no—please!" he gasped out.

Please what? In terror, Ann turned again, running straight into another body.

She let out panicked shrieks as if every demon in hell was after her.

"Ann!" She could hear Jon calling her, racing toward her.

But if Jon was coming to her now. . . .

She looked up at the face on the solid block of human wall that had stopped her.

"Ann! It's Mark, stop it."

"Mark?" she whispered weakly.

People were running in from all around her. She turned in Mark's hold. There was Jon.

There was Harry Duval.

And there, coming from another path, was Jimmy Deveaux.

They all stopped dead, staring awkwardly at one another. "What the hell is going on here?" Mark demanded.

Ann tried to disengage herself from his arms. "What—what are you doing here?" she demanded suspiciously. She saw Jimmy Deveaux over his shoulder. She didn't trust him.

"What do you mean, what am I doing here?" He turned to Jimmy himself. "Did anyone get Jacques?"

"The boys must have. I'll go back and check," Jimmy said.

"Jacques?" Jon said, watching Mark. "You came here—because you knew Jacques was here?"

"We're bringing Jacques in for questioning in

the murder of Ellie Trainor—Jane Doe," he explained. "Jacques' secretary told us where he could be found on the night of a full moon," he added. "You slipped the guys watching you at the hospital, Jon."

"Were people watching me?" Jon asked innocently.

"And you!" he said, arms tightening angrily around Ann. "You haven't got the sense of a stupid person!"

"Hey," Jon protested in Ann's defense.

"What the hell were you doing out here?"

"Trying to solve a murder—since the police aren't doing so well with it!" Ann informed him.

"Come on," Mark grated angrily. "We're all getting out of here."

As it happened, they certainly didn't need a cab ride back.

They left the cemetery in police cars.

They all went to the station.

Jacques Moret, admitting that he took part in cultist rituals at the cemetery but denying that he knew anything about the murder of Ellie Trainor, was booked into jail for the night anyway, pending charges from the D.A.'s office. Jon, Harry Duval and Ann sat sipping coffee in a room that offered nothing but a table and a few chairs, until Mark at last reappeared to be with them.

He leaned against the door, arms folded over his chest. "You first, Duval. What were you doing in the cemetery?"

Harry shrugged. "I had heard about the rituals. I told Jon about them earlier this evening. I thought, since he remained a prime suspect in Gina's death, that he should know. Then I worried. I thought that he would rush to the cemetery, and his wife was with him. I came to help if I needed to do so."

"Jon?" Mark said.

"You heard him. I'm a desperate man, La-Crosse. And I'm looking for whatever I can find before you get me into a cell. Unless you think that Jacques Moret killed both women? Am I still here with my neck half in a noose?"

"We haven't any real proof against anyone yet," Mark said. "Your blood on Gina is still pretty damning."

"I rest my case."

"You dragged Ann into a very dangerous situation. I should book all of you for breaking into the cemetery."

"Waste of taxpayers' money, don't you think?" Harry asked him.

He didn't seem to hear Harry. He was staring at Ann. "Jail might be the safest place for you."

Ann just stared back. So far, she hadn't told anyone that she'd been attacked in the Manning tomb.

"Jacques Moret—is being held for murder?" she pursued.

"Yes," Mark said. "For the time being. However, all I have right now is the fact that he dined with Ellie Trainor and he was the last known person to see her while she was still alive."

Had Jacques been in that tomb—searching

for whatever damning correspondence he might have last carried on with Gina?

Had he watched her tonight . . .

Waited for her, planning to bludgeon her?

As Gregory had been struck, on the night of the storm?

It must have been Jacques Moret! she thought. God, yes, it had to have been. And now he was under arrest, and pray God, the evidence would now accumulate against him, proving him guilty of both murders and more.

"If you're not charging me, Mark, may I leave now?" Harry asked politely.

"Yeah, yeah, you can go," Mark told him.

Harry made a quick getaway.

"Then Ann and I are free to go as well?" Jon said hopefully.

"I'll take you," Mark said.

Jon led the way out; Ann followed him. She could feel Mark behind her all the way.

On the street, he ushered her into the front passenger's seat of his car, leaving Jon to his own resources to enter in back.

"I'll drop you at your place first, Marcel," Mark said.

"No, that's all right. Just take me to Annie's. I don't think she should be alone."

"You're her *ex*-husband."

"I'll be in Katie's room, if that's any of your business. She shouldn't be alone."

"She won't be alone," Mark said.

"What?" Jon said sharply.

"I'll be on her couch."

"Oh, really? Isn't that taking police work a little above and beyond?"

"Would you two please quit talking about me as if I wasn't even here?" Ann demanded furiously.

"Oh, my God!" Jon breathed. Ann felt his hands clamp on her shoulders. "You're sleeping with him!"

"Jon, what I choose to do—"

"You're the ex-husband. You don't sleep with her anymore. You were in love with Gina; you were going to marry her, remember?" Mark taunted.

"Yeah, well, ex-husband rates higher than newly met casual lover," Jon insisted.

"Stop this!" Ann hissed. "Stop it immediately; I swear I'll lock you both out—"

"Katie's room?" Mark said.

"The couch?" Jon demanded.

"We're here," Mark said.

"Yes, and I'm going up alone," Ann said.

"The hell you are," Mark said.

"Not on your life," Jon told her.

Ann let out a furious cry of frustration, and started up the stairs to her apartment. They were right behind her.

The two of them.

All the way.

Twenty

Mark watched as Ann slammed her way into the kitchen, poured a glass of wine, and disappeared into her bedroom—then slamming her shattered door the best she could.

It closed. It just wasn't going to lock.

Of course, that probably didn't matter much. Not with both him and Jon Marcel in the house.

"Maybe we should have some wine, too," Jon muttered. He walked on into the kitchen area, getting glasses. "Are you off or on duty? Do you mind me helping myself in the kitchen? Just how far has this gone? Tell me, did you get Annie while you were on or off the first time?"

"Marcel," Mark said irritably, "it's none of your damned business, but if you must know, it all came about when I went after her in the swamps while she was risking her own fool neck to try to prove someone else a murderer."

Marcel didn't respond to that. "Wine? You are officially off duty, right?"

"What else does she have?" Mark asked. "Bourbon on ice would be damned good right now."

Marcel grinned. "Bourbon on ice coming up."

He poured the drink, handed it to Mark, then noted Ann's easel. He walked to it, throwing up the sheet that covered the sketch she'd been working on.

He whistled softly. "Nobody, nobody, does faces like my Annie." He looked up at Mark. "Come see."

Mark walked over to where Jon stood and studied the sketch on the easel.

There were three faces in the sketch, drawn together, like a family portrait.

His face, his son's face, Brit's face.

All the similarities were shown in the sketch, all of the differences. All the dreams in Brit's eyes, steadiness in Michael's, wisdom in his own. The sketch was far from complete; it was wonderful, telling, and more. The emotion was striking; the affection between the three of them was quite obvious. Somehow, that drawing promised beautiful things for the future, while being a tribute to the present.

"Okay, so maybe you're not such a casual lover," Marcel commented.

He looked at the pad Ann had set aside. He picked it up, setting it on another easel.

"Cindy. She was doing a good job with her, too. Going for the same thing, the beauty in movement, the sadness of what it can all fall to . . ." He paused, looking at Mark. "I didn't kill Gina. I swear it; I didn't do it. Tell me honestly—did Jacques kill her?"

"Honestly—I don't know. We'll spend most of tomorrow questioning him regarding every step of what happened. The same way we did with you. I won't be able to hold him long unless I get something else. You had blood all over you and I didn't hold you, if you'll recall."

"Yeah. But if Jacques didn't kill her, who the hell did?"

"There's still Harry Duval."

"Or your partner," Jon pointed out.

"My partner?" Mark demanded, startled.

Jon offered him a wry grin. "I just found out about that one myself. Duval told me tonight. Jimmy Deveaux found out about those meetings in the cemetery. Apparently, he was bribing Gina."

"I don't believe it."

"Why? Because he's a cop?"

"Because—he's a good man."

"I'm a good man, whether you want to believe it or not. That didn't keep me from wanting Gina."

"You're talking about blackmail and things much uglier than wanting someone."

"Oh, man, LaCrosse! Hell, I wanted to marry Gina, but I knew the truth about her. She was a prostitute. Cops are human. They pay prostitutes, too. Okay, you didn't. It was a relationship you formed. The first time with me—I paid her. Our relationship developed from there. Maybe your partner just paid her."

Mark swallowed down his bourbon. His head

ached. God damn Jimmy. Why the hell hadn't he ever said anything?

"Jimmy—Jimmy didn't kill her," Mark said.

"You know, LaCrosse, to me, you make just as good a suspect as anyone else."

"Do I now? I remind you—I wasn't the one wearing the blood."

Jon Marcel lifted a hand, wincing. "I shouldn't have said that. I don't think that you're guilty. I . . . I don't know. I just know that there's something I saw that should help, but I can't remember what!"

"Are you willing for me to arrange for a hypnotist to maybe help you find out what it is?"

"A hypnotist?" Jon queried.

Mark nodded. "Yes, I've seen hypnotism work. People can recall things under hypnosis that their conscious minds have closed off."

"I'm willing to try anything that might help," Jon assured him.

"Fine. We'll get someone tomorrow."

"All right."

"If I'm gone in the morning, don't leave here until I get back."

"All right," Jon said, quirking a brow.

Mark didn't owe him an explanation. He decided to give him one anyway.

"I want to talk to Jimmy before he goes in tomorrow."

"Ah. Well, I won't go anywhere, and I won't leave Ann. Good night then." He grimaced, pointing to the door down the hall from Ann's. "Katie's room."

Mark nodded. He pointed across the room. "Sofa."

"Yeah." Jon started for Katie's door, then turned back. "I sleep like the dead, you know. You've been damned decent. I—well, I can tell from Annie's sketch. I really shouldn't be here."

"Good night," Mark told him.

"Good night."

Jon disappeared behind Katie's door.

Mark sat on the sofa.

Jacques.

Damn him.

Jane Doe was Ellie Trainor, and she'd done business with him and had dinner with him the night she'd been killed. Further testing would probably prove they'd had sex together as well.

So what did that prove?

Who else was connected with Ellie Trainor except for Jacques Moret?

The answer was simple and frightening.

Anyone who might have been at the club the night she'd been killed.

He drew his fingers through his hair. Son of a bitch, but they had to have some answers. He'd been so damned scared when he'd heard Ann screaming in the cemetery. He'd had terrible—if absurd—images in his mind of Ann stretched out on a tomb, her throat bared to a voodoo priest's knife as if she were a long-necked chicken.

He looked to her door.

Shook his head. He couldn't take any more of this. He was too involved.

He was in love with her.

He shouldn't be here tonight.

He stood up and walked uncertainly to her door. Barge it open, take the assertive approach! he told himself.

Barge it, and it would fall apart completely, and Ann and Jon would both be out here staring at him as if he were some kind of a complete idiot.

Open it, just open it. Tell her that you act like an ass when you're scared stiff that something is going to happen to her.

He opened the door. Quietly, carefully.

She wasn't in bed. She was dressed in a thin, white sleeveless nightgown, her wineglass in her hand. She was sitting in a wicker chair that looked out the window to the small garden area on the side of the house. Night lights on the street illuminated a gardenia bush, a hammock, and a little cupid fountain. It was a pretty, peaceful sight.

She heard him come in; he knew it. But she didn't turn around.

Neither did she protest.

He walked to her. Hesitated. Slid his hands beneath her hair, lifted it, and pressed his lips to her shoulder, nape, and throat.

She still didn't speak.

He took her wineglass from her and set it on the windowsill. Her eyes met his.

He pulled her against him, kissing her lips.

She kissed back.

He slipped his fingers beneath the thin shoulder straps of her nightgown and let it fall to the floor. He drew his hands down the length of her back, curving his fingers around her buttocks.

He kissed her lips, and her breasts, and felt her begin to quiver.

He went to his knees, drawing her against his face.

He knew when she was about to cry out. He came to his feet and quickly swallowed any sound with his kiss as he swept her up, and took her into her bed.

It was much better than the couch.

In the morning, Ann heard the phone ringing.

She was entangled with Mark, his limbs atop and beneath hers and vice versa, but she bolted up like a streak of lightning, grabbing her terry bathrobe from the foot of the bed and flying out to the counter to pick up the phone before the machine could announce the caller to everyone within hearing distance.

"Hello?"

There was a lot of static on the other end. Then she heard a low voice speaking. It was a frantic, female voice.

At least . . .

It sounded female.

"Ann?"

"Yes!"

Static again. "Mama Lili Mae wants to see you. She says not to trust anybody near you, not to trust anybody you think that you should trust, do you hear?"

"I, yes, but—who is this? April, Cindy?"

"Oh, God, I can't talk long, I'll be heard. Don't trust anyone at all, get to Mama Lili Mae. As fast as possible. Hire a boatman, get to the bayou. Oh, God, you can't imagine—"

The line went dead.

Ann hesitated, then hung up. She should tell Mark. Or Jon.

Don't trust anyone. Don't trust anybody you think you should trust.

Jon had been in the hospital when Ellie Trainor had been killed!

The murder hadn't necessarily been committed by the same killer!

Mark had been seeing Gina, too.

No, not Mark. Not Mark.

What about his partner? The blood hound?

What if someone on the force was guilty? Would Mark refuse to believe, refuse to see, cast her into danger himself by insisting she be with the wrong person?

"Who was that?" Mark called from the bedroom.

"The—dry cleaners!" Ann called back. "My suits are ready."

"What the *hell?*" she suddenly heard Mark say.

She hurried to the bedroom door. He was still naked, on his stomach, his body angled so that he was staring off the bed, looking at something on the floor.

She came into the room. His head jerked up, and he stared at her.

"What?" she demanded.

"Get me a plastic bag."

"Why?"

"Do it."

"I'm not your maid or your lackey—"

"God damn it, Ann, please get me a plastic bag!"

Muttering furiously, she returned to the kitchen for a plastic bag. She brought it to him, then gasped when she realized what he had found.

A bloodied knife.

It was at least ten inches long, and the blood was now dried and crusted upon it. He wrapped the plastic around the handle, picking it up carefully, wrapping it completely. Ann stared from him to it in horror.

"I didn't put it there."

He didn't say anything.

"Damn you, Mark, I didn't put it there. And neither did Jon."

Mark rose, reaching automatically for his clothes, not saying anything as he dressed. Ann felt cold. "Mark, he didn't do it. Anyone could have gotten in here. The cops were in here, all over the place the night Gina died. Then—I've been out! I was in the swamp one night, and I was at your place one night. Anyone could have gotten in here."

"Isn't that convenient."

"You son of a bitch! How dare you."

"Get Jon."

"Listen to me, you're not a damned drill sergeant, and I'm not your private—"

"Ann, please get your ex-husband for me. I'm not hanging him; I need to talk to him!"

At his last furious outburst, Ann determined to do as bidden. Biting her lower lip and shaking, she hurried down the living room to reach Katie's door. She knocked on it. "Jon?"

He didn't reply.

"Jon!" She knocked again.

He still didn't reply.

"Jon, damn you!"

She pushed open the door.

The bedroom window, facing the garden as her own did, was open.

And Jon was nowhere to be seen.

Ann exhaled on a long, shaky breath. Oh, God, was she so wrong? Was Jon a murderer? It couldn't be; it couldn't be.

What about Mark? a voice tormented her. He'd found the weapon—when he'd been in her bedroom.

"Ann!" Mark called sharply.

She strode back to the bedroom.

"Where's Jon?"

"He's—"

"He's what?"

"Gone," Ann admitted.

"Son of a bitch!" Mark swore. He leveled a finger at her. "No more bull from you. When I get my hands on him, he's behind bars this time.

And I hope they prosecute him to the absolute full extent of the law!"

He started out of her room. Ann hurried after him, catching his arm. "Wait! You don't know anything yet—"

"I know he's gone."

"But—"

"I've got to bring this in, Ann."

"Please, just—"

"God damn it, Ann, I'm a cop!"

"This is a setup. It has to be."

"Right. That's why Jon Marcel ran."

"He probably heard you breathing fire and bolted."

"He left you."

"He left me with you."

He shook his head. "I have to go."

"Please don't bring that knife in yet. There's got to be an explanation—"

"Ann, I've got to go. And don't you leave this place, do you understand me? I mean it."

He didn't ask to use her phone; he had a new cellular. He pulled it from a pocket and pressed a number. "Dispatch, this is Mark LaCrosse, get someone over to Ann Marcel's. Have an officer come straight up to her damned hallway—since she managed to elude her guard yesterday. I need someone now, all right? See if you can get Jimmy for me."

"No!" Ann cried. "Don't. Don't get Jimmy over here. He makes me uneasy."

"Jimmy didn't kill Gina or anybody else."

"You can't just say that—"

"You say that Jon didn't kill her; well, I say that I know that Jimmy didn't!" He started to the door to the hallway, then turned back to her. "Don't leave, damn you, don't you leave here, do you hear me?"

"Go to hell!"

"I'm going to tell Jimmy or whatever officer is there to arrest you if you so much as set foot outside that door!"

She stood dead still. Eyes narrowed, furious, she stared at him. He returned her stare.

"Ann, I'm sorry—"

"Go to hell."

"Ann—" he started back toward her.

"Go to hell! And don't you dare touch me, do you understand?"

He stopped. His gray eyes seemed filled with anguish for a number of seconds.

Then they just seemed cold. Glittering silver.

"Don't leave here. I will have you brought down and booked. There are plenty of charges I can level against you."

He spun on his heel, and left her.

The second the door closed, Ann spun around and raced for her bedroom, dressing as quickly as humanly possible. She had to get out before Jimmy Deveaux came to stand guard at her doorway.

She dressed for the bayou.

"Hey! Mark, where are you going?"

To Mark's amazement, he saw Jon Marcel

hurrying to him from the cafe across the street from Ann's place. He was balancing a bag of pastries with a cardboard tray filled with coffee.

He stared at Marcel until the man reached him. "I thought the point was that someone should be staying with Ann. You're a cop; I'd think you'd have checked to make sure that I was there before you just upped and left her."

Jon realized that Mark was staring at him oddly.

"What is it?"

Mark produced his plastic bag.

"Oh, Jesus," Jon breathed.

"Under Ann's bed."

"You can't possibly believe Ann put it there."

"Maybe not."

"Oh, man, come on! You can't believe I did that either. Gee, please feel free to go sleep with my ex-wife; I've hidden a bloody knife in her room?"

"Maybe that's the point. Hide it where it's just too damned obvious."

"And I went for coffee for you and everything," Jon said disgustedly. "Fine. Frigging fine, just arrest me then. I didn't do it, and you're going to let the real killer walk free."

Mark stared at him. Gut reaction—Jon Marcel didn't do it. Why go off the deep end about the knife? He was a cop—he had to turn in evidence.

Maybe it was a hoax. Maybe the blood on this particular knife would turn out to be chicken blood.

He shook his head in disgust. "When you were barely conscious, you said to her—"

"Annabella's. If I could just see . . . see beyond the shadows. Damn it, I must have seen the killer."

"Let's go up. We'll all discuss this. Calmly. I think," Mark said. "Maybe it won't make any difference if I arrange for the hypnotist, then turn in the knife."

"Yeah. Thanks. Let's at least drink the coffee. It's the good kind."

They went up the stairs to Ann's, went in. Jon set the bag of pastries and the tray of coffee down.

"Ann!" Mark called.

Ann didn't reply.

"She must be changing," Jon said.

"Ann?"

She still didn't answer.

Frowning, Mark hurried to the door. He threw it open. The broken door shuddered, the hinges gave, and the door slammed to the ground, nearly catching Mark's feet.

He barely seemed to notice. He felt ill. Gut-feeling. She was gone.

And she was in real danger.

"Where?" he grated out raggedly.

"I don't—" Jon began. He broke off cleanly, staring at Mark. "The club?"

"Let's try it," Mark said.

They hurried out of Ann's house. Mark called dispatch as they drove, telling the operator that Ann Marcel wasn't in her house, but that he wanted a man in her hallway anyway. "Did you get my partner yet, Janey?" he asked the operator.

"Not yet—sorry."

"If you do, tell him to meet us at Annabella's."

But Ann wasn't at the club.

Harry Duval's one-eyed bouncer met them at the door. "The boss is in the back, but I haven't seen the pretty little artist lady either. She's not here. I mean, I'm sure, but I'll make positive. No one's in today yet, not Jen, April, Marty, Cindy . . . they must think it's the damned Fourth of July come early or something."

"See if Ann Marcel is back there, please?" Jon prodded.

"I'll have someone check back in the dressing rooms."

They wandered in. Mark leaned against a bar stool. It happened to be the stool by the phone. There was a notepad sitting there.

He glanced at the notepad. Ann's number was doodled on the pad.

As he stared at it, Harry Duval made an appearance. "Gentlemen! You're here early."

Mark stared at the notepad. Ann's number had been written there not just once.

But over and over.

"Duval!" he said sharply.

Both Harry and Jon moved over to him.

"Whose writing is that? Do you recognize it by any chance?"

"I'm not sure, I don't really recognize it—" Jon began.

Duval whistled. "Yeah, I know it."

"Oh, God, I know it, too!" Mark exclaimed. "Oh, hell, I do recognize it."

"She was lured out this morning!" Jon said. "Oh, God, where would you lure a woman to . . ."

"Kill her?" Mark finished, feeling ill. He stared at Jon.

"The swamp," Jon said.

"Wait!" Harry Duval said. "Maybe there's something else you should know."

"What?" Mark demanded.

"Well, I never thought it mattered much, but here goes."

Both men listened.

Then they all started out.

One-Eyed-Jack returned to the bar area to tell them that the back was completely empty.

There was no one to tell. Even his boss was gone.

Twenty-one

Ann had planned on hiring someone to take her out to the bayou, but she wondered if that wouldn't take her too long—she wouldn't have much time before someone realized she wasn't home—and if it wouldn't become too complex.

She drove straight out to where the boats were kept and selected the best one. She was afraid she wasn't going to be able to start the motor, but three little pulls on the cord and it was humming away.

It was a long ride, shooting across the open water. Long enough for her to warn herself that she was an idiot. She shouldn't be out here alone.

Who should she be with?

In all of this, it seemed, there was only one totally trustworthy person. One person who hadn't been involved with Gina. Who had loved Gina, not with passion, but with tenderness.

Mama Lili Mae.

And Mama Lili Mae had warned her not to trust the people closest to her. The people she should trust.

She was a fool. She knew Jon, and she knew

Mark. She hadn't known Mark long, but she knew him well.

Or did she?

The doubts plagued her as she pressed on relentlessly across the water, glancing up at the sky now and then.

She swore as she did so.

There was another storm coming. The sky was already turning gray.

She had to hurry.

But there was no way for her to hurry. Once she'd crossed the open water, the hard part started; going the right way within the tangle of the bayou. She'd been out here only once. Thank God for Gregory's clear-cut manner of going places. It had, at least, been easy to traverse the main body of water.

Then, of course, she had to cut the engine, and hope to find the landing spot for Mama Lili Mae's property.

The first channel she took was completely wrong; she came all the way back. She took another wrong turn, then another.

She passed Mark's cabin, and grew excited to realize that she was at last on the right track. She rowed around and saw what she was certain was the proper landing.

There were three boats drawn up there already. She rowed her own carefully up alongside the others.

She shivered. The rain was imminent. The day was dark.

Mama Lili Mae's was right up the path. Jacques Moret wouldn't be there; he was in jail.

She had to be safe.

Ann stepped out of the boat and into the shallow water, drawing her boat up. She started up the path she'd learned from Gregory and Cindy.

After a few feet, she paused.

She was being followed.

Ann started to run, then paused again. Her fear had sent her crashing into the bush.

In the wrong direction.

Hold, pause, get your bearings, she told herself. Oh, God, she was so ridiculously close! *Find the right path, and walk fast!* she warned herself.

"Ann!"

She heard a hushed whisper, very near her. A female voice, she thought.

"Ann!"

The soft, feminine voice again.

Then a louder voice.

"Ann! Sweet Jesus, Ann, are you out there?"

It was Jon. Calling to her. Jon Marcel. Her ex-husband. Who had been covered in Gina's blood.

She hunched down in the bushes. Oh, God. There were rustlings in the foliage everywhere, so it seemed.

The thunder clouds were rolling in all around her.

She heard swearing. She ducked low, and looked through the branches around her.

She sucked in her breath. A man was walking by. She couldn't see him. Was it Jon?

Or someone else. She heard the swearing again.

Jimmy . . . ? Jimmy Deveaux? The cop she didn't trust?

"Ann!" She turned, crashing right into Cindy McKenna.

"Cindy!"

"Ann!" Cindy drew a finger to her lip, then beckoned to Ann. "It's Jimmy!" she warned Ann.

"Jimmy Deveaux?" Ann whispered back.

Cindy nodded strenuously. "Let me get you out of here."

"You can get to Mama Lili Mae's?"

"Yeah, but we've got to shake Jimmy first. Please, Ann, be quiet. Did you know—he slept with Gina. He was blackmailing her. He—I think that he killed her."

Ann couldn't breathe. She felt as if a tremendous weight was crushing down on her chest.

"Come on!" Cindy said.

They started off. They could hear Jimmy thrashing around the bushes.

"Mrs. Marcel? Mrs. Marcel! It's Detective Deveaux. Please, can you hear me? We've come to help you. We've—"

"Don't listen!" Cindy cried, tugging at Ann's shirt. "Come on, come on, run!"

Ann followed her, carefully skirting the area where Jimmy was flushing the bushes, looking for her.

"How can you be so sure it was Jimmy?" Ann whispered nervously.

"I—I don't know. But it doesn't matter. They're all over! Oh, God, one of them is a killer."

"Who's all over?"

"The two cops. Mark and Jimmy. They were both sleeping with her, you know. And Jon. Jon is here. He slept with her the most. Come on, let me get you farther away; we've just got to get out of here. Someone is trying to kill you, Ann."

Cindy caught Ann's hand. She started to draw her along a path through the bushes. They ran, going faster and faster. Ann began to lose her breath. She tugged on Cindy's hand.

"Wait, stop! We've got to stop for a minute. Cindy, this is crazy. They surely aren't in on this together. And one man could hardly kill us both that easily. Maybe none of them did it; maybe Harry Duval did it!"

"Harry just likes sex," Cindy said.

"Men do seem to like sex," Ann said dryly. Her side was killing her. She forced Cindy to stop.

"And women!" Cindy blurted angrily.

Ann bent over to slake the ache in her side. She looked up at Cindy. Her pretty face was twisted in a strange mask.

"Cindy, we need to just go back. They can't kill me if they're all together. We'll go to Mama Lili Mae's. Make some sense out of this."

"They all thought Gina liked sex with them. Like Harry. He thought that Gina couldn't really leave him, just because he thought he was such a stud. He used to make us come to him

together, because he got such a kick out of
watching. And when she was alive, he wanted
Gina."

Something about the way Cindy was speaking
made Ann acutely uncomfortable.

"Cindy, you don't have to tell me about this—"

"It's all right. You remind me of Gina, a little
bit. Oh, you're from the pure side of town, of
course. But Gina could have been so much more
than what she was. . . . They did it to her. We
were going to get out together."

"You were friends," Ann said carefully. "But
then Gina fell in love with Jon."

"We were more than friends," Cindy said. "I
really didn't want Jon to have to pay for her
murder; he was decent to all of us. Most men
aren't. But then again—it was Jon's fault, and it
might have been best if he'd just died. I killed
that idiot dikey bisexual just because they told
me that Jon had survived. I had to make it look
like someone was killing strippers or club girls.
Who the hell would have known it was probably
the prig's first time in such a place?"

"Cindy, you can't mean—"

"Oh, Ann! Yes, I do mean! I didn't want to
kill Gina; she just wouldn't listen to me. She was
going to leave me, and marry Jon. Just walk
away! She was all that I had. We'd hated men
together forever, even though she kept sleeping
with some guys because she wanted to. She had
a hang-up on the cop for the longest time . . .
but it wasn't right. She'd tell me about him.
She'd tell me about him when we made love

together. She did the same when she first started out with Jon; then she got quiet; then she was fooling around more and more with that stupid voodoo stuff in the cemetery with Jacques Moret . . ." Cindy paused, smiling broadly. "I tried to kill you last night, you know. Jacques could have taken the blame real easy since he was running around in stupid voodoo robes. That would have worked nicely. But this will do okay. They'll find the knife in your room soon enough. And Jon Marcel will be out here, so that when you're found, it will be a real tragedy. The ex-wife who tried so hard to prove her marauding guy innocent of murder—a victim herself. It's too bad—I really wanted someone to pay besides Jon, but he'll have to do."

Ann barely breathed, just staring at Cindy.

It was unbelievable.

She'd been afraid of Duval, of Jacques Moret. She'd even had doubts about Mark's partner— her own ex-husband, and even Mark.

And here was Cindy. Telling her about an affair that she'd never imagined.

Telling her that she'd killed the two women.

"Did you knock Gregory out?" Ann asked her. What the hell did she do now? Keep Cindy talking? Hope someone would stumble upon them? How far had they run?

"I tried to kill Gregory. He had just left Gina when I killed her. I was afraid he'd seen something."

"He didn't. But Jon did. It will come to him soon enough."

"Who's going to believe him when he's locked up for murder himself?"

"It's not going to be that simple."

"They needed a murder weapon to convict him. Now they have it."

"It still won't be that simple! Even if he's here now, he's with Mark. Mark will know that he didn't kill me. Cindy, you can't run forever. You can't keep killing more and more people because you will get caught!"

Cindy laughed.

"Sweetie, don't you bet on justice being so damned just!"

Cindy reached into her pocket then. Ann tried to tell herself that she was small, but strong.

You can beat her! she told herself.

But Cindy's hand came out of her pocket, and Ann heard a *ker-plunk* and then a whistling sound.

She saw the switchblade in Cindy's hand.

And her mind was made up.

She had to run. She dropped to the balls of her feet, grabbed up a handful of dirt, threw it into Cindy's eyes, then sprang into action.

Screaming as she started out.

"I hear her!" Jon shouted.

"From where?" Duval demanded.

Mark was already running, beating his way through the trees and brush, sinking into the mud, crawling out of it.

"Damn!" he swore, as the rain started.

It pounded down. He kept going.

Ann ran and ran. Her hair fell into her eyes, soaked, blinding her.

She paused, grasping hard to a branch to draw the hair and water from her eyes.

She inhaled.

Closed her eyes, opened them.

Cindy was there. She made a swipe at her.

Ann cried out, ducking. The switchblade stuck into the tree. Ann made a dive for Cindy.

The switchblade slipped out of the tree just as they fell to the ground together. Cindy raised it over Ann's head. Ann brought her knees in, kicking out hard, throwing Cindy off her.

Gasping, winded, she made it to her feet. She threw mud at Cindy, then started to run again.

"Ann!" Mark shrieked. The wind was carrying his voice away.

Damn that Duval! It had never occurred to him to tell anyone that the girls had been closer than even he had realized. Damn Duval, damn himself! He should have remembered the way Gina talked about Cindy, how careful she tended to be regarding the other girl's feelings.

Another scream ripped out on the wind.

"Ann!" he cried out in anguish again.

He ran through the brush and the blinding rain.

Ann stumbled over a tree root and went rolling into the mud. Gasping, she tried to drag herself out. The mud was grasping at her, holding her.

Cindy sprang into view, rain and wind slamming into her. She didn't seem to notice. She smiled despite the stinging pellets, walking almost casually to where Ann battled the suctioning mud.

"There you are!" Cindy said happily.

"Cindy!"

The sharp call sent Cindy's head spinning around. Ann saw Mark approaching the woman, soaked himself, fighting the onslaught as he neared her.

"Mark, Mark! Be careful, she's got a blade!" Ann cried. With tremendous effort, she pitched herself out of the mud, and went racing desperately toward Cindy, who held the blade behind her back now.

Waiting.

"No!" Ann cried, almost upon Cindy.

Cindy turned, the switchblade raised.

Ann shrieked, throwing herself to the side.

Cindy came crashing downward then, into the mud herself. Mark's fingers were wound around her wrist.

The switchblade fell.

There was a slurping sound.

The mud sucked up the switchblade. Facedown in the mud, Cindy sobbed.

The rain continued to fall. Ann just stared down at her. Then at Mark.

"Can't you ever just stay home when I ask you to?" he demanded wearily.

Very, very, very slowly, she smiled. The rain sluiced over his handsome face. His eyes were steady and gray, with just the slightest silver glitter. She didn't know how he'd managed to be here again, he just had.

Jon, Jimmy and Duval made it into the clearing. They saw Ann and Mark, and Cindy down in the mud, still sobbing.

"I'll get Cindy," Duval said. "Jimmy, give me a hand?"

The two men picked her up.

Jon stared at Mark and Ann.

"Hey, folks, it's raining, you know."

"Yeah, we know," Mark said.

"Go get out of the rain, Jon!" Ann told him.

Jon muttered, and departed.

Mark came over to Ann. He drew her into his arms and lifted her chin.

"Don't you ever, ever listen?" he asked.

"Marry me," she told him. "I make a really good wife. Ask Jon."

"Why don't I believe that marrying you will make you listen more to what I say?"

"Well, it may not. But then again, I really do like a good discussion. And I am willing to take advice. Most of the time."

"Is that an invitation?" he queried.

"It's an invitation for you to come up with a proposal," she told him.

He smiled, lowering his eyes. Then he lifted her up, out of the mud, into his arms.

"Are you all right?" he asked anxiously.

"I'm all right." But she shivered fiercely. "Oh, God, Mark! I knew Jon was innocent, but I was even afraid of him today. I was really afraid of your poor partner."

"My poor partner was really innocent in all this. We had a long talk. He wasn't blackmailing Gina, or sleeping with her. He was trying to convince her to give up the voodoo business in the cemetery before she wound up in real trouble over it."

"I feel so guilty. I thought he was a slime bucket."

"And he really did say great things about you."

"I'll have to apologize, huh?"

"Well, not necessarily. I don't think that anybody ever told him you thought that he was a slime bucket. Just be nice to him in the future, huh?"

"Oh, I will. Of course, you do owe Jon an apology."

"He'll definitely get one from me."

She smiled, then grew grave. "I was even nervous about you—for a very brief spell, of course."

"Of course."

"But then, you had the audacity to think I might have hidden that knife."

"I knew that you hadn't."

Ann sniffed.

"All right, so I was pretty damned sure that you hadn't."

"Oh, God, Mark, I never suspected Cindy!"

"None of us ever suspected her. We assumed it was a crime of passion."

"It was a crime of passion. She loved Gina. I don't think she ever intended to kill Gina, but once she had done the deed, she was caught up in it." Ann shivered. "She killed that poor Trainor woman just to throw suspicion! Oh, God, no one knew! Mark, she's not sane."

"No."

"What will happen to her?"

"I imagine she'll be judged mentally incompetent. And she'll be institutionalized."

"Mark, what she did is so horrible. But . . ."

"But she's sad herself."

"Yes. Her dreams were broken. It sent her over the edge. It cost Gina her life, and that poor innocent Trainor woman. And it might have cost both Jacques and Jon their freedom, or their lives."

"But it's really over, Ann. The truth is justice, and you discovered the truth. You fought for Jon, and you proved him innocent. And you nearly lost your own life in the effort!"

"Well, you wouldn't listen to me."

"I was listening to you! Jon didn't go to jail, did he? He came out here with me, you know."

"I know." Ann realized then that they were moving. He was carrying her through the swamp.

The rain was still falling down upon them.

And they weren't heading for Mama Lili Mae's.

"Where are we going?" she demanded, then

realized their destination. "But, you're going to have a mound of paperwork—"

"It will wait 'til the storm subsides."

"But—"

"They'll take Cindy to Mama Lili Mae's to wait it out. If it clears before we get back, Jimmy will bring Cindy in, and start the paperwork without me."

"Are you sure—"

"Will you shut up? I'm going to need just the right atmosphere to propose."

Ann went quiet, staring at him.

He arched a brow. "You're all right?"

She nodded, and kissed him.

"Ann . . ."

"You did just tell me to shut up, didn't you?"

"Yes, I just didn't believe it was possible for you to listen to me."

She smiled and leaned against him. It didn't seem long today before they reached the cabin.

Ann stayed on the porch and showered while he started the fire.

She poured wine while he showered.

When he came in, she strode across the cabin to meet him, shedding the towel she'd worn.

"Invitation?" he queried.

"Definitely," she told him.

"Will you marry me?" he asked.

"Definitely," she repeated.

He laughed, and lifted her up.

And outside, the rain continued to fall, the wind to blow.

Inside . . .

Passion flared. Within it, the new-found sparks of trust ignited.

And love became the flame.

They made it back to Ann's house just minutes before ten o'clock.

The phone started ringing as Mark and Ann entered, Jon right behind them.

"It's Katie!" Ann cried, and dived for the phone.

Jon made it first, flashing a smile to Ann.

"Katie, sweetheart! It's Daddy, how are you?"

Ann could dimly hear her daughter's anxious voice going on and on.

"Well, we've had a bit of excitement here, but nothing that isn't all right now. What's that? I'm fine." He flashed a smile. "Yes, Mom's fine, she's right here. It's quite a long story, but honest to God, honey, Mom and I both are really, truly, just fine. Don't worry about it now—I mean, you're coming home soon, right? Yes, well, you'll have to. Mom is getting married. Yep, you heard me right. Your mom is getting married. And can you believe this?" He winked at Mark. "She's marrying a cop! Here's Mom."

"Katie, sweetheart, are you all right?" Ann gasped, grabbing the phone.

"Mom, I'm doing great, but you gave me an awful scare, calling, then not being there; then I heard rumors down here and saw a little tiny piece in a copy of the *New York Times* . . . Mom, is everything really okay. Wait—are you really getting married. To a cop? This is all so damned confusing!''

"Katie, yes, I'm marrying a cop. He's great—you're going to love him. Dad even loves him. Here, say hi.''

She thrust the phone over to Mark.

"Hi, Katie.''

"Hi.'' Katie was quiet a moment. "Umm . . . do you have a name?'' she asked politely.

He laughed. "Mark, Katie. Mark LaCrosse. And I can't wait to meet you.''

"Sure—you, Mom and Dad are all there, right?''

"Yeah. Well, your dad is leaving soon. I'll let him explain a bit more. Bye, Katie.''

"Bye . . .''

Mark passed the phone back to Jon Marcel.

Jon took the phone.

Mark kissed Ann.

Jon sighed and turned his back on them. "What was that, Katie? Yeah, honey, he's really an all right guy. Well, I guess I kind of have to like him. He's—he's got good taste in women. All right, all right, honey. I'll try to start at the beginning . . .''

Mark cleared his throat, taking the phone back. "Your dad wants to know if you can call him at his place in about thirty minutes?'' He nodded at whatever Katie said, smiled, and hung up the receiver.

"Well?'' Jon asked.

"She's not going to call. She's on her way to the airport. She's coming home. She says she just can't trust you two on your own at all anymore."

"Oh," Jon said.

Mark escorted him to the door. "Go home, Jon."

"Yeah. Sure." He smiled at them both. "Thanks, guys."

Ann nodded. She walked over to him and gave him a big, warm kiss on the cheek. "Thank you," she told him huskily.

Jon smiled, and nodded. Hugged her back.

Mark caught her arm, pulling her back against him. "Ann, he's the *ex*-husband, remember?"

Jon departed, pulling the door closed behind him.

"And I'm the new lover," Mark reminded her.

Ann nodded.

She gave him a big, warm kiss . . .

And it wasn't on his cheek.

In fact . . .

It was an invitation.

And slipping his arms around her, Mark accepted it.

Most gladly.

The night breeze swayed.

From somewhere, a jazz trumpet played its melody into the night.

And the smell of chicory wafted on the air. . . .